Lord Lucan
A Strange Encounter

by
Clive Payne

Grosvenor House
Publishing Limited

This book is published by
Grosvenor House Publishing Ltd
28-30 High Street, Guildford, Surrey, GU1 3EL.
www.grosvenorhousepublishing.co.uk

A CIP record for this book
is available from the British Library

ISBN 978-1-78623-752-1

My best wishes

Clive Payne

ACKNOWLEDGEMENTS

My thanks are due to my friend Martyn Gay, a bookseller with Waterstones who gave me great help and encouragement to relate this adventure. Also my brother, Bryan, a director at the historic Crockfords casino in Mayfair, with thirty years of experience in the trade, who provided me with invaluable information about the world of casino gaming, together with past and present laws and technicalities.

Thanks also to Grosvenor House Publishing for proofreading and editing my manuscript. Lastly, to my friend Tony Abraham who passed away suddenly before I was able to give him a copy of my novel.

CHAPTER ONE

Danni had seen me coming and was already selecting the model of bike I preferred from the rows of cycles lined-up neatly outside his shop. I always went for the sturdy model with a large basket strapped to the front where you could store your bits and pieces. Danni and his Dutch wife had run this bike-hire shop, tucked away a few blocks from the beach, for as long as I could remember.

While I waited for the saddle height to be adjusted I reflected how tough this business must be for them, especially out of season. They opened from eight in the morning till eight at night, seven days a week, and at nine euros a day hire-fee there could not be much of a living out of it. But there were plenty of bicycle-hire shops in Mallorca and the competition was fierce.

The saddle height was perfect, and having paid my euros I peddled away towards the seafront. I planned to do my usual run into Palma, which was a nice easy ride with hardly an incline for the whole ten kilometres. Being long time retired from a job sitting at a computer all day and now in my mid-sixties I was not looking for anything too strenuous while on holiday. An easy ride like this, a coastal walk, or a set of tennis was about it now.

I slipped into the cycle lane that skirted the coast road and headed south. The riding here was wonderfully safe with dedicated bike lanes and was now the only place I felt comfortable to engage in this type of sport. I had a bike back home in London, but it had been collecting cobwebs in the garden shed for many years. After some near accidents I had come to the conclusion that I was too old for cycling on the London streets and that it was a long way from being conducive to my wellbeing.

I stopped about a mile along the track to don a hat and apply some sun cream. It was only March but it promised to be a fine warm day. I soon left the sprawling resort of Can Pastilla and weaved my way round the old quarry works and headed towards the small town of Molinar. The faster riders coming from behind would ring their bell to let you know of their approach but most cyclists on this route were holidaymakers like myself, peddling along at a nice sedate pace.

After the quarry I passed some derelict hermit cottages on the beach, their roofs long since gone and the ruins now home to a multitude of noisy sea birds. The cycle paths only slight incline opened out to a little headland with views across the Bay of Palma. Here the local municipality had, for some reasons best known to themselves, erected a rather odd modern art folly of polished steel and wooden poles that sprouted from the ground at crazy angles.

Soon I arrived at the quiet little town of Molinar and the Café Plaza, my usual half-way stop for a coffee. I found a railing near the outside chairs and tables where I could chain my bike and keep an eye on it. It was easy to find a nice table with some shade as business for the café looked pretty slow, the holiday season, such as it was for this small resort was not yet underway.

A young waitress greeted me with a friendly smile. I braced myself for an attempt at the language, which always gave me a little satisfaction for at least having a try. 'Un café con leche e un botella agua pequeno, thank you,' I uttered sheepishly. She gave me a sweet, understanding nod-of-the head at my attempt at Spanish. Timidly, I always said 'thank you' rather than 'por favor' to confirm that I was English and would be totally befuddled and embarrassed in the unlikely event that I might be mistaken for someone who spoke the language.

I lit a cigarette and congratulated myself that it was the first of the day.

The café was the main focal point of this seaside town and was mainly home to locals, a few of whom were still wearing coats despite it being a warm day.

Molinar is not really a tourist spot despite having a good sandy beach. There are no hotels, clubs, or holiday apartments. In the middle of the communal square was a children's play area with swings, a sandpit and some climbing frames. Surrounding the square were a few small cafés, a couple of shops, and an estate agent. Most outsiders who stumbled on this resort were usually people like me cycling into Palma.

My order arrived and whilst sipping a welcome coffee, I pondered how the Spanish love their dogs. Some poodles and small terriers with leads tethered to table legs rested disinterestedly in the shade by their owners. I stretched my legs and took out some pamphlets and mobile phone from my rucksack and saw that my phone provider had decided that I was in France rather than Spain and listed various tariffs for sending texts. I cast my eye over some literature about Palma Cathedral, which I was thinking of visiting.

I read with interest that in the autumn of 1229, King James I and his army sailed to Mallorca to defeat the Arabs. A storm raged so violently during the three-day journey that the young king feared for his life, so he made an oath to God promising, should his enterprise succeed, to erect a temple dedicated to the Virgin Mary. He was lucky, not only did he arrive safely but he also defeated the Arabs. As a God-fearing Christian he did not forget his promise and quickly set about putting his oath into practice.

On New Year's Day 1230 the foundation stone was laid on the site of where the main mosque originally stood.

The king decided that the site for his new church was obvious. The Muslims were already using the perfect position for their mosque. So by razing the mosque and constructing a house of God on its foundations, King James knew he would be highlighting the victory of Christianity over Islam. But in doing this he also created one of the great, all-time historical paradoxes; anyone kneeling at the altar does so in the direction of Mecca like a Muslim not, as should be the case for a Christian, towards Jerusalem.

As the centuries went by no fewer than fifteen architects worked on repairs and improvements to the cathedral right up until 1901 when Antoni Gaudi, who had already established his reputation with his work on the cathedral of La Sagrada Familia in Barcelona was called in to finish the job. For three years he studied and sketched until finally in 1904 he presented his drawings and work could begin. Then, for another ten years he laboured without interruption, completing some incredible work, until suddenly one day he decided not to finish. Why this happened was not quite clear, but it was probably due to criticism he received at the hands of the Mallorcans. Whatever the reason, it left the then Bishop frustrated. The cathedral had now exhausted 16 generations of architects and was still not finished.

Whilst reading this most interesting story I became vaguely aware that perched on a stool at the bar, a neatly attired old-boy seemed to be taking an interest in me. He puffed on a cigarillo between sips of brandy while every so often stealing an inquisitive glance in my direction. It seemed he had made a decision to come and speak to me for he slowly got to his feet, and with brandy in hand, gingerly made his way over to me. He stooped forward over my table like a waiter ready to take an order.

'You are English?' he enquired in a soft, polite manner, his face holding a warm enticing smile.

I nodded. His voice was low and refined, and this along with his smart appearance lent him an air of mild gentility.

'Do you mind if I join you for just a moment?' he asked pleasantly, 'I don't get to speak to many people from back home.' I gestured to a chair. 'Please,' I said, whilst being somewhat perplexed as to why he had sought me out. He settled himself and placed his brandy on the table. I guessed he was about eighty. He was tall and dressed very smartly in a blue lightweight suit with a red handkerchief tucked neatly in the top pocket. His good head of grey hair and neat beard worked-well with the sharp features of his broad tanned face with fine prominent cheekbones and inquisitive grey eyes. It crossed my mind that he would have cut quite a dapper figure in his day.

'Where are you from in England?' he enquired.

'From London,' I said, still feeling a little apprehensive as to who he might be and why he had made a beeline for me. 'From Finchley,' I added, 'Mrs Thatcher's old constituency.'

His face brightened with a knowing smile. 'London was my home town, It's where I was born,' he said eagerly. 'But

I lived mostly nearer the centre.' He looked past me in the direction of the sea, his eyes momentarily glazing over as though recalling a memory. He turned back to me. 'I miss London you know, I miss the place so much.'

'Do you not go back?' I asked, suddenly warming to this courteous stranger.

'I used to,' he said, with something of a resigned sigh, 'but not any more. My health has not been too good these last few years.' He gestured a hand in the direction of the neat little houses that surrounded the communal square. 'This is my home now and I am content to see out my days here.'

He took a sip of brandy and rested his arms on the chair rests. 'I get the English papers so I keep in touch with life back home,' he said, his mood suddenly lighter.

'What on earth is going on with house prices in London? It's unbelievable what people are prepared to pay these days. I don't understand how anyone can afford that sort of money.'

I looked to see that my bike was safe. 'It's all pretty crazy.' I said. 'But so many people are moving to the capital. Supply and demand I guess, along with a lot of wealthy foreign buyers.'

He shook his head and smiled grimly, 'I dare not think what my house would be worth now.' he murmured. He lit a small cigar and blew a puff of smoke skywards.

'But I must not complain,' he said slowly and thoughtfully. 'I've been fortunate to live in the sun all these years and feel quite settled here now. Mallorca is a lovely island and this is a nice little town with friendly people.'

We chatted away amicably and to my surprise I felt quite at ease talking to this old boy who came across as having an easy affable charm about him. His voice was low and soft and unhurried, which at first seemed a bit strange and a little irritating – a sort of Prince Charles deliberation – but as we talked I realised that this slightly upper-class voice was not feigned but simply the way he had always spoken.

His considered speech along with his bright and fresh appearance gave the impression that despite his age he still clung proudly to some sort of countenance and bearing that he had probably enjoyed in former times.

We discussed house prices and the weather and such before we somehow got round to talking about the sporting scene back in England. He asked me with twinkle in his eyes if I liked horse racing, which I did, and went on to tell me that he had once owned some good thoroughbreds. He reminisced fondly how he and his friends would travel all over the country to watch his runners and that while he had won some good quality races, being an owner was incredibly expensive and had cost him a lot more than he ever received back in prize money. I found this conversation most interesting, as I had always been fascinated with the sport of kings from a young age.

Settling back in his chair, and in a bright mood, he told me that he had also owned some greyhounds which he had raced at the now defunct Harringay dog track. This amused me as I used to visit the track when I was a young lad. We swapped fond memories about the old stadium with its dog racing, speedway and the absolute mayhem of stock car racing.

It was pretty clear talking to this engaging character who had owned racehorses and greyhounds that he must have had a fair bit of money at some time in his life.

He sipped his brandy and sent another puff of smoke in the air. 'I've been following that casino case back in London,' he said quietly, while shuffling his chair a little closer to me to gain some shade from the sun that had been gradually creeping over our canopy.

'Did you read about that high roller who won a fortune playing baccarat and the casino refused to pay him?'

I nodded, and told him that I had.

'I can't believe that American chap nearly got away with it,' he said, warming to his narrative with raised eyebrows. 'The case intrigued me enormously because I loved playing baccarat and so the story brought back memories. What he was up to is an old trick that I have seen many times. You spot a small blemish on one-side of the back of the playing cards and if they are the ones you want you simply get those cards turned one-hundred-and-eighty degrees.'

He shrugged philosophically and relaxed back in his chair with a knowing smile. It was an odd coincidence that he should mention this story, as I had more than a passing interest in the impending court case. A friend of mine worked at the casino in question and had explained to me why they had refused to pay the famous gambling guru and poker champion, Phil Ivey, seven million pounds.

'I have been following the case,' I said. 'At first they couldn't work out what he was up to, only that something was very suspicious, so they quite rightly withheld the money.'

'I'm glad they refused to pay him,' he said with a wry expression. 'I loved gambling more than was good for me, but I never tried to gain an unfair advantage.'

We talked a little more about London life before I beckoned to leave. I delved into my rucksack for some euros.

'No, no,' he protested firmly, 'I will get this, it will be my pleasure. It's been so good to talk to someone from back home and I hope that I have not detained you. By the way my name is Sidney, Sidney Ainsworth.'

'I'm Adam,' I said, 'and thanks for the drinks Sidney.' I picked up my bottle of water and headed for my bike when, as though he had suddenly thought of something, he called after me.

Chapter One

'Adam, will you be coming back this way?' he enquired quietly.

I unlocked the bike chain and moved towards him. 'Yes,' I said, a little hesitantly, thinking what might be coming. 'I'm cycling into Palma, then back to Can Pastilla.'

He looked a little anxious and eyed me nervously. 'I know I shouldn't ask this Adam, but I have enjoyed talking to you so much that I feel inclined to take a chance and ask if you might oblige me with a huge favour.'

He looked shy and uneasy before asking: 'Would you stop by here on your way back and collect a letter from me? I know it's unfair to waylay you like this, and please forgive me; it's not something I would normally do. You see I am desperate to get a letter delivered to a London address and I was wondering whether you could post it for me when you get back home.'

I hesitated, this was a strange request and I felt suspicious. 'Can you not post it from here?' I ventured politely but a touch warily.

'It's a little difficult to explain,' he said softly, his face solemn. 'Rather a long story I'm afraid. It's just that I need to feel assured in my mind that it gets delivered.' He paused for a few seconds before adding with polite emphasis. 'I would be more than happy to pay you for your trouble.'

I was feeling confused about this and he must have read my mind.

'I assure you it's just a letter,' he hastened to say, 'composed on my old typewriter. I don't know about all that modern computer business and printing machines and the like. I'm a bit of a dinosaur when it comes to modern things.' He offered me a nervous smile. 'I would be very pleased to show you the letter just so you know there is nothing untoward. It's simply to a very old friend, someone I wish to contact after a long absence.'

It was still lost on me why he couldn't simply post the letter himself and I felt unsure of what to say to him, but I had enjoyed chatting with him and he seemed a most genuine and likeable character, and so why, I thought, should I refuse what seemed a simple favour. 'Okay Sidney,' I said, after some hesitancy 'I'll stop by on my way back.'

He rested a hand on my arm thanking me most profusely and repeating that he would like to pay me for my trouble.

Cycling into Palma had been easy and carefree. On arrival I was surprised to see that despite it being early season the town was gay and lively with plenty of tourists mingling with the street artists and enjoying the Spanish guitar players in the main square. I pushed my bike through the crowds and past the performers that pose as Robin Hood, Quasimodo and the like, and who stay motionless as though statues rather than real people. There were also the ones dressed as shepherds, cowboys and Charlie Chaplin who cleverly support themselves with concealed metal rods that seem to make them hang in the air without any support – a trick that I thought was now slightly overplayed everywhere from rainy Trafalgar Square to Tenerife. But these artisans certainly earned their wages trying not to blink for hours on end. The sketch artists also deserved whatever they might earn in a day charging just twenty euros to draw the face of some girl from Tokyo who was trying to keep an even pose while her friends giggled nearby. I always admired these artists who are so highly-skilled but certainly wouldn't get rich in their chosen profession when it can take the best part of an hour to achieve the perfect likeness of a holiday tourist.

I made my way past the crowds queuing to get into Palma Cathedral, which I decided to give a miss, and crossed the waterside esplanade to the Palau de I'Almudaina, originally a palace for the Moorish governors but now a palatial residence housing a series of state apartments kept in readiness for visiting dignitaries and the Spanish Royal Family.

I crossed the Park de la Mar and headed for the lovely Old Town with its cobbled squares, fountains and narrow lanes. I found a safe place to chain my bike and took a seat outside a small ornate bar for some tapas and a cold beer.

After a nice break and refreshments I wheeled my bike along meandering back lanes of the city before eventually emerging at the Passeig Mallorca where I made my way down a series of terraced gardens to the harbour front. As I descended, I passed the huge column erected by Franco in honour – as it's said – to some Balearic sailors who were loyal to the fascist cause.

I was near to Bellver Castle with its imposing towers and fortifications but decided against a visit, as it was a steep climb to reach the top and would be hard work while pushing a heavy bike. Instead I chained my cycle to some railings and popped into the museum Es Baluard and studied, somewhat absent-mindedly, some works by Picasso, Maigritte and Miró that were striking but also bewildering and thought provoking at the same time.

From the museum and out into the bright sunshine I collected my bike and crossed the busy Passeig Maritin to the harbour and took a few snaps on my mobile of the gleaming white yachts and speedboats neatly lined up in their hundreds, waiting for the day their owners might show up and take them out to sea.

As I cycled along the front passing row after row of these magnificent yachts I reflected how many millionaires there must be knocking around.

But of course these boats were no more than modern day interlopers resting up on the shore of a city with a thousand years of rich history. I contented myself with this thought as I cycled along the front stealing a last glance over my shoulder at Palma Cathedral with its massive exterior buttresses, now bathed in early afternoon sunshine and no less a great sight despite having been built facing the wrong way.

As I cycled east I wondered if I should stop and see Sidney and collect that letter of his or just cycle past and forget all about him. Then I thought it would be pretty mean of me not to do him a simple favour. In any case, to my surprise, I had really enjoyed chatting with him. It was clear that he had been something of a gambler in his time but he came across as a most likeable chap and it was clear that he had led an interesting life. As I peddled at a steady pace, listening to the rhythmic sound of the wheels beneath me I began thinking deeply about my own liking for a bet. Perhaps it had been talking to a one-time gambler, and someone who liked a drink, that had triggered in my mind thoughts about myself.

I had started betting when I was about seventeen. I had discovered a very astute tipster called Supernap who gave occasional tips in the now defunct *Daily Herald*. There were no bookmakers in those days but I had somehow managed to open an account whereby I could bet by post. This entailed sending off selections along with a cheque, which would have to bear a timed postmark before the race meeting. I did very well following this tipster who became a scourge of the bookmakers, but my bank manager was not best pleased. He pulled me in one day wanting to know what I was up to with so many cheques flying around and how I had managed to show a healthy profit. I told him I had been lucky, but thereafter used postal orders instead of cheques as the bank manager had threatened to close my account. Perhaps it's better to lose when first attempting to gamble so that its seductive nature gets quickly extinguished, but I had caught the bug. Nobody quite knew who Supernap was, but one day he wrote a sad note in the *Herald* informing his followers that he would no longer be offering advice and tips. The bookmakers had moved the goalposts. From now on they would only pay one-fifth, instead of one-fourth, the odds for a placed horse. It was only a slight difference but enough to take away the edge that Supernap worked to. Such are the fine percentages between winning and losing in the betting arena. Supernap was more of an accountant than a tipster. For days on end he might not offer a selection if no horses fell within the strict parameters of his system. In the five years he wrote for the *Herald* he showed a profit of over 30 points for each season. A remarkable achievement, the success of which was based on a very clever system, but most importantly – patience; something that gamblers do not possess in abundance. After Supernap I was on my own, and it was pretty much downhill from then on.

I married my wife Jane, when I was in my early twenties, and at first we lived in rented accommodation until we managed to put enough together for a deposit on a house. We were both working hard. Jane was training to become a midwife and I was working as a store manager. Our deposit for a house would have come about sooner had I not been gambling away a proportion of my wages each week, losses which I kept from my wife.

My drinking habit had also become problematical. I had, from a young age, liked a drink and pubs had always held an attraction for me. When I was very young my mum and dad would take me and my brother and sister to a pub in Camden Town where my parents would meet up with their friends and relations. Of course we were too young to go inside the pub and so we huddled in the back of my dad's big black Wolseley car.

Every so often my mum or dad would come out to check on us and hand over bags of crisps and orangeade. We were strangely happy and I would stare out of the car at the brightness and warmth coming from that huge pub window and imagine the merriment inside. Across the road my Aunt had a little stall, selling cockles and whelks.

Soon after leaving school, my mates and I sought out pubs in the Holloway Road that were prepared to serve us despite our being under age. The fare was, Watney's Red Barrel, bottled Light Ale and Double Diamond. Alcohol was very much a part of my growing up.

By the time our first child arrived, Anne, I decided to keep a tight rein on my drinking and gambling. I had started a growing company selling batteries and this was going well and I was working long hours trying to build up a client base. That I was fully occupied kept me away from the pub and I was more settled with my family.

My problems began many years later when I sold my business and all of a sudden had time and money on my hands. After working so hard building up the business I had convinced myself that I deserved a break and a new type of lifestyle, away from the drudgery of long hours and worry about the company.

It had been a hot summer and with plenty of time on my hands I had taken to drinking at lunchtime and this would then often carry on through the rest of the afternoon and into the evening. Also I was gambling heavily and trying to chase my losses – something that is the worst thing you can do. Up until that time and that summer I had been quite disciplined, but I seemed to lose my way and it all became a problem and a habit that I found difficult to prise myself away from.

Chapter One

The next couple of years were something of a blur as I tried to get my life back on track. With coaxing from my wife and despite regarding myself as not being that far down the road I reluctantly attended Alcoholics Anonymous and Gamblers Anonymous. I thoroughly enjoyed these meetings, as to my surprise and delight, the talk was never about giving up drink or gambling but were comforting discussions where complete strangers opened up to each other. Talking about your demons and listening to other people's problems was uplifting and helped me to think more clearly and confront my own weaknesses.

Later on a friend managed to get me a job in the print, but I had to spend a year going-cap-in hand to the union begging them to accept me. My drinking and gambling was now under control and how this had come about was odd. It was not as though I had made some sacrifice or summoned up great will power, it's just that I couldn't do it anymore. If you don't have the money you can't gamble, and as for drink, I had grown tired of not being in control and hangovers.

Now retired, and with a couple of small pensions, I am lucky enough to have a little bet if I so desire and I can still enjoy a drink without it being a problem.

Reflections on my past came to a sudden and abrupt halt. With my mind totally elsewhere I had run slam into the back of a woman cyclist. I apologised most sincerely. She seemed quite aggrieved and shot me a withering look before scooting away. I shook my head to clear my mind and told myself to cycle with a bit more care and attention. Ahead of me, and round the next bend, Molinar would come into view. Yes, I would stop; I would do Sidney a favour and collect that letter of his. The sun was shining, I was on holiday and in that relaxed mood one feels more open to an act of benevolence. All the same, I still felt suspicious as to why he wanted me to post a letter for him when he could easily do so himself.

As I approached the Café Plaza I could see Sidney sitting alone at a table under some shade. He smiled broadly as I wheeled my bike towards his table. Most of the customers that had been here at lunchtime had now departed.

'Thanks so much for stopping by Adam,' he said, his voice soft and enthusiastic as I pulled up a chair. 'Let me get you a drink dear boy. What will it be, beer, brandy?'

'Thanks Sidney,' I replied, 'but I won't stop as I should be getting back.' I said this knowing I was in no real hurry, but did not want to get involved in too long a conversation.

'Of course, of course,' he said, cheerfully. 'I have the letter and I would like to pay you for taking up your time and asking such a favour.' He delved into his inside jacket pocket and produced a wad of notes.

'Really Sidney,' I said, trying not to sound reproachful. 'I'm happy to do you a favour, there's no need to pay me.'

'You won't take anything?' he murmured, looking disappointed.

'Definitely not,' I said.

He picked up an envelope that had been resting on the table and extracted a letter, which he held up to me like an auctioneer might show an exhibit.

'Does it look alright?' he enquired in a low voice. 'I use an old typewriter.'

'It looks fine,' I said.

He held the envelope upside down to show that there was nothing hidden inside and then replaced the letter which he sealed and then handed over to me. This little ritual was by way of assuring me that this was just a letter and I was not being asked to handle anything dodgy. I noted the address on the envelope.

Colin Hedley-Davies
c/o Warren Hedley-Davies
London House Publishing Ltd. Bedford Square,
London WC2

'As I mentioned Adam,' he said in a slow soft voice, 'the letter is to an old friend, someone I have not seen in forty-years. For now it's best I stay in the background but at the same time I wish to let him know that I am still around.' He gave a deep sigh and added almost in a whisper. 'I know that must sound odd. Please forgive an old turkey like me.'

While he had been speaking I had considered him thoughtfully, trying to sum him up. There was something about this man, but what that something was I couldn't pin down. I had met all sorts of characters that were living in Spain for one reason or another but Sidney was not like anyone I had come across before. He was very different. But beneath that refined exterior one thing was for sure – he had something to hide.

I put the letter in my rucksack. 'I understand Sidney,' I said matter-of-factly. 'You would rather the envelope did not show a Mallorcan post mark – is that it?'

He looked a little uneasy and gazed at the floor for a few moments. Then he turned his eyes to me, eyes that were now dull and faraway.

'You see I have a story, but…' He left the sentence unfinished.

I rose from my chair. 'I had better get going,' I said, feeling that his melancholy made for a timely exit.

Sidney raised himself and looked at me thoughtfully. 'Before you go Adam,' he said quietly, 'could I ask one last favour?'

He now looked contented and his expression gave me no cause for alarm.

'If you should pass this way again, would you stop and have a drink with me? This is my local and I'm always here.'

'Of course I will Sidney,' I replied, 'It would be my pleasure.'

I set off on the cycle path and gave him a farewell wave. I had to admit I liked the old chap; he was a most intriguing character and generous in wanting to pay me for doing him a favour. Very doubtful though, I thought to myself, that I would ever see him again.

Chapter Two

It was my last night in Mallorca. After returning the bike and saying my goodbyes to the Dutch couple I returned to my hotel for a quick shower and did a little packing.

After a buffet dinner I sauntered over to the Manchester bar thinking they might be showing a football match on the big screen. It wasn't football but rugby, the rules of which have always baffled me. The bar was packed and I had to admit that rugby, as back home when the pubs were screening a match, was hugely popular, more so than football.

I preferred football to rugby but contented myself with the thought that not every sports enthusiast loves every sport. An American wit had described cricket as a game invented by the English to make all other human endeavours look interesting and lively. Something I couldn't go along with.

I had a couple of drinks and watched the match to the end, cheering along with the enthusiastic fans, sharing in some banter and pretending I knew the rules. Altogether it had not been a bad way to finish my last night on holiday.

I said my farewells to the friendly bar staff, telling them I would be back soon and headed to my hotel. Tomorrow it would be a taxi to the airport and goodbye to Mallorca until the next time.

The journey back to London was uneventful and once home I soon busied myself with the humdrum jobs I had taken a break from. I emptied most of the contents of my suitcase into the washing machine, put my passport somewhere safe and after putting a stamp on Sidney's letter added this to some bills I needed to post.

I then got down to dealing with some mail and phone messages that had cropped up while I had been away. My brother and I were in the process of selling my mothers house and it was proving to be really frustrating. I was getting vague enquires from surveyors asking questions like: Where does the rainwater drain to? and when was the boiler last serviced? On top of this we could not find the deeds to the house and these had not been lodged with the Land Registry.

My mum had died some months earlier at a ripe old age. The little break in Mallorca was by way of taking my mind off things and coming to terms that she was no longer around. She had always been there for me through life's ups-and-downs.

During the Spring I involved myself with the ongoing politics at my tennis club, enjoyed some good country walks with friends and took some trips down to the south coast whenever the weather was good.

In June, along my with brother and his wife, I went on a mini-cruise to the Channel Islands. It was my first ever cruise and it was brilliant. From Guernsey we hopped over to the remote island of Herm and walked the whole perimeter of this enchanting place.

There was an added incentive to this little trip as we intended to cast our mum's ashes into the sea on the way back to Southampton. Her father had been lost at sea towards the end of the war, his merchant ship having been sunk by a German mine not far from where we would be sailing home. There is a strict rule not to throw anything from a cruise liner, not even a cigarette butt so we planned our deed carefully, finding a quiet deck that hardly anyone ever visited and a choosing a time when most guests would be at dinner.

We made our way to the deck and having checked that nobody was around cast my mum's ashes into the dark and foaming sea – It was, if you believe that sort of thing, my mum's final voyage to meet her dad.

After the cruise I was pondering whether to take another little holiday. My mind was made up when I met an old friend who looked wonderfully tanned who told me he had just spent a great week in Spain sunbathing and watching the football.

The World Cup was being staged with great razzmatazz in Brazil. The England team had made their usual poor start, not surprising really as they had won nothing in the last fifty years, but there was still plenty to come from this competition and I thought it would be a good time to have another break from London.

Once again I decided to visit Mallorca and so opened up Travel Republic on my computer.

Thanks to the Internet, booking a holiday anywhere in the world nowadays is an easy pleasure. Everything you need to know is at your fingertips. I always sorted the flights first and then surfed around for a hotel.

As was often the case, Ryanair had the best prices and flight times, which was good and bad at the same time. I always felt a bit nervous at their check-in desks as to whether I had complied fully with their rules and regulations.

To their credit Ryanair have in recent times decided to improve their image and I had to admit I had never had a bad journey with them.

Having booked a flight for the following day I looked at a map of Mallorca and thought about a location. I wanted a hotel near the airport as I had experienced some tiresome transfers trying to get to the north or west of the island.

Over the years I had learned to be selective when booking somewhere in Mallorca. Parts of the island like Magaluf and Palma Nova were like clones of Benidorm and the Germans had their enclaves such as Arenal and Peguera although not with the same degree of garishness.

After some research I plumped for the town of Illetas, a pretty little resort that I had visited many years before. It was near the airport and I remembered it as an attractive, if somewhat quiet place.

In fact Illetas is a secret gem. From the motorway a road winds up the cliffs and then levels out to reveal a series of coves far below separated by promontories. Each cove having a couple of hotels built directly into the cliff face that spread up from the beach to the road above.

I arrived at the Riu Palace hotel just after midday. The flight was fine and we had landed to the fanfare sound of a pre-recorded klaxon blaring the news that yet again Ryanair had arrived at its destination on time.

My room was on the second floor and rather than wait for the lift I decided to take the stairs. Oddly, this brought me out onto the roof. I was confused and decided to get the lift and simply press the number two button. The lift sped me downwards from there, and still feeling a little disorientated, I found my room. It turned out that the entrance from the road and reception was on the eighth floor and the ground floor was down at beach level. It took me ages to get my head round this layout.

Chapter Two

I spent the days lazing around the swimming pool, going for long walks, reading the latest C.J. Sansom novel and watching the World Cup matches at various bars on the main drag.

On my penultimate day I decided to take a trip into the capital. This was easy as the bus stop for Palma was right outside the hotel and the buses were frequent.

The city proved much too crowded for my liking. I felt hot and sticky caught up amongst so many sightseers. I thought about visiting the cathedral but, as usual, there was a long queue to get in and the idea of trying to appreciate the building in the company of so many tourists clutching cameras was not appealing.

After a little aimless wandering I decided to take a stroll along the coast to Molinar and escape the crowds. It was a fair distance but once there I could have a beer, relax for a while, and then bus it back to my hotel. It would be a nice way to kill a few hours as well as a good bit of exercise.

As I approached the little town I wondered if that intriguing old boy, Sidney, would be there. I had no real desire to meet him, but should he be around I would say hello and ask how he was getting on. I arrived at the Café Plaza and found a nice table with some shade but there was no sign of Sidney. As I ordered a beer the waitress looked over my head and began smiling at someone behind me. There was a tap on my shoulder and I turned to see Sidney. He was carrying a plastic bag and had been shopping.

'Adam my boy,' he said, with a little chuckle. 'What a lovely surprise. How nice to see you again.'

He looked most happy to see me and had remembered my name. He gestured to a chair at my table. 'May I join you?'

'Please do,' I said. He exchanged a few pleasantries in Spanish with the waitress who obviously knew him well and ordered a brandy. He sat down and studied me with a keen steady expression for a few moments.

Sidney was dressed very smartly, just as the last time I had seen him, but behind those fine leather tanned features I noticed that he looked a little frailer.

'Well well, what brings you this way Adam?' he enquired, in that slow, refined voice of his.

'I've been enjoying a nice little break up at Illetas,' I said. 'But I'm back home tomorrow. By the way Sidney,' I added. 'I posted that letter for you.'

He leaned forward resting his arms on the table as though to speak in confidence.

'Thank you so much Adam,' he said quietly, 'I felt sure you would do me that favour, it was most kind of you. I just wish you had let me give you something for your trouble. I have lived alone for a very long time now and friends that I could once turn to have long since gone. It was a bit of a cheek to ask a favour out of the blue like that but I decided to take a chance that you might oblige me.'

Our drinks arrived and we sat in silence for a while. Sidney lit one of his small cigars and settled back in his chair. 'Tell me Adam, where are you staying in Illetas?'

'The Riu Palace,' I replied. 'It's a lovely hotel built up against the cliff-face in one of those coves.'

'I know the Riu Palace,' he said slowly and thoughtfully, as though searching his memory. He took out a handkerchief and blotted some beads of sweat from his forehead. 'I think I stayed there once, but that would have been a long time ago. Nice little place Illetas,' he added gently.

We talked about London for a while and places we both knew. He was keen to steer the conversation around to sport and the horse racing scene back home. He was keen to know about the recent Royal Ascot Meeting and what the new

Grandstand was like. I told him I had spent a nice day at the meeting, that the weather had been lovely and the new grandstand was fabulous. One of the best courses in the world I told him.

While we were talking about racing I got round to telling him about the explosion of betting shops in London and how, near me, in North Finchley, which was only small shopping area, there were two Paddy Power shops, two William Hills, one Coral and two Ladbrokes. This spread of outlets I explained was all down to the gaming machines that all the bookies had installed in their shops and where you could now play any number of casino games. These terminals had revolutionised betting shops, which were no longer a male preserve. Now, many women were popping in to Ladbrokes to play roulette. Most of the bookmaker's profits were coming from these terminals, rather than the traditional punter having a tenner on a horse at Sandown.

He laughed and reminded me that before 1961 there had been no such thing as a high street betting shop. 'You had to have an account in those days,' he added dryly.

We had a lively chat for about half an hour before I made a move, saying that I should get going as I needed to catch the Palma bus and then another to my hotel.

He shook my hand warmly and thanked me for spending some time with him and said how pleased he was to see me again. He then added somewhat cautiously. 'I know I shouldn't ask this Adam, and once again it's a real liberty, but would you oblige me with another huge favour and post a document for me when you get back to London? It's a very important manuscript and I need to make sure it gets delivered safely.'

He had taken me by surprise and I was caught in hesitation, just as I had been the last time we met. 'To the same place?' I mumbled, for want of something better to say.

He nodded shyly and raised a hand in a little gesture of benediction. 'I feel terribly embarrassed asking this of you Adam,' he said softly. He pointed across the square.

'My place is near your bus stop, so I won't be taking you out of your way and I would dearly love to pay you for your trouble if you could do this for me.'

He then raised both hands in a gesture of surrender. 'I will understand if you cannot to do this.' he said meekly, his grey eyes looking straight into mine.

I felt uncomfortable as we crossed the square and turned down a side street which was lined either side by unattractive three story apartments. Sidney walked slowly and deliberately while all the time thanking me for the favour and saying that he would get the document quickly and not delay me.

The climb up the two flights of stairs to his apartment had left him a little breathless as he fumbled around for his latchkey.

Inside, I followed Sidney through a narrow hallway that led into a small lounge. As Sidney slumped into an armchair I quickly scanned the room. Against the far wall was a drinks cabinet containing mostly Spanish brands of liqueurs and brandies. There was a writing desk propped in the corner sporting an old Olivetti typewriter and reams of paper stacked neatly to its side. Sidney was sitting in one of the two high-backed armchairs that were placed either side of a large window that looked out onto the Palma road and the scorched landscape and hills that lay beyond.

The room was a little hot and musty. On the floor by each armchair were stacks of books, old magazines and newspapers. In the corner was an old television collecting dust that I guessed had not been used in years.

Sidney was still catching his breath after the climb up the stairs. 'Adam,' he said, his voice low and strained as he pointed to the hallway. 'In my bathroom above the sink there is a little bottle with yellow pills. Would you be so kind?'

I fetched him his pills and he swallowed two without water. 'I'm on all sorts of things these days,' he croaked. 'I must not hold you up dear boy, I know you have to catch your bus.' He gestured towards the desk holding his old typewriter. 'The document I would like you to post for me is in the right hand drawer.'

I found a large brown envelope and checked the hand written address. It was to Loudon House Publishing in Bedford Square, as before.

I was wondering to myself how I had ended up in Sidney's apartment and that the walk into Molinar was maybe not such a good idea. Sidney was, after all, a stranger to me and now I found myself doing him a rather dubious favour for the second time. But I was here now and might as well show some sort of empathy to the old boy. It wasn't going to hurt me. It was pretty clear that Sidney was lonely, and was trying to be generous in wanting to pay me for doing him a favour.

'Adam,' he said, his voice still hoarse. 'In the bottom drawer there is some money, please take whatever you wish. I really do insist on giving you something.'

'It's no problem Sidney,' I said, waving a dismissive hand to express that I would not take any cash. 'You don't have to pay me, and, by the way, you should not be so trusting with your money.'

He shrugged and shook his head sadly. 'I have reached the point where I have to take a chance on someone Adam, and considering you hardly know me, you have been more than kind.'

'I will post this for you when I get back,' I said. He looked tired and on the point of dropping off to sleep. I gently touched his shoulder and bade him farewell. 'You take it easy Sidney,' I said, and then quietly let myself out.

I got a couple of good bus connections back to my hotel and placed Sidney's large brown envelope in my travel bag.

After a quick shower and dinner at the hotel I made my way to the Illetas bar to watch a dismal England performance and their exit from the World Cup. I drank a little more than I had intended, but told myself that I had to raise my spirits after the England show and also it was my last night in Mallorca. All the same I felt guilty and admonished myself for drinking more than the strict limit I always imposed on myself. Back at my hotel when walking past the reception desk a young girl called after me. 'Excuse me sir,' she said with a nice smile. 'Are you Adam?' My first thought was that I might be asked to settle my bill as I was leaving early the next morning.

'We think this is for you. It came by taxi.' She handed me a small white envelope. On the front it simply said: 'By hand. Riu Palace hotel, Illetas,' and then my name.

'You are the only Adam staying here,' she said, still smiling.

I recognised the handwriting. It was from Sidney. 'Would you please sign for it?' she asked politely, while searching below the counter to find some sort of form, which was a problem, as she could not find something for this eventuality. After some rummaging she handed me a slip of paper that was for towel-hire and asked me to sign anywhere.

In my room I opened the letter. I pulled out a quantity of notes and counted them. Five hundred euros. Wow. I exhaled a loud whistle. I read the enclosed letter, which had been typed on Sidney's Olivetti.

Chapter Two

Dear Adam.

Please accept the enclosed money by way of a thank you for being so considerate towards me. Your acceptance will give me some comfort for taking up your time while you are on holiday. As I mentioned, I have to take a chance on someone and I hope that you might be that person. I know I have no right to ask this and if you should simply want to post my manuscript and forget that you had ever met me, then I will, of course, fully understand.

Perhaps you might like to read the manuscript that is now in your care and maybe follow it up once it has been delivered. I will leave this entirely up to you.

All I ask is that you keep my whereabouts to yourself. I beg you not to tell anyone where I am. In that respect I have a deep feeling that I can trust you.

(It's that old gamblers instinct in me and my final throw of the dice).

(The envelope is not sealed, just a clasp)

Give my love to London. Sidney (John)

I was feeling tired and just wanted to get to bed. I put the euros and the letter in my rucksack. It was too late to return the money, which he must have known, so I would just have to keep the cash, which would more than cover the cost of my holiday.

This was all a bit cloak and dagger stuff and that was a hell of a lot of money for a simple favour, but for now, I just wanted to get to bed, sleep off the drink, and be ready for my trip home in the morning.

Palma airport was very busy. I queued for a takeaway coffee, which made me late arriving at the boarding gate. This turned out to be a blessing as I quickly scurried past a couple of families who seemed to have about ten tearful infants in tow. I was relieved to find a seat at the back of the plane well away from those crying tots, as that noise and my hangover did not quite marry.

I made a welcome gesture to the lady sitting next to me who shot me a thin indifferent smile.

I arranged my bags under the seat and stared blankly at the Ryanair steward who was waving her arms and going through the flight safety procedures. She donned an inflatable vest and demonstrated how to blow on a whistle. I glanced round at the other passengers and could see that not a single person was taking a blind bit of notice of her.

Not surprising really, as I had recently read an amusing Bill Bryson article where he had pointed out that nobody in aviation history had ever been saved by one of these inflatable vests.

I checked on my reading material. I was about half way through the C.J. Sansom book and although I loved his novels I was feeling that this latest tale was being unnecessarily stretched out and I would never finish it on a two-hour flight.

In my travel bag was a copy of *The Times* tucked against Sidney's large brown envelope. I decided to read Sidney's papers and get them out of the way; after all he had paid me five hundred euros in the hope that I might do so.

I opened the clasp of the manila envelope and extracted about a dozen A4 sheets that had been typed on his Olivetti.

I settled back and started to read.

MY NAME IS RICHARD JOHN BINGHAM, SEVENTH
EARL OF LUCAN.

I slammed the papers down on my lap nearly knocking my coffee over Mrs strict women sitting next to me who gave me a hard agonised stare.

As the plane nosed into the sky I felt as though someone had punched me above the heart. Had I read that line of type wrong? I read it again. No mistake, that's what it said. I was utterly flabbergasted. Had Sidney gone a little potty in old age and being lonely? Was this some sort of joke or an attempt at a silly scam to lighten up his life?

It was crazy and I felt somewhat let down and bemused that he had sought to include me in such foolishness. I had liked him and couldn't believe this old chap was attempting to pull off something so silly and outlandish. It was not only outlandish, it was down right irresponsible and could land him in huge trouble.

I leaned back and tried to run this through my mind. He had struck me as a highly intelligent and dignified man and definitely not someone showing signs of madness. Or had he fooled me? Was he a very clever imposter or someone sadly deluded?

Did he really expect me to believe he was Lord Lucan?

That letter I had posted for him, and these papers were for a publishing house in up-market Bedford Square, not some dodgy PO Box in Tottenham Court Road and so how did he think he could convince a top-notch publisher that he was Lord Lucan if it was not true? Something was not adding up. This was all very eerie indeed.

My heart was beating fast. I picked up Sidney's papers and decided that I had to read his document. I started again at the beginning.

Chapter Three

THE STORY: PART ONE

MY NAME IS RICHARD JOHN BINGHAM, SEVENTH
EARL OF LUCAN.

Part One of my manuscript.

It is said that a story should have a beginning, a middle, and end.
  This is how I shall present my manuscript in order to give
a wider perspective of my life and to provide absolute clarity.
My story is not a nice one. It is a tragic tale of murder and lives
ruined – for which I am totally to blame.

PART ONE: Will be an outline of my early life: Eton College
and an introduction into the world of gambling, military
service, employment, relationships with my parents and my
social life and beliefs.

PART TWO: In this part I will outline the break-up of my
marriage, the court case relating to the custody of my children
and, for the first time, put on record the lead up to and the true
facts relating to the murder of Sandra Rivett.

PART THREE: Will be a full account of how I managed to escape,
who helped me, and my life thereafter.

For some time I have wished to tell my story and put the record
straight, and now, with failing health, the time has come to put
an end to all the wild speculation that has surrounded me for
over forty years.
  In doing so I would like to make it clear that I fully accept
my guilt and will in no way try to excuse my crimes. However,
I will endeavour to protect my friends and family from any

more hurt so must relate my story with a degree of care and prudence. This will in no way detract from the truth.

Some of the major players involved in my life, John Aspinall, Jimmy Goldsmith and Dominick Elwes, along with other dear friends are no longer alive but they have left behind loving families and I feel a responsibility not to cause further embarrassment to these people along with my own brother and sister, my wife, my three children and their children. Should there be a higher court than in this world then I realise that my escape from justice may simply have been a postponement for the inevitable punishment that may still await me.

It is to this court that I shall answer, for I do not intend to give myself up, stand trial amid a media circus, and end my days in prison, which at my age would serve no purpose and would only bring further distress to those associated with me. In any case, I am too old and unwell to undergo such an ordeal. Forty years of hiding and a dark conscience has taken its toll.

I have sent a letter prior to this manuscript which details certain events which I believe are indisputable proof that I am the person who I say I am.

Over the years much has been written and said about me as to what happened on the night of 7 November 1974, my life before then, and my subsequent disappearance. Most of the stories concerning me have either been vastly exaggerated, improbable, or more often, totally false. My intention is to correct all the many errors, theories and speculative tales written about me so that all parties can have closure as to the truth once and for all.

Furthermore, I wish to express my deep remorse for my actions all those years ago and put on record that it was for the love of my children and concern for their welfare that drove me down such grievous path.

However, and in no way trying to excuse myself, I would like to state that I made every effort through reasonable and legal means to rectify an impossible situation and that I was comprehensively let down by the judicial system.

Throughout the years I was able to obtain books, press stories, magazine articles and even a film about me. It has continued to amaze me how totally wrong the police and the media at large were about my actions. It has always been clear to me that even with certain evidence staring them in the face, the police and journalists alike, were totally unable to piece together some logical conclusions as to what actually happened on the night of 7 November 1974.

In my three part manuscript I intend to come clean and tell the whole truth about my gambling, my concerns for my children, the torment of my marriage and the events that led to murder at my house. I will explain exactly what took place on that terrible night and put on record how I managed to escape and evade justice for all these years.

PART ONE:
I was born at Marylebone, London, in December 1934.

My father was George Charles Patrick Bingham, 6th Earl of Lucan. My mother was Kaitlin Elizabeth Anne.

It goes without saying that I was born into a life of wealth and privilege, an advantage and responsibility that I shamefully failed to live up to.

During the Second World War my parents evacuated us children off to Canada and then on to America where we stayed until 1945. I was with my brother, Hugh, and my sisters, Jane and Sarah. In the States we stayed with Marcia Brady Tucker, a banking heiress. It was a taste of wealth and luxury that few children would ever experience.

We had our own house at Marcia's summer estate at Mount Kisco, Winchester, complete with servants to look after us. In this vast estate were tennis courts, swimming pools and magical woodlands and lakes where we explored and played. During the summer I was sent to the Adirondacks for summer camp. In the winter we stayed at Marcia's grand residence on Park Avenue, New York. Marcia also had properties scattered around Florida and owned an ocean going yacht.

Our time in America was a far cry from what was happening in Europe and that world of wealth and luxury cast a lasting impression on my young mind.

Back in England I went to Arnold House prep school in London before following in my fathers footsteps and attending Eton College. It was here, between Greek and Latin lessons, that I developed a passion for gambling, which would turn into a lifelong addiction.

I must take time out to speak of my stay at Eton for it was here that my gambling habit took root and led me to believe that betting could be an exciting career path and would serve me well throughout my life.

At first, myself and fellow Etonians, played games for fun and the simple reward of trying to win and being perceived as a smart player. We played bridge, poker and backgammon quite happily, until one day, and taking a lead from some of the older boys, we slipped into the habit of giving these pastimes a volatile edge and playing for money. Now these games took on an entirely new dimension with the tension and thrill that goes with the chance that you might lose your weeks spending allowance or, if you were fortunate, improve your finances.

It was my first entry into the world of betting and after some dreadful and embarrassing losses I decided that these setbacks should act simply as a lesson to me and that gambling was not some frivolous game of chance but something that had to be studied and taken seriously. To be a good gambler, I told myself, was an undertaking that you had to work hard at. Much harder than any Greek or Latin lessons which I decided would have to take a backseat. I read everything I could about strategy and probability on games like backgammon and poker. As time went by and pursuing every chance to learn more about tactics and systems I slowly became a better player and what were once depressing losing encounters with my fellow pupils now gradually turned into winning sessions.

Between lessons my chosen field of study was the psychology of gaming. I trained myself to remember a sequence of cards, to employ maximum concentration, but, and most importantly, to appreciate fully the law of probability.

Foolishly, I had determined that for me gambling was not to be a pastime, but a profession, and while others might leave Eton to study engineering or the law I would immerse myself in a much more exciting and, hopefully, profitable occupation.

Around this time I became aware of a fellow gambler at Eton whom I must speak of in detail, for he would become a major player in my story. He was a year older than me and in a different house and although I never actually spoke to him it was clear that he had gained something of a reputation. His name was James Goldsmith, the son of a Jewish banking family that had fled France on the last overloaded ship to get away when the Nazis invaded the country. An act that probably saved their lives.

Chapter Three

Goldsmith's father, Frank, who's business empire had been rivals to the Rothschilds, changed the family name from the German Goldschmidt to Goldsmith. Apart from banking the family had owned hotels and property in France that they had been forced to leave behind and so by the time Jimmy Goldsmith started out in business there was little left of the family fortune.

Although I did not know it at the time our lives would later be inextricably linked and he would become a good and loyal friend to me.

Jimmy was handsome, well-built, and very much the leader of those that flocked to his circle. He was cocksure and possessed a confidence that belied his age. He also liked to gamble and by all accounts was a skilled backgammon and poker player. Jimmy also took horse racing bets from the lads that he relayed to a bookmaker in London and, it was said, sometimes kept the wagers himself in the hope that they would be losing bets and thus pocket the money himself. A sideline that I soon involved myself with.

These gambling instincts and acts of bravado were to be the hallmark of his incredible success in the world of business that awaited him.

Just before he left Eton his stock was to rise to an all time high. Jimmy invited a group of students to go racing with him at Lewes and it was here that he won a small fortune by backing three horses to win a treble bet.

They all won at good prices and he milked the occasion to the full. His entourage celebrated with much champagne and free bets paid for by his windfall. It seemed he could do no wrong, that he had the Midas touch which marked him out from others.

Many years later while dining with him at the Clermont Club he confessed to me that his winnings that day at Lewes had been highly exaggerated and not really the bet of the century that he had proclaimed. Certainly, he had hit a treble, but as he explained to me he had wagered on lots of trebles that day in various permutations and so there was a good chance that one of them would come in. That was how the young James Goldsmith operated, he wanted to impress, to have people look up to him. It was desirable that people perceived him as someone who was naturally lucky.

He would later employ similar tactics in business and relationships to get what he wanted. To Jimmy, gambling was just one way of making money, but even at that young age he knew that on its own it would never be enough. He would also have to venture into the jungle of trade if he wanted to gain the influence and riches that he had set his sights on.

The staff at Eton did not take to him and regarded him as an arrogant ne'er-do-well who was unappreciative of the privilege bestowed on him, but then Jimmy disliked the masters as much as they disliked him.

He was a free spirit, a sort of rootless person. Half German Jew, half French Catholic. The ritual and long history of Eton meant very little to him. His Jewish family had settled in countries and built up businesses only to have to flee and start all over again in another country. Thus he was aware that historic roots to a particular place and patriotism did not apply to him at that time in his life – something the staff at Eton never really understood.

There was one little cross that I had to bear while at Eton which invariably came as a jibe from a pupil that I had relieved of his cash at backgammon or poker. It was that my great-great-grandfather the 3rd Earl of Lucan had given the fateful order for the Charge of the Light Brigade at the Battle of Balaclava and thus into the Valley of Death as later immortalised by the poet Tennyson. I always responded to these insults by stating that my ancestor in question was a very brave soldier, carrying out a command to attack, and despite the debacle of Balaclava was respected to the extent that he was promoted many times after the battle, eventually gaining the rank of field marshal.

Sad to say, that some 160 years later, myself, the 7th Earl of Lucan, would attract considerably more adverse publicity than was ever levelled at the 3rd Earl.

In the summer months the gamblers amongst us would skip lessons and make the small trek over to Windsor Racecourse. It was at this venue I developed a lifelong passion for the turf. I loved these days out. The sport of kings was so colourful and exciting. The jockeys' silks, jugs of Pimm's served from tents on the lawns and the unique sound of horses hooves pounding towards the winning post. We were probably under age to gamble but the bookmakers were prepared to turn a blind-eye and take our money. It was at the Windsor races I promised myself that one day I would own a racehorse and stand in the

privileged area of the paddock before a race chatting to my
jockey and trainer. A dream that I would later realise.

In 1953 I once again followed in my fathers footsteps and joined
the Coldstream Guards, the oldest regiment in the Regular
Army. Because of my family connections I was accepted
without question.

I enjoyed my three years with the Guards as a Second
Lieutenant and for the first time in my life settled into a
regime and discipline that I had not known before.

We were posted to Krefeld in West Germany, where the
British Army of the Rhine was stationed as a defence against
the Soviet threat. I witnessed the re-building of the country
after the ravages of war and the desire of the people to distance
themselves from the past and create a new and democratic
land. There were many Regiments serving in Germany in this
cold war era and I never felt any hostility by the German
people towards us and, if anything, they seemed happy with
our presence.

The discipline and way of life with the Guards should have
been a platform for me to follow later in life, but sadly, the
gambling instincts that had gripped me from my time at Eton
were never far from my thoughts.

In our leisure time we enjoyed small poker sessions and some
of the Guards were also keen on gambling at backgammon.

Of course I was only too pleased to join in with whatever
wagering was taking place but it was clear that I had an
advantage over my fellow soldiers who, unlike me, had never
spent their days studying the strategy of betting. I wanted to
play to keep my hand in but rather than divulge myself as
something of a technician I would deliberately lose games and
keep my friendships intact. As soldiers, we all shared a sense of
closeness and camaraderie and for me to win too often would
have gone against the grain and alienated me from my
colleagues.

After my time with the Guards I decided that I needed some
independence from the strictures that had been my life at Eton
and then the military.

I rented a flat in Wilton Place, my very first home, and for
the first time in my life felt completely liberated. It was also a

time to see more of my family and I spent many weekends with my parents at their weekend retreat in Essex.

My father and I would play golf and go for long ambling walks. At this time my father was interested in what career I intended to pursue but when I explained that I wanted some time to myself and maybe travel a little he was understanding and did not try to put any pressure on me.

My father, despite his wealth and title, was a socialist with a regard and concern for the less well off in society. He joined the labour party under Clement Attlee and was later opposition chief whip in the House of Lords for ten years, a position he held up until his death.

He served in two world wars with distinction and in 1918 was awarded the Military Cross. Along with many others in the Labour Party including Hugh Gaitskell he sent messages of support to anti-apartheid activists kept under house arrest in South Africa. He supported the integration of foreign students into British Society and spoke out against the bad housing conditions that affected so many people. He wanted to see a more equal society and would take every opportunity to speak up for the working classes.

My mother was also a socialist and a member of the Labour Party and was probably more left wing in her beliefs than my father.

I believe their political affiliations had brought them together in the first place.

My parents shunned away from exhibiting any signs of wealth or title. As children our summer holidays were pretty basic and unexciting and my father would not replace his old car that had a leaking roof. My mother who seemed to be embarrassed by her title and standing in society stubbornly refused to indulge in any spending on herself that might be deemed extravagant.

Many years later I was to learn that my mother, when she was not delivering Labour Party pamphlets, was studying Russian in her spare time. (Waiting for the revolution as my friend Bill Shand Kydd, saucily quipped).

On those country walks with my father he related to me why he believed in socialism.

He had spent a great deal of his life with soldiers from all different walks of life. They had served and supported each other, regardless of class or background. In conflict all men are equal with a responsibility to help each other, he explained. An exploding shell or a bullet had no regard as to whom its intended victim might be. The fear of being carried away on a stretcher was the same for all men, be you an earl or a coal miner.

He also told me that the brave working class soldiers returning from the First World War were treated badly by their country with slum housing and mass unemployment.

This, he told me, had left an indelible mark on his thinking and he had thereafter believed it his moral duty to support a movement that would make Britain a more equal and fair society.

My father, whilst not wanting to push me in any direction, politically or otherwise, was concerned that his eldest son should not end up being what he called 'one of the idle rich.' He believed the title he had inherited, and which would eventually pass down to me, bore with it an obligation of duty, and that like him and past earls, I would carry on the Lucan tradition of responsibility and earnest endeavour.

Of course I understood my fathers wishes that I would be a good role model and not abuse the privilege that I had been born into. But having served three years in the military I wanted to enjoy my new found freedom and taste the finer aspects of life.

With some of the ex-Guards and old friends from Eton we arranged racing days out. There were plenty of courses near London like Sandown, Ascot, Lingfield and the soon to be defunct, Alexandra Palace.

After the races we would head back to town for dinner and invariably end up in Soho for drinks at little private clubs we had discovered.

We always made a rule that whoever had been successful on the horses would bear the brunt of the expenses, an arrangement that acted as a sort of insurance for those who had lost their money at the races. A redistribution of wealth as my father might aptly have put it.

It was at one of these race-days that I met Caroline my first real affair. She was a bubbly blonde, the daughter of a prominent Harley Street doctor. We both had our own places and enjoyed the freedom of living independently. We partied together, had weekends away and liked each other's company.

However, Caroline had ideas of marriage and children which was, and something she accepted, the last thing on my mind at that time in my life. We parted on friendly terms, so much so, that I was a guest at her wedding some two years later.

After Caroline, I had a few fleeting affairs but they were no more than that for I was spending most of my leisure time either at the races or wagering with Old Etonians and like-minded gamblers at various houses that arranged poker evenings.

In the Autumn of that year I travelled to Paris with a plan to broaden my gambling horizons and test my skills on a higher level in the Paris casinos. I had a limited amount of money at this time and in any case there were rules on how much cash you could take out of the country so I planned to be careful, bet small, and learn as much as I could. I had no interest in roulette, which is a game that has no skill attached to it and is simply a lottery that I have never played, or wanted to play. I knew blackjack was a popular casino game and that the good players would always employ an underlying strategy of knowing when to hold or whether to ask for another card depending on what the dealer was showing.

I had read everything I could about the game and together with the mental practice I had taught myself over the years felt prepared to pit my wits against the house and see how I would fare.

But the game that I really wanted to play was baccarat, chemin-de-fer, the game immortalised by Ian Fleming in his very first novel *Casino Royale*.

Later in life I would make friends with Ian at the Clermont where we would pit our wits against each other at backgammon. I had loved reading *Casino Royale* with the all or nothing high stakes battle at the baccarat table between Bond and the powerful soviet agent Le Chiffre.

However, it would be another, little known Fleming short story that I would read much later which would have a profound affect on my thinking and confirm to me the utter hopelessness of my situation and prompt me to make such a shocking decision.

In the Paris casinos I did reasonably well, winning just enough to pay my expenses before moving on to Deauville.

Chapter Three

Here, I booked into a cheap hotel and then familiarised myself with the town and its casinos.

At this time, Deauville, with its racecourse, marinas, villas, and top class hotels was regarded as one of the most prestigious resorts in all of France and the closest seaside town when coming from Paris.

Deauville had staunchly held firm to its rich history of being the most fashionable resort outside the southern Riviera and had always attracted the wealthy international upper classes and high stakes gamblers. I was determined to pit my wits against them.

I spent my evenings at the wonderful Casino Barriére de Deauville and it was here, amid the sumptuous elegance of brass-studded leather, chandeliers and croupiers in immaculate suits that I first played baccarat.

The atmosphere inside the Casino Barriére was heady and intoxicating. The clientele were immaculately attired, the waiters wore green baize aprons that matched the colour of the playing tables. This is where the fabulously wealthy hung out and only champagne and gin martinis seemed to be the drinks of choice.

I felt a dizzy sense of home and belonging. I played baccarat for two nights and came out even but it was the experience and thrill of the casino world and that particular card game that so caught my imagination.

Back home in London I was quickly brought down to earth. My father, through a friend of a friend, had arranged an interview for me at a merchant bank in the City. Of course I had to go for the interview to appease my parents but I was pretty sure they would not employ me as I knew absolutely nothing about City Institutions and had no interest whatsoever in working for a bank.

To my surprise they took me on at £2,000 per annum. It was an old school tie thing and perhaps they considered that a future earl would be a nice addition to the board at some later date. I stayed with William Brandt's for three years and was reasonably good at the job as I had a good head for figures and an awareness of risk.

During this period I was flitting between my parents home in St. John's Wood and my own flat in Wilton Place. My gambling habits had been somewhat curtailed as for the first time in my life I was having to hold down a job and also keep my parents happy.

My main entertainment during my time at Brandt's was greyhound racing. Along with friends from the bank we would go racing at Harringay and White City. It was great fun and an escape from the world of banking and finance.

Harringay was Monday and Friday nights after which we would make our way back to town for drinks and dinner. I loved the gritty atmosphere of dog racing and Harringay attracted a fascinating cross section of the gambling fraternity. I was so taken by the sport that I bought a couple of greyhounds from a trainer who had a yard near Epping Forest. Whenever they ran he would tell me whether they were worth a bet or not. This was the only way an owner could get some sort of return because the prize money for winning a race was almost non-existent.

This little escape into the world of greyhound racing was wonderful fun and cost me very little as myself and friends managed to win some good bets when my trainer gave me the nod for one of my dogs.

However, and on a higher level, the memories of the enchanting atmosphere at the Casino Barriére de Deauville were never far from my thoughts.

In the Spring of 1958 I returned to Deauville with a plan to play baccarat for fairly large stakes and see where it would take me. By now I had accumulated a fair bit of money from my job at Brandt's and wanted to test my skills at the highest level.

I stayed in Deauville for a couple of days before moving on to La Touquet, a quieter and less glamorous town than Deauville.

On my first night playing at the historic Casino du Palais I was up 14,000 francs. The following night it seemed I could do no wrong and hit some wonderful coups. My tactics were to always take a third card if I was holding five or less and this turned out to be very lucky for me.

The chances of bettering or worsening your hand with a count of five are mathematically about even. But my luck was holding up on virtually every hand where I used this tactic.

At two in the morning I signalled to the chef-de-partie that I wished to cash out. The croupier raked in my chips and skilfully clicking his fingers arranged five neat columns of high denomination plaques which he slid across the green baize towards me. I had won over twenty thousand pounds. I was hooked for life and would henceforth acquire the inappropriate tag of 'Lucky Lucan.'

It is widely believed that the Casino du Palais was the venue that had inspired the setting that Ian Fleming used for his casino at the fictional Normandy town of Royale-les-Eaux.

Among many of the crazy stories attributed to me was that I had been screen-tested by 'Cubby' Broccoli for the role of 007. I did meet 'Cubby' many times at the Clermont and we got on very well and he once jokingly remarked that I had the demeanour of a Foreign Office Diplomat. But I was never offered any acting role and this was just another silly myth that journalists seemed to revel in.

As I left the casino that night with a surge of adrenaline running through me I could not help but feel a little like Mr Bond.

I had won enough money to change the course of my life and now was the time to enjoy myself and break away from the drudgery of the bank and fog-ridden winters in London. The plan was to spend some time in the Caribbean. Snorkel, play golf, take up sailing and generally behave as what my father might describe as one of the idle rich.

At this time there were two things I would relinquish – my rented flat in Wilton Place as I now intended to travel, and my job at William Brandt's.

With a few friends that I had met through the banking world we set out to explore the high life.

We spent a few weeks island hopping in the Caribbean including the aptly named Lucayan Archipelago. We played golf, hired speedboats and, of course, played poker in the evenings where we would try to entice others to join in our games. From the Bahamas we ended up in San Francisco where we hired a car and slowly motored our way down the West Coast spending time at places that took our fancy.

My friends, at various times had to return home and back to their professions in London until the last of our band, my uncle, left me to my own devices in Florida.

I enjoyed Florida immensely and rented an apartment in Pompano Beach. Here I spent my days sea fishing off the main pier and my evenings at the various bars and clubs scattered around the beach area. It was easy to make friends in this holiday fun town and there were quite a few attractive women who seemed strangely taken by my English accent.

While in the States I took the opportunity to travel to New York and meet up with my elder sister and our former guardian Marcia Tucker who had cared for us children during the war. Marcia was a multi-millionairess and treated me like a long lost son. I stayed with her in the lap of luxury for a while before meeting up and spending some time with my sister. New York had become my second home and I enjoyed everything about this great city. But with the savage winter about to descend I flew back to Florida and the sunshine and where I felt equally at home.

I returned to England in early 1959 and rented a nice flat in Park Crescent, opposite Regents Park.

England seemed dull and the weather was poor but I felt a responsibility to stay close to my parents and give the impression that I was soon to settle down and be employed in a meaningful profession.

While I had been away in Florida, Marcia had sourced a couple of oil paintings for me as a present, which she had shipped to my parents for safekeeping. She had enclosed a letter for me saying the paintings were by English artists and that they would prove to be a good investment.

It did not take me long once back in London to pick up the threads of the social gambling I had embroiled myself in before my travels and I was soon back with friends playing poker, bridge and backgammon.

In the summer of that year, at one of these poker evenings, a friend told me of a new and exclusive world of gambling that had been slowly evolving in the upper-tier of London society. The game was baccarat, chemin-de-fer. This most seductive game, which had been most lucky for me was being hosted with sumptuous aplomb at prestigious locations by a certain John Aspinall.

It did not take me long to gain an invite to one of these chemmy events that were taking place at a house in Eaton Place, and it was here that I met John Aspinall for the first time.

Although I had never set eyes on him before, John greeted me like a long lost friend and told me that I was most welcome. The chemistry between us was immediate. Aspers, (as he was known), would become one of the best friends that I ever had.

Chapter Three

He was the most remarkably talented and complex person that one could imagine.

No longer did I have to hop over the channel to feed my addiction for chemin-de-fer. I had found John Aspinall and John Aspinall had found me.

At these chemmy evenings I would go on to meet, and befriend, Dominick Elwes, Mark Birley and Jimmy Goldsmith. Along with John Aspinall we would later become known as the 'Clermont Set,' a term coined by the national press. Also I got to know Ian Maxwell-Scott, a lifelong friend of Aspers and an expert on food and vintage wines. Often the gambling would stop while Ian laid out tables for the guests to enjoy the very best cuisine he had carefully sourced. Ian and his wife Susan would become very good friends of mine. Added to the culinary delights and fine wine on offer were very special game pies cooked by Aspinall's mother who, like Ian, was a lover of good food.

It was strange that Ian, later to be a Clermont director, was not labelled one of the 'Clermont Set,' for he was Aspinall's inspiration and right-hand man and very much part of that inner circle.

Aspers chemmy soirées were attracting wealthy high rollers who were prepared to gamble on a scale that I had not come across before in London and many of them were reckless players who relied solely on luck, and if luck should desert them they would simply fall back on the excuse that fortune was not with them but the following evening would be different. Of course you cannot win all the time at chemmy, but by and large these events proved a happy hunting ground for me.

My bank accounts continued to be healthy and stable, which enabled me to pursue a certain type of lifestyle.

Between 1959 and 1963 my life was independent, carefree and indulgent. There was the winter sports – bobsleighing and skiing, in Austria and Switzerland. Also I was a keen sailor and had purchased a nice powerboat, White Migrant, that was moored at Hamble near Southampton, and which I raced at every opportunity. I also indulged in my passion for horse racing, both over the jumps and the flat and I bought my first horse, a lovely grey mare, picked up quite cheaply from a trainer friend.

There was also now a whole host of gentlemen's clubs that had sprung up in Mayfair with the relaxation of the gaming laws and betting shops had come into existence.

Of course my lifestyle did not sit well with my socialist parents and my visits to see them diminished over the years. My father had, quite reasonably, enquired how I was able to finance such an expensive way of life. When I told him that I was a proficient gambler and had won a lot of money at La Touquet he was horrified. In his book, to gain rewards in such a way was not much better than robbing a bank. To him, it was unearned and undeserved income and gambling was no more than a capitalist enterprise whose ultimate purpose was to relieve the poor and foolish of their cash.

However, the big problem with my parents was their odd political views. The way I saw it, they were supporting a party that would happily do away with their standing and titles with no regard to the centuries of tradition and service that my father, the 6th Earl, and all those before him had contributed to the history of the country. Without wanting to be unkind to them, I thought their affiliations were deluded and that the very party they were supporting would come back and bite them. They were supporting a system that would, logically, lead to their demise.

What they believed in, and how I thought, were totally at odds. I had once tried to explain to them that in my view wealth and prosperity could only come from the top down. This view did no more than provoke an argument. When meeting my parents I had to keep my politics to myself for fear of alienating myself from them further.

However, I have to state that I loved my parents dearly and they were always kind and supportive to me, which was much more than I deserved.

Aside from the differences with my parents, life was pretty good for me in these early years.

Having said that, there was one very important thing still missing. I was approaching 30 years of age and I wanted to have children and fulfil my duty and, hopefully, have a son that would carry on the Lucan line.

Chapter Three

To this end, fate was to play a massive part in my life. My dear friend, Bill Shand Kydd, had invited me to a golf club function in Surrey. However, on the night in question I had also been invited to an art preview in Chelsea. I was not over keen about either invitation as there was a bridge competition that very same evening at the Portland Club.

I decided to spin a coin. Heads I would go to the golf club party, tails it would be the art preview in Chelsea.

The coin could have come down tails in which case my life might have taken a totally different direction and you would probably not be reading this, or indeed have ever heard of me.

But the coin came down heads, and so it would be the golf club party. It was here, whilst mingling with the guests, a glass of champagne in hand, and making small talk about golf handicaps that Bill Shand Kydd took my arm and introduced me to his pretty sister-in-law and, as it would transpire, my future wife – Veronica Duncan.

signed

Richard John Bingham

January 2014. part 1/3

Chapter Four

Once back home to my flat in north London I propped Sidney's document on top of a kitchen worktop where it could continually hold my eye in all its strangeness. I was wracked by indecision. I wondered whether to tell someone about this as I was feeling shocked and bemused. It was very spooky and possibly menacing. My mind was in a whirl trying to decide whether I should treat the manuscript as genuine or not. And if it should turn out to be true, what the hell then?

For the moment I was unable to think straight. This was way over my head and too disturbing for me to take in. I needed time, a lot of time, to work out what to make of this incredible story.

I resolved not to rush into anything, I had all the time in the world. There was no need for me to do anything quickly, no need to jump to conclusions or make a hasty decision. Let the problem lie for a few days. Wait for my senses and nerves to settle down and then I would decide what to do – if anything.

It was hard, but I determined to close my mind-off completely from the mystery and just get on with my life until I felt able to think straight and give the matter some clear-headed reasoning.

I got down to some issues I had to deal with. Mail to sort out as well as messages left on my answering machine. Also there were a number of e-mails waiting for a reply regarding the sale of my mum's house, which was dragging on and proving to be awkward.

One of the messages was from a committee member at my tennis club asking if I would meet him to discuss the possible sale of the club with some land developers. I had been a member of Swan Park Tennis Club for about thirty years. The club had been built from scratch by the original members after losing their first home when the lease expired. A plot of land was purchased in Whetstone for a risible sum and a brand new club arose out of nothing. The members chipped in with various skills and with the help of a builder created a new club with three courts and a clubhouse.

When the club opened in the early sixties a constitution was drawn up stating that the club would be owned by a few shareholders but with some eighty per cent of the shares going to the members, who would own the club.

When all this was being drawn up, nobody could have foreseen that land prices would rocket in London. The developers told us they were willing to offer four million pounds for the freehold.

If the club accepted this offer then the members would come into a small fortune, and this was more than tempting as the club had been in terminal decline for many years and attracted few keen players.

A sale would not be easy though, as some members were intent on saving the club despite the fact that the place was falling apart. Many others would be more than ready to cash in. Eventually it would have to go to a vote, but in the meantime the politics and arguments about greed and money grabbing would rumble on.

While I had been away my garden, which I had ignored for months, had gone mad and looked sadly disowned and jungle like. I braced myself for some hard work and decided to spend a few days getting it back into shape.

Lone gardening proved to be just what I needed. Perhaps it's being close to nature that allows your mind to slow down and relax. After a couple of days of backbreaking work I was feeling pleased with how nice it was coming along. As I had hacked away mercilessly at weeds and overgrown shrubs my thoughts and jitters as what to do with that incredible manuscript had settled and I felt a little more confident with myself about making a decision.

Did that envelope hold the identity of Lord Lucan? Could it possibly be? The thought still made me shudder but I had decided to keep this to myself for the present as getting advice from others and perhaps being ridiculed about the affair would only confuse me more.

I had come to the gradual conclusion that the manuscript had to be one of three things. It could be a load of nonsense by a lonely deluded man. A very intricate hoax or con trick, or it might be genuine. It had to be one of those three. But there was something fundamentally odd about the whole affair. If it was a hoax then it was very, very clever indeed.

I had met Sidney twice now and chatted with him at length. I had even been to his apartment, seen the way he lived, collected pills for him from his bathroom. He in no way came across as a trickster or someone who had gone a little potty. That, or I am someone who is easily fooled. Whatever the truth, I could not escape the fact that I was gripped by curiosity. Could it possibly be that Sidney really was the missing earl? He had an air about him and certainly sounded the part.

Returning home from my local one evening, some four days after reading Sidney's manuscript, I lit a cigarette and gazed at that big manila envelope that was staring back at me on the kitchen worktop. After days of considered thought I had decided there were just two options open to me. I could simply post the document and forget all about it. Then as time went by Sidney would realise that I had not been hooked and would no doubt look out for another Englishman to come into his sphere at the Café Plaza and try his luck again. But then I might spend the rest of my life wondering if, by some miracle, I had really encountered Lord Lucan.

The second option was to let curiosity take over. To follow up that document and try to discover if there was any truth in all this. I would have to be very careful though, and not act naively if I wanted to unburden my mind from what killed the cat. If by some chance this story was true then it had to be remembered that the man in question is wanted for murder. On the other hand if this was a scam I could be in big trouble for having anything to do with it. No matter what the truth might be, one thing was for sure, I would be taking a huge risk if I was to involve myself in this affair.

Nevertheless I decided on the second option.

I drove out of my postal district and posted the manuscript. I had to be careful and cover my tracks. Nobody had any idea who I was – and that's the way I intended to keep it.

It had darkly crossed my mind that maybe it was me that was the target of some clever sting. Get me interested, string me along, make me believe it's all true and then set some sort of trap. It was a remote possibility. I had told Sidney where I was staying in Illetas, and that hotel would have all my details – my name, address, everything.

Hotels are not supposed to give out details of their guests but with computer hacking these days anything is possible. I had to watch my back and be aware.

A couple of days after posting the document I took the tube into town and meandered into Covent Garden. I wanted to buy a mobile phone, as I did not intend to use my own.

I found a phone shop and asked for the cheapest model they stocked. I knew they had one for about thirty pounds but the sales assistant directed me to their latest smart phones and went into raptures about the new Xperia M2 with back and front cameras and video and a host of things I did not want. I thanked him and asked for the basic pay as-you-go model. But sir, the sales assistant rattled on, 'the M2 has Sony technology.' 'Thanks,' I said, 'but I'll have that bog standard one.' He refused to look me in the eye as he bundled the cheap device into a bag and shoved it towards me with an abject sigh. I resisted the urge to be rude back to him for it seemed I had already ruined his day.

I was going to phone Loudon House Publishing, but was not going to use my own mobile and risk they capture my phone number. I had to be on my guard. They might simply tell me to get lost and put the phone down on me. On the other hand if this was a scam, then they might try to lure me into the hands of the police. If I smelt a rat I would quickly end the call. If I was careful I had nothing to lose and the exercise would settle my curiosity once and for all.

On the corner of Charing Cross Road I popped into a Ladbrokes betting shop and unpacked my new mobile. While there I had a tenner on a Mick Channon trained horse that failed to come out of the stalls. Not a good omen.

Outside the Ladbrokes shop I went down a side alley away from the traffic noise. I phoned the publishing house.

Chapter Four

A chirpy female voice answered.

'Can I speak to Warren?' I said.

'Who's calling?' she asked briskly. 'He doesn't know me,' I replied. 'It's to do with a document he received by post from Mr Bingham.'

'Ingham, did you say?' she enquired.

'No, Bingham,' I said.

After a long pause came a loud voice. 'Warren here,' the voice cracked. 'What do you want? What's all this about?'

'You don't know me,' I said calmly, 'It's regarding a document from Mr Bingham.'

'I gathered that! Who the devil are you?' he demanded angrily.

'My name is Adam,' I said, trying to keep cool but feeling an edge of panic in my voice. 'I'm simply a messenger. I posted that document for him, and out of pure curiosity I thought I would give you a call to see what you thought about it.'

There was another bellowing. 'Well you can tell that old bastard if it really is him that he's come to the wrong address.' The voice was aggressive and loud as he blustered on in the same rude tone. 'That letter he sent to my father scared the shit out of him, made him ill. Bloody dangerous, bloody irresponsible.'

I resisted the urge to ring off as he blasted on, swearing and his temper rising.

'How do you know this person? What the hell is he up to?' Then, after a seconds pause, he barked coldly. 'And what's your role in all this? What are you after?'

I still kept calm but my hand was sweating on the mobile and I was wondering how it was that I had not ended the call by now. 'As I say,' I repeated, but with a little more emphasis in my tone. 'I'm just the delivery guy. I don't really know him. I've only met him a couple of times on holiday when he asked me to post that letter and then the manuscript, which by the way, I read with utter astonishment.'

'I bet you did,' he snapped. 'Where is he?'

'I only know him as Sidney and he has asked me to keep his whereabouts a secret.'

'So you're not going to say where he's holing up?' he asked bluntly.

'Not right now,' I said with a slightly rising confident tone. 'His health is not good and I've no desire to get him into trouble.'

'Well listen to me,' he said, the edge in his voice easing off slightly, 'I don't know what this Sidney is up to but you can tell him from me that if he thinks we can print that stuff then he's off his rocker. If he really is still knocking around and we had anything to do with him the authorities would come down on us like a ton of bricks. The bloke we are talking about is wanted for murder.'

Despite all this shouting at me I was prepared to stay calm and not end the call as this dialogue was not going quite the way I had been ready for. I had told myself to be careful if there was any hint that this was a hoax but the tone of this conversation was not heading that way and not once had Warren tried to dismiss the story.

'As I say, Warren,' I said, keeping my voice level as a direct repost to his rudeness. 'I assure you that I contacted you in good faith. I'm sorry to have troubled you.' My lowering voice gave the clear impression that I was about to end the call when he suddenly barked back at me urgently.

'Wait, wait. Don't ring off whatever you do. I need to talk to you. There could be something in this. My father says that letter is genuine and could only have come from one person. Mind you, I can't go overboard on what he says, as my father is not the whole pack of cards these days. We have to meet. I need to explain our position to you. This is a very delicate and dodgy situation. Can you come to my office?'

I baulked at this suggestion, especially as he sounded so arrogant and rude. My head was spinning. I needed to think quickly. I had planned making this call with care, making sure that I did not get myself into trouble, but I had not really thought how I would handle things if the conversation sounded positive.

'I'm not happy with that idea,' I said. My heart was beating fast and Sidney's face suddenly flashed up in my mind. There had been no talk of deception and so it was a possibility Sidney was telling the truth, and if that was the case, bizarre as it might be, then it was me who was now in the driving seat.

'Meet me on the steps of the National Gallery at twelve noon tomorrow.' I did not give him a chance to answer and ended the call.

I had no worries that he might arrive with the police, the conversation had not gone like that, and in any case, I had told him that I was just a messenger, which was the truth. As it stood nothing much could be laid at my door.

In any case it was a risk I was willing to take. I had now involved myself in a mystery and would stick with it so long as I could remain safely anonymous and try and find out if this crazy story was true.

The one person taking the biggest risk and a staggering gamble was Sidney. He was taking the punt of his life that I would not 'shop' him, that I would not tell the publishing company where he was living or contact the police. It was clear that he had decided to take a big chance on me. He was lucky, I had no intention of throwing him to the wolves, no matter whether he was deluded, or a clever hoaxer – which

I was now thinking he might not be. But I was confused and totally unsure what to think.

I arrived early at the National Gallery. At the top of the steps I leaned over the balcony wall and took in the scene below. Trafalgar Square was its usual buzzing self. Hundreds of tourists mingled with the street performers and pavement artists. The weather was typically English summer, a light blustery drizzle was interspersed with fleeting glimpses of hopeful rays of brightness that intermittently flashed across the Square.

I saw a chunky guy climbing the steps, he had a swagger about him and I knew it was him. He was casually dressed in a three quarter length coat over a crew neck sweater, jeans and brogue shoes. I walked towards him. His piercing eyes scanned me up and down.

'Adam?' he said bluntly. I nodded. 'Lets not talk here,' he said brusquely. He turned quickly on his heels and I followed him, darting through the crowds across the square to a pub on the corner of St. Martins Lane. It was quiet inside the cavernous lounge. 'What's yours?' he asked, without looking at me.

'Lager,' I said.

With pints in hand we settled at a table in the far corner of the bar.

He took a big gulp of his beer and eyed me coldly and cautiously. He was stocky with a wide ruddy-red face, small eyes and sharp thin lips. I guessed he was in his mid forties. He reminded me of a posh country type, the sort that sit proudly upright on a horse holding a stirrup cup before setting out on a fox hunt. I braced myself to be on my guard with this guy.

'I wanted to speak to you to explain our position,' he said with an air of determined authority. We eyed each other for a little while before he continued. 'You told me you just posted stuff for this man. Is that correct?' he said, looking me hard in the eye.

I had made my mind up to stay calm and cool while speaking to Warren and that I would keep my voice low and casual and not allow him to get on top of me. After all it was him who wanted to speak to me. Also I was the only one who had met the mysterious Sidney and I was the only one who knew where he could be found.

'That's right,' I replied in a steady voice. 'He introduced himself to me at a café while I was on holiday telling me his name was Sidney and asking if he could talk to me for a while. He told me that he was English, originally from London. The man came across as being very charming and polite. We talked about London life and sports and things like gambling and horse racing. He told me that he kept in touch with events back home by reading the English newspapers.

I took a good drink of beer and settled myself to tell the story plain and simple.

'Anyway, he asked me if I would post a letter for him when I got back to London. I wasn't particularly happy about this and asked him why he couldn't send it himself.'

Warren took a long gulp of beer and then leaned towards me, 'Is that right you won't say where he is?' he asked snappily.

'I'd rather not say at the moment.' I said. 'He asked me not tell anyone of his whereabouts. If this man is who he is claiming to be you can see why, can't you?'

Warren cocked an eyebrow. 'You bet I can,' he said loftily, leaning back in his chair sporting a sly knowing smile.

'So, go on,' he said, with a note of mischief and a wave of his hand.

'Anyway,' I continued, determined not to get flustered. 'I did post the letter for him and then forgot all about it.

A couple of months later I bumped into him again at the same café. He looked a little weary but told me how pleased he was to see me again. We talked for a while and he then asked me if I would post the document you have. He insisted on giving me some money for the favour, which I refused. I had told him where I was staying and that I was returning to London the next day. I collected the document from his apartment. That night a letter arrived at my hotel.'

I took the letter out from my pocket and handed it to Warren who read it greedily.

'He enclosed five hundred euros,' I added casually. I noticed a sudden steely intensity in Warren's eyes. 'Yes, he's in the euro zone,' I said matter-of factly, as he slid the letter back to me.

'On the plane home I read his document and nearly had a heart attack. I was totally shocked. It was surreal, crazy, unbelievable – you name it. And so, as I have said, my curiosity got the better of me and I just had to find out what this was all about.'

Warren drained the last of his beer and pointed at my glass. 'I'm okay,' I said. 'I have to watch my drinking.' He gave me a short animal laugh. The man returned with a fresh pint, took a huge gulp and slumped into his chair.

He gazed at me intensely. 'I have to ask you,' he said with an edge to his voice, 'what's your angle? What are you looking to get out of this?'

I marshalled my thought and shrugged. 'I really don't know,' I said quietly. 'I've met this guy twice now and he seems very genuine. I'm not really sure what to think. Truth is he does look the part and that manuscript was highly compelling. That's why I phoned your office. I had no idea what you would say, but just had to contact you.' I relaxed back in my chair, drink in hand and continued speaking in a slightly cautious tone. 'But of course all this is so fantastic and queer that you have to pinch yourself and wonder if there is a catch somewhere. It's all very improbable.'

My suggestion that this might not be all it appeared immediately put Warren on the back foot. His expression and mood seemed to change all of a sudden. If I was some shadowy agent acting on behalf of Sidney, then highlighting some doubt about this story would be the last thing I might propose.

His hard demeanour seemed to reign back somewhat. He peered at me curiously for a few moments before taking a mighty gulp of beer. He liked a drink I thought.

'So Adam,' he said in a more harmonious tone, 'let me get this straight. You have met this complete stranger twice, and as a favour to him and because you liked him you have made two postal deliveries on his behalf to our offices. Is that right?'

'That's about it,' I said evenly, while looking him straight in the eyes.

He smiled at me as though summing me up and then gazed away towards the bar, his mind preoccupied. We sat in silence for a while before he turned his attention back to me.

'Have you told anyone else about this?' he asked with a lowered voice.

'No,' I said. 'I've been keeping things to myself while trying to figure this out and make sense of it. After all,' I added uneasily, 'from the few articles I've read, Lucan was a heavy drinker and smoker, and if he did escape hardly anyone would believe he was still alive. The man I have met could be Lucan but I simply don't know. At the moment I'm not sure what to make of it. I'm totally bemused.'

'Okay,' he said abruptly and decisively. 'This is our position. If this is real it's absolute dynamite and we couldn't touch it with a bargepole. It's against the law for a criminal – especially a criminal on the run – to make money from their deeds. Besides which, we would have the police crawling all over us.' He threw a dismissive hand in the air. 'We could print his story as a novel of course, portraying all this as fiction, but there are dozens of books like that already on the market and we would be lucky to recover our printing costs. There would be nothing in it for us. Anyway, as I told you on the phone, he's come to the wrong address if he thinks we can get his story into print.' He took a good gulp of beer and continued.

'But like you, I'm intrigued. The reason we are here talking about this is because of that letter he sent to my father identifying himself. My father was distressed when he read the contents; in fact it shocked him to the core and made him feel really queasy. He told me the letter has to be genuine, as only the two of them could possibly know about some of the things that were mentioned. My father assures me he has never spoken to another soul about the details in that letter. So, if Sidney is not the real McCoy, how the devil did he write that bloody thing? I should tell you that my father knew Lucan well. He was a long time member of the Clermont Club when the place was owned by John Aspinall. My father was not one of the big gamblers that were about in those days but he was very friendly with Lucan. They played bridge and went to the races together. They part-owned a couple of horses and were good buddies for many years. Mind you, as I mentioned on the phone, my father is not the whole ticket these days. His memory is not what it used to be.'

Warren finished his beer and looked towards the bar wondering whether to get another pint.

'Would you do me a favour?' he asked, his tone suddenly low and considered. 'I have not talked about this to anyone other than my father and have kept the papers locked away in my office safe. But I would like to run this by my business partner to see what he thinks. He's in New York at the moment but should be back tomorrow. He might have some ideas on how to handle this.'

He produced a business card from his wallet and handed it to me. 'You can reach me on that number at any time Adam. Would you give me a few days to discuss this with my partner?'

He gazed at me keenly. 'I'm sorry we got off to a bad start but I would like you to trust me to do the best thing. We both have the same agenda to be careful with this. Will you give me your phone number? I think it's important we keep in touch.'

I hesitated, but could see no reason why not. I rang his number from my spare mobile. He took his ringing phone from his jacket pocket and checked the screen.

'You have my number,' I said casually and made to leave. 'It's Thursday now. I will ring you early next week.'

'That will be great,' he said. We shook hands. Our meeting had ended more amicably than when it had begun. As I left the pub I glanced back to see that Warren was at the bar ordering another pint.

I retraced my steps back to the National Gallery. I would relax for a while and look at some of my favourite paintings. The Canaletto's and the two that I loved best and which I could look at all day long – Delaroche's *The Execution of Lady Jane Grey* and Joseph Wright of Derby's *An Experiment on a Bird in the Air Pump*.

After a couple of pleasant hours sauntering around the galleries I felt refreshed as I made my way up to Leicester Square tube and home. It had been an interesting day I was thinking. I did not have to do anything for the time being and my conscience was clear. The ball was firmly in the court of Warren, his father and Loudon House Publishing, and it was now for them to come up with some answers.

As far as I was concerned this mystery was about one thing, and one thing only. Is Sidney Ainsworth really Lord Lucan? It was mad.

CHAPTER FIVE

I did a check on Loudon House Publishing and they were a well-established set-up with posh offices in a very exclusive part of town. That they would be party to anything underhand seemed totally out of the question.

As things stood nobody knew my surname or where I lived, so for the time being I could play along with this story and see where it was going – if anywhere.

I had been running the details of this strange affair over, and over, in my head and trying to decide if, after all these years, the vanishing earl could still be alive and, if so, could Sidney conceivably be that person. Whatever my thoughts, I would have to act and think with a certain amount of suspicion for, as I kept telling myself, you would be more likely to win the lottery than bump into Lord Lucan while on holiday.

With that in mind, and if Sidney was a fake, it still left the question as to what this was all about.

The only proof that any of this was true hung on the word of Warren's father who had received that letter proclaiming it to be genuine and stating that it could only have come from one person. Could it be that he and Sidney, both ex-Clermont Club members, and privy to clever knowledge about the Seventh Earl, were cooking up something between themselves and attempting to use Warren's Publishing house as a conduit for some sort of unknown plan? It was a possibility of course – but what would they be looking to gain? What would be the point?

This was one hell of a conundrum. For now I would be careful and play it by ear and see what Warren had to say when I phoned him. So far, all I had done was post a couple of items and met Warren for a drink. I was no more than a delivery person in all this. If I smelt a rat then I could just disappear and ditch the mobile phone that was the only tenuous link between myself and Loudon House Publishing.

As it transpired I had no need to contact Warren, for early the following week he phoned me and left an excited message on my mobile. There had been none of the rudeness this time.

'Adam,' he had bawled with enthusiasm. 'My partner and I have handed over the documents to Paul King. He is a top investigative journalist, the best in the business. He wants to run with this and see where it leads. Look him up on the Internet, he has a great reputation. If this story is genuine then Paul is just about the only journalist out there who could persuade one of the big newspapers to run with this. Anyway,' he continued, in a lively, animated voice, 'I have shown him all the papers and he is very eager to speak to you. You can trust him, believe me.'

There was a pause in the message before he added determinedly. 'Make sure you ring him Adam. As soon as possible.'

A text message followed with Paul King's phone number.

He had sounded very keen. I wondered what sort of kickback Warren would expect if there was any truth in this. The man would want something that was for sure.

Chapter Five

I looked up Paul King on the Internet. It was clear that he was known and respected in journalistic circles. Paul was a freelance and from what I read about him it seemed he was not shy in digging the dirt on the more powerful elements in society. He had been at the forefront of exposing some MP's in the expenses scandal and had ruffled feathers with the Met on racial prejudice and had even taken on the Serious Fraud Office on some high profile cases where they had been dragging their feet.

I phoned him not knowing quite what to expect.

His manner was business like, but friendly when we spoke. He was eager to see me and discuss, as he put it, 'This Sidney affair.'

I told him that I had already explained where I stood in all this and that I was not prepared to go through justifying myself all over again and fending off all the suspicions I had encountered with my meeting with Warren.

He assured me that having met Warren and spoken to him at length, he appreciated that I had simply been acting as a courier and, whilst knowing that I was not ready to disclose my details or Sidney's whereabouts at this juncture he was happy in the knowledge that I could be trusted and was acting out of pure curiosity. He went on to say that he understood my reservations about the legal implications of the matter.

There had been an offer to meet me for lunch or come to my home to discuss the affair. In the end I settled to meet him at his house the following day.

Paul lived in a terraced house in a leafy avenue off the Fulham Road. I was greeted with a warm friendly handshake. I took him to be in his late thirties. He was tall and thin with a slight stoop of the shoulders. A mop of straw-coloured hair swept his forehead flopping down to his thick-rimmed glasses.

His face and demeanour bestowed an impression of studiedness along with a touch of geniality.

Paul ushered me into what would normally be a front lounge but was now serving as his office.

'Please, make yourself comfortable,' he said gladly, pointing to a battered old leather chair on the other side of a busy looking desk. I quickly took in the surroundings of his office, which contained a few filing cabinets set against one of the walls with folders piled on top. The rest of the room had been shelved-out and was brimming with books and old newspapers. Above his desk were some framed certificates with big red stars, which I guessed were journalistic awards.

He read my eyes and smiled indulgently. 'You'll have to excuse the mess,' he said, sweeping a disinterested hand around the room. 'I keep meaning to have a tidy-up. I'll get round to it one day. I've got some coffee on, will you join me?'

He scurried out of the room and quickly returned with two mugs of steaming coffee. 'Just instant, I'm afraid,' he said apologetically.

Once settled behind his desk he smiled and looked at me reflectively.

'Well Adam,' he said, in a calm tone, 'I should kick off by saying that I am not going to quiz you on your role in this as I have been through all that side of it with Warren and I am happy with his appraisal of you. So between us we can talk together in an open way and try to get to the bottom of this. I'm sure that's what we both want.' He wiped away hair from his forehead and moved his chair closer to the desk.

'I appreciate you want to keep a low profile for the moment which is fine by me. That is by and large how I operate. I get information from wherever, and whoever, and I have never betrayed a confidence. I'm a freelance journalist and have a certain freedom to get to the bottom of a story by any means I can. That's my job. It's what I do for a living. As far as the law is concerned we could be sailing pretty close to the wind and so I understand your reservations.'

Paul took a sip of coffee before continuing in an easy business-like voice.

'I have built up many contacts during my career, people trust me and I can sometimes get information from sources that others don't have access to. I look after my contacts, they are a very important part of my trade.'

Paul relaxed back and fixed his eyes on me from over the top of his glasses.

'I know you've had a long conversation with Warren but would you allow me to ask a few questions so that I might get a handle on this?'

I nodded.

'What does this Sidney look like?' he asked mildly.

I took a sip of coffee and settled myself. 'Well I guess he's about eighty. He has grey hair and a neat grey beard. The two times I have met him he has always been smartly dressed. The man likes a drink and a smoke and he comes across as being well educated. We have talked about gambling and he seems to know his stuff. But he's pretty frail, I don't think his health is too good.'

Paul removed his glasses and began cleaning them with a handkerchief. He gave me a considered look. 'What about his height, his voice, facial features?'

'Well that seems to work judging by some old photos I've seen of Lucan. Sidney – as we should carry on calling him – has fine cheekbones and his voice is quite refined. Although he is somewhat stooped I guess he would be about six foot.'

Paul put his glasses back on and swept a mop of hair away from the rims.

'This is where I'm at, Adam,' he said, his voice precise and unhurried. 'That letter sent to Warren's father intrigued me and that's why I have taken an interest in this case. With Warren's permission I drove down to Surrey and spoke to his father, Colin. Contrary to what Warren says I found his father to be most lucid and reliable. He is adamant that nobody other than Lucan could have known the details contained in that letter. As for the other stuff.' He tapped his pen on Sidney's brown manila envelope that rested on the side of his desk. 'That document,' he continued, 'is a very interesting read but of no real importance at the moment. Anyone could have written that. You could get most of the information from the Internet and then just chuck in a few made-up stories to juice it up.'

I leaned forward and absent-mindedly tapped my fingers on the desk. 'Could it be,' I asked falteringly, 'that Sidney and Warren's father have cooked this up between them, maybe as some sort of joke to play in their old age?'

Paul raised his eyebrows and made a little chuckle. 'Don't worry, I've already thought of that. I have contacts you know,' he said, shooting me a conspiratorial smile. 'I had Colin checked out. The man is as honest as the day is long. He's never so much as received a parking fine.'

This journalist is good I thought to myself.

'No.' Paul continued. 'All we have to go on at the moment is a very clever letter sent to someone who knew Lucan well and who can vouch for him. But that alone is not good enough by a long chalk. I could never persuade a paper to show an interest in this story based on such flimsy evidence, no matter how compelling and intriguing it might seem.

Have you heard of the Hitler Diaries?' he asked, in a low voice.

'I'm not sure,' I mumbled, thinking that I was soon to find out. Paul settled back in his chair, coffee in hand.

Chapter Five

'In 1983 *Stern* Magazine paid three million quid for what they believed were the secret diaries of Adolf Hitler which had been smuggled out of East Germany by a certain Dr Fischer. The story was that they were part of a consignment of documents recovered from a plane crash near Dresden in 1945 and had been secretly stored away ever since. *Stern* had carried out handwriting tests in Europe and the States which confirmed that the handwriting was that of Hitler.'

Paul sipped his coffee and continued in an even voice. 'Well, you can imagine the worldwide excitement in the story, soon the big boys in publishing were falling over each other for a piece of the action and a chance to bid for the serialisation of the diaries.

The *Sunday Times* sent their World War Two expert and historian Hugh Trevor-Roper to Switzerland to authenticate the diaries and *Newsweek* did likewise with one of their own experts. It was reported back that the diaries were genuine and the *Sunday Times* and *Newsweek* paid goodness knows how much for the rights to publish. So convinced was Trevor-Roper of the diaries' authenticity that soon after returning from Switzerland he wrote in *The Times* that he was convinced that the documents were authentic and that they would shed new light on our understanding of Hitler's habits and personality.'

Paul took a little break and gazed past me at nothing in particular. After a few moments, no doubt recalling events in his mind, he continued.

'Despite all the ballyhoo there were those who doubted the diaries' genuineness. But it was too late for the *Sunday Times* who had been duped big-time. Just days before going to press it became pretty clear that the diaries were fake. Trevor-Roper and Weinberg had now got cold feet and were desperately trying to disentangle themselves from their previous endorsements.

The writer David Irving ridiculed the diaries producing papers exactly similar to the Hitler Diaries and confirming that they were forgeries and had almost certainly come from the same source as *Stern's* material.

The hoax was blown wide open and what made it worse was the fact that these forgeries were not even clever. It emerged that the paper and ink were quite modern and that the contents of the diaries had simply been lifted from a book of Hitler's speeches and were full of historical inaccuracies. Later, when the diaries were scrutinised by a handwriting expert it emerged that the forger's had failed to observe the most basic characteristics of his handwriting. It was all pretty amateur, but had somehow managed to fool the biggest names in publishing.

In the full knowledge that they would be the laughing stock of Fleet Street the *Sunday Times* went to press with the first part of the serialisation but would have to pull it after that.

The fall-out was awful. Top people lost their jobs and their reputations to boot. The *Stern* editors had to resign, as did my old friend Frank Giles, editor of the *Sunday Times*. The *Newsweek* guy had to resign and Trevor-Roper's reputation was in tatters. On top of it all the *Sunday Times* took a real kicking from their rivals and were made to look stupid.'

Paul took another little breather and a sip of coffee before continuing. 'You know,' he said quietly. 'Being an editor is a bed of nails these days. Just recently Rupert Murdoch was asked at the Leveson inquiry about his role in the Hitler Diaries and admitted that it was his decision to go to press. But at the time Murdoch stayed silent and let Frank Giles fall on his sword. How unfair was that? What more can an editor do than listen to the experts that advise him?

Chapter Five

I relate all this simply to show you how dangerous big stories can be. Since the Hitler Diaries, editors have been on their guard and now you hardly ever get a big exposé, simply because top management and lawyers are reluctant to risk their jobs. There is also the threat of litigation. If you printed Lucan material that was found to be fake then his family could come after you complaining that they had been subjected to hurtful and unwarranted publicity.'

Paul shrugged his shoulders. 'So you see Adam,' he continued, somewhat defensively. 'This is an absolute minefield. It would have to be established without a shred of doubt that Sidney is who he purports to be.'

'So how convincing is that letter he sent?' I asked with keen interest.

Paul opened the top draw of his desk and produced Sidney's letter, which he pushed across to me. 'Be free,' he said.

I searched for my reading glasses, which, as usual, were in the last pocket I looked in. Then I remembered the letter Sidney had sent to me. 'We can do a swap,' I said eagerly. I found Sidney's letter in my jacket pocket and handed it over to Paul. He thanked me and we both proceeded to read.

I laid the letter sent to Warren's dad flat the on the desk.

Dear Colin.
I hope this letter finds you in good health old friend and please forgive me for contacting you out of the blue like this but I am wondering if Warren's publishing company might be interested in hearing from me with the understanding that I can remain safe.
I have not been in great health these last few years and now feel the time is right to put the record straight while I can. I appreciate that this letter will come as a huge shock to you and will fully understand should yourself and Warren wish to ignore my unsolicited, and possibly unwelcome approach.

As you will realise, I am still alive, if not exactly kicking, and now I wish to put on record what happened all those years ago.

Apart from clearing my chest, I would like in some way to ask for my children's forgiveness. Should my sad tale be worth something then it is hoped that my children might benefit. I wish nothing for myself other than to relate my story.

While I am still able, I wish to tell my children how much I have always loved them and that they have never been far from my thoughts throughout all these lonely years.

Without naming names, I was most fortunate that my friends continued to support me for a long time after I left London.

As the years passed my friends, one by one, sadly passed away. There came a time when I found myself very much alone and with no further contact with London. I had outlived everyone who had come to my aid. Before he died, Jimmy arranged a handsome payment for me. Money was put in secure accounts that could not be traced back to him and that I could withdraw cash from and move to other accounts in other countries with ease.

But this money would not last forever and so I had to make a decision. This entailed moving to a quiet place and living a frugal lifestyle (no more silly gambling).

I have missed you Colin, and my family and the wonderful friends I once had, but are no longer with us. All these years I have been a prisoner on the outside.

Do you remember that day at the Cheltenham Festival. We were staying with Toby and Michelle at Churchdown. We had backed different horses in the World Hurdle and your horse, Four Aces, and my one Berkeley Square (of course) crossed the line together. We had no idea which horse had won. As we waited for the judges photo we shook hands and agreed whichever was called the winner we would share the winnings. As it turned out your selection won by a short head.

At the end of the afternoon we played up our luck and found the winner of the last. We decided to head back to London and miss the following days Gold Cup as it was sure to be too crowded for comfort.

After dinner at the Criterion we popped into the Club for a quick drink before moving on to the Stork Room, and then to Boodles where Reg tipped us the winner of the following days Gold Cup. (Fort Leeney).

While at Boodles we shared KD's (keep down). I told you what I had heard about Burmah Oil and you gave me some information about the Downes House yard where some of us were thinking about buying a yearling from an owner there.

That year we dealt with the 'Nicole' problem, and between us sorted out that issue without anyone knowing why she left London in such a hurry.

I relate all this only to verify myself. So, Colin, as you can tell, I am still around dear friend.

Again, I would like to say that I hope this letter finds you in good health, still playing a good game of bridge and that Warren is a good son to you.

As you will appreciate my position is precarious, as it has been for the last forty years. I wish to tell my story which I have been working on for some time.

However, how I go about this I have yet to determine. With time running out I will probably have to take a chance on someone to act on my behalf (my last gamble).

I hope to make contact with yourself and Warren again in the near future in the hope that you may be able to help me. If this is not possible I will fully understand. Yours truly.

John

I thought for a few moments about what I had just read. I looked up at Paul. 'What's this about any money going to his children?' I asked curiously.

'That's not on,' Paul said firmly. 'Criminals can't be seen to profit for themselves or their family. In any case if he tried to push money their way he would simply be incriminating them. Anyway, his children have all done well for themselves.'

'So we can rule out that they have anything to do with this?' I offered.

'Absolutely,' he replied firmly. Paul held up the letter I had given him. 'Do you have the envelope?' I shook my head. 'I did not think to keep it. Silly of me.'

'No matter,' he said easily. He then tapped his finger on Sidney's manila envelope addressed to Loudon House Publishing. 'I'm getting that handwriting checked out by an

American expert. A persons handwriting can change over the years but it could give us another clue to his identity.'

This journalist certainly does have ways and means I said to myself.

'Do you know,' I muttered hesitantly, with a slight feeling of unease. 'I've always thought it a million-to-one chance, but something is telling me that this old chap I've met on holiday might be Lord Lucan. A scam is all about getting money from someone, that's the sole aim. But he's not asking for any money. That it's a trick seems to be something that can be ruled out.' I shuddered. 'Could it possibly be? Could he still be alive after all these years?'

Paul leaned over his desk, his face carefully composed. 'The feeling amongst most commentators was that Lucan committed suicide. The only problem with that theory is that his body was never found and it was well known that he had powerful and wealthy friends who were more than willing to help him escape.'

I took a deep breath. 'So where do we go from here?'

'Let me interview him,' he said decisively. 'I would do my homework. I have ways and means,' he added, with a wry smile. 'I would ask him a series of questions that would be pretty fool proof in checking out his identity. I would also want his fingerprints. The fingerprint angle is a bit of a long shot but I might get lucky. In any case, if he shied away from any of this, then we would know right away that he was a phony. I understand his obvious need to keep his whereabouts a secret, but if he's genuine and wants to tell his story then he must realise that he has to be thoroughly investigated to prove beyond any doubt that he is the person who he is claiming to be. Other than that I couldn't go any further with this story. I need to find out for sure whether this man really is Lucan.'

Chapter Five

'So you want me to set up a meeting with him, is that right?'

'That's it Adam,' he replied crisply. 'If it's a ruse I'll know within ten minutes. And if that's the case I might have a story anyway.'

This last statement hit me hard. How naive was I being? Whatever way this turned out this journalist was looking for a story – I imagined the headline.

"Paul King exposes outrageous attempt by Mallorcan pensioner to pass himself off as Lord Lucan." I felt deflated and decided to change tack. So far Paul had been pushing all his chess pieces in my direction. Now I moved my imaginary queen out to the centre of his desk.

'Look Paul,' I said matter-of-factly. 'If this story isn't true then I shall just walk away. I'm not going to hand this old guy to you on a sacrificial platter.'

I could see that Paul was taken aback. He raised his eyebrows at me.

I pointed at Sidney's manuscript. 'You can keep that,' I said. 'Along with the letter and do what you like with them, but I will simply take my leave. I have no appetite in getting this old boy in trouble if it turns out that he is deluded or worse. He has taken a liking to me and put his trust in me. I can't explain why, but I have taken a shine to him and don't want to see him in hot water. Regardless of who he might be we should remember he's old, lonely and in poor health.'

Paul eyed me narrowly and raised his hand in a small gesture of penitence.

'I understand,' he said softly. 'That was wrong of me. It's the journalist mentality coming out. Even so, I will still need to see him and check out his story. I will give my word that however this turns out I will respect his anonymity.'

I decided to continue while I felt the tables had turned slightly in my favour.

'If this story is true,' I asked, 'how much is it worth?'

He gave a hollow laugh and raised his hands in the air and let them fall helplessly to his sides.

'It's impossible to say Adam. I would have to speak to editors and lawyers and haggle for all I was worth. I would have to give a guarantee that I had thoroughly checked the story and that I was sure it was genuine beyond reasonable doubt.'

'A million pounds?' I asked with an air of mischievousness.

He frowned, his eyes narrowed. 'You must be joking,' he said flatly. 'If I could give you a figure I would, but I can't. You'll just have to trust me to whip up interest and go for the best offer. That's if I could ever get an offer. But what you must understand Adam, is that ever since the 'Hitler Diaries,' newspapers are reluctant to pay big money for a scoop. At one time a story like this would be worth a fortune, but not any more. I might get one of the Sunday's to take the story but they would only pay so much. And I will tell you why. Firstly, there is the concern that the story might not be true and careers would be at risk. Also, what guarantee can we give a newspaper that someone else does not hold the same manuscript? Added to that, there is the risk of litigation and possibly being leaned on by Scotland Yard.'

Paul removed his glasses, laid them on his desk and shrugged philosophically.

'So you see,' he continued quietly, 'I might be able to sell this, but a newspaper will only risk a certain amount of money no matter how exciting the story might seem. Everyone will want to cover their backside. If the story went belly up, then those that made the decision could tell their proprietors that for the small amount they paid it was worth the risk. They will always look to cover themselves. It's also a possibility that a newspaper might pay for this story simply to hold on to it and keep it under wraps. Wait for future events to unfold before going to press. Something that might take years or never happen. People talk about the freedom of the press, but believe me, editors are often handcuffed as to what they can print for fear of getting something slightly wrong and being sued.' He paused and thought for a few moments. 'But lets not jump the gun Adam,' he said with a sudden spark of enthusiasm. 'When can you arrange a meeting with our Mr Sidney Ainsworth?'

'I'm on holiday in the south of England for a few days,' I said. 'I'll try and sort something out as soon as I get back.'

I raised myself to leave. Paul came across to me and offered his hand with a warm and sincere expression. 'You can trust me Adam,' he said. 'We should work together on this. I think we can make a good team and get to the bottom of this.'

I headed for the tube and home. I was not going to see Sidney hung out to dry if all this went wrong. To that end I had already formulated a plan in my mind.

However, for the first time, I felt a slight chill running through me. Pointers were leading me to believe that this man I had met while on holiday was indeed the person he was claiming to be.

And that thought was frightening in the extreme.

CHAPTER SIX

My good mate Dave, had invited me over to his place on the Isle of Wight, and with the weather set fair I was looking forward to a break and a chance to forget all about the very strange goings on in my life. For a few days I would relax and do some coastal walks with my friend and refresh my mind and thoughts.

I had not been to the Isle of Wight since my parents took us children there when we were all very young. We had stayed somewhere on the island that was unique for its different coloured sands. Having played on the beach all day in the glaring sun we ended up with awful sunburn. My parents took us to a local chemist where they looked at our burnt skin with horror and probably regarded us as silly Londoners who had never seen a beach before. We spent the rest of the holiday as little white ghosts smothered in calamine lotion. It had not been the best of family holidays.

Dave had invited my to stay at his house in Ventnor but as I knew he was working on his place I decided to book a hotel and let him get on with his DIY.

Chapter Six

I checked a few Internet sites and eventually settled on a hotel in Sandown. The photos of the hotel looked good. It was more of a pub, which I liked and it looked a bit olde-worlde, which I preferred to the more clinical Holiday Inn type places.

The journey to the Isle of Wight was most interesting. From Ryde there was a train that chugged along the coast as far as Ventnor. But this was not a train as you would know it. These carriages were old London underground stock that had been shipped to the island in the fifties. They were rickety and loud and the doors would open and close with grinding reluctance, but amazingly they were still doing a great job.

Arriving at my hotel, I realised immediately that I had made a bad choice. A dull woman asked for payment up front before handing over the keys to my room.

The room was musty and grim. The shower had the dimensions of a coffin and the bed and tatty furniture looked as though they had been bought from a charity shop. The window looked out onto a filthy yard full of old beer kegs and rubbish. I was not feeling great, as I knew I had a heavy cold coming on and this hotel had done little to raise my spirits. I cursed myself for not asking to view the room before paying. After unpacking I set of to meet my friend.

Dave was going to walk towards Sandown along the front while I would head towards Ventnor and we would meet halfway. I had nearly reached Ventnor before we met up.

Dave was keen to show me the resort and so we set off uphill. Ventnor I soon realised was a cut above Sandown. The town boasted good hotels and a charming theatre. We eventually winded our way along the cliff edges to a little café in a park overlooking the sea. We ordered a cream tea and sat back admiring the wonderful view across the Solent.

I told my friend that I would skip the walk we had planned for the following day as I needed to take it easy and nurse what I was sure was an oncoming chest infection.

Back at the hotel I had a little rest before venturing out for a couple of drinks in the evening. Alas, I was not feeling very well and so decided to have an early night.

At breakfast the following morning, and still feeling unwell, I pondered how this bizarre hotel could make a living because you would never willingly book this run-down place and anyone that had stayed here would certainly never return.

The answer was apparent when I stepped out into the lobby and found myself engulfed amidst hundreds of pensioners many with Zimmer frames that had just been deposited at the entrance by a row of coaches. This hotel made a living by catering for the 'holiday by coach' firms. The ones that advertise three days in the Isle of Wight or Devon, or wherever, for a knockdown price. I spent the morning wandering around Sandown, which proved a disappointment. The place had little appeal and the pier was nothing more than a series of wooden sections, each of which housed a multitude of incredibly noisy slot machines.

Back at the hotel I packed my stuff, left the room key at reception and headed home to London to see my doctor and get some advice and medication.

I phoned my friend and apologised for having to abandon the holiday so abruptly. In the doctors waiting room I flicked through some magazines while waiting for my name to come up on the TV screen they had recently installed.

I saw a lovely lady doctor who simply asked me if I was still smoking. I told her that I had recently packed up for which she gave me a knowing smile that silently said, 'I know you are lying, but it's really up to you.' She confirmed that I had a chest infection, told me to rest indoors and duly gave me a prescription for some antibiotics.

Chapter Six

I would stay peacefully at home for a few days and take it easy. It would give me time to do some research. It was an unplanned, but ideal opportunity for me to read up on the Lucan case. To learn everything I could about the man accused of murder who apparently vanished into thin air.

From the doctors surgery I headed to Finchley High Road to see if I could get any books on Lord Lucan. I checked Waterstones, WHSmith and some charity shops but had no luck. I would, for the time being, have to use the Internet.

If Sidney Ainsworth was the real McCoy – the genuine article – then he would have to prove it beyond a shadow of doubt if his ambition was to get his life-story into print and tell his side of this unsavoury tale.

When I was ready I would return to Mallorca and tell Sidney that I did follow up his story and had duly arranged a meeting with Warren, of Loudon House Publishing, who informed me he was unable to help but had, instead, passed the letter and manuscript to a top class journalist who could be trusted and had the reputation and influence to possibly sell his story to a newspaper.

However, I would explain to him that you could not simply come out of hiding after 40-years hankering to tell your story and not to expect an enormous amount of scrutiny as to your real identity, which you would have to prove to this journalist. You would have to back up your claim that you are the Seventh Earl of Lucan. I would also inform him that his handwriting was being examined by an expert and that his fingerprints were required.

An idea that I had been pondering was that I could do something similar to what Paul King had in mind. I would don a Detective Poirot hat and put to Sidney some very searching questions and try to establish if he was telling the truth. I would thoroughly research the Lucan investigation and forearm myself with as much information as I could and then check Sidney's incredible story in my own way, and on my own terms.

When meeting him next I would try and be canny, let him do most of the talking, but every now and then throw in some questions about the case to get his reaction and body language. There was nothing to stop me determining whether this man really was Richard John Bingham. What was to stop me doing what Paul King had in mind?

If it turned out that all this was a ruse, for whatever reason, I would tell him how lucky he had been in taking a chance with me as his messenger boy for someone else might have set a newspaper man on him, who would have taken his picture, and armed with that clever letter, would have exposed him as a fraud and got himself a juicy little story for the daily papers back in England. If, after my determined research of the case, Sidney failed to convince me that he was the man he claimed to be, I would not feel bad about this little adventure, as Mallorca was my second home, and in any case, I had received five hundred euros from Sidney which had more than paid for my previous holiday.

I would give him a friendly pat on the back and simply say – nice try Sidney – you are a very lucky man as I do not intend to embarrass you, but I must advise you not to try this again. Back in London I would phone Paul King and tell him that it was all a fantasy. Sidney was not Lord Lucan. It had been most engaging but now it was over. He could shred that manuscript and forget all about the affair. In a way it might come as a relief, as I could free myself from something that, had it been true, would have been one of the most astounding stories in recent years, but would also have been most disturbing and dangerous to be involved with.

Chapter Six

However, if it were the other way round, and I was convinced that he was the real thing, then I would have to ask myself how far I was prepared to go in helping Mr Sidney Ainsworth get his remarkable and disturbing life-story into print.

And why should I help anyway? And if I did help, what was I looking to get out of this for putting myself in peril? At this moment in time I was at a loss to answer these questions.

CHAPTER SEVEN

There was plenty of Lucan material on the Internet, press cuttings, magazine articles and even a Lord Lucan official website. There were also about a dozen books on sale with Amazon.

I checked out the reviews of the various publications, which revealed just how many authors had tried their hand at unravelling this murder mystery together with theories as to how this peer of the realm managed to pull off the most baffling disappearing act in British history.

There were a few titles which seemed to be pretty much tongue in cheek accounts sprinkled with others that looked at the mystery from a scientific and painstakingly researched point of view. Some of these titles I downloaded to my tablet.

I was in my mid-twenties and working in North London when the Lord Lucan murder case hit the headlines. After that, and as time went by, it was no more than rumours, so called sightings and pub tittle-tattle as to whether he had got away and if he might still be alive somewhere. The residue of an unsolved crime like this is that every Tom, Dick, and Harry, feels obliged to give a view as to what might have happened, no matter how outlandish, safe in the knowledge that their opinion cannot be readily disproved.

Having downloaded a mass of reading material, and with a notepad to hand I began my research. I was determined to learn everything there was to know about the elusive Richard John Bingham.

I was a few days into my studies when I received a text message from Paul King asking if I had any news for him. It was pretty clear that he, and Loudon House Publishing, were showing a great deal of interest in this very curious affair.

Although I was keen to know who exactly Sidney Ainsworth was, and had absorbed myself in this mystery, the fact that a publisher and a top class journalist were thinking that maybe this story could be true was intriguing, but at the same time somewhat alarming. It had crossed my mind frequently that I had involved myself in something devious that was way over my head and for which I was totally unqualified to handle.

I texted Paul back saying that I was laid low with a heavy cold, but would definitely contact him as soon as I was able.

Paul King would have to be patient as I pursued my interest and studies into the investigation surrounding the slippery Seventh Earl of Lucan.

Once into my reading it soon became apparent that as far as the police were concerned the person responsible for the murder of the nanny, Sandra Rivett, was pretty obvious and straightforward.

With the total breakdown of his marriage, Lucan had moved out of the family home at 46 Lower Belgrave Street, first to the mews cottage held in trust at Eaton Row that nestled directly behind number 46, and then a little further afield to a large apartment at 72a Elizabeth Street.

He had fought a bitter court case against his wife to obtain custody of their three children and possibly regain his house with all its valuable contents. Having lost the legal battle he was a desperate, broken man, added to which the costs of the court proceedings had brought about financial ruin.

Having tried through legal means to get custody of his children and in a state of morbid depression and hatred he decided on an alternative, deadly course of action. On the night of Thursday, 7 November 1974, the earl decided to take matters into his own hands. He knew that the nanny, Sandra, took Thursday nights off, her one night away from the house. He was also aware that his wife followed a customary ritual of asking Sandra to make her a cup of tea around 9pm. With Sandra away, it would be his wife who would descend to the basement kitchen to put the kettle on. Well away from the children who would be asleep upstairs Lucan intended to seize the moment.

According to the police, at around 8.30pm, Lucan entered the house at 46 Lower Belgrave Street, armed with a cudgel and a large US canvas mailbag. He went down to the basement, removed the overhead light bulb and waited in the dark. The mailbag was intended for his wife's body which he would later dispose of out at sea.

Just before 9pm a figure appeared in the semi-darkness of the kitchen. Lucan struck out with great ferocity, but as the body hit the parquet floor he soon realised his horrendous mistake. Blood and bone and cerebral tissue had sprayed everywhere, across the floor on walls and the ceiling, but the slumped, pitiful body, was not that of his wife, but the nanny, Sandra Rivett, who had changed her usual night off.

Lucan panicked. He went about cleaning the blood from the floor and attempted to bundle Sandra's body into the mailbag that had been intended for his wife.

Chapter Seven

It was to no avail. Wondering where Sandra had got to, Lady Lucan came down the stairs calling her name. Lucan's plan to murder his wife had turned into a shambles and probably in a state of utter confusion and despair he now attacked his wife. He landed a couple of blows to her head before they ended up in a fight on the basement landing. She fought for her life and managed to kick him in the groin before almost escaping to the front door. The earl grabbed her, and now coming to his senses and realising that the game was up, tried to pacify his wife. For a few surreal moments they sat at the bottom of the stairs talking and crying. Then Lucan guided his wife up to her bedroom. All this commotion had roused their eldest daughter, Frances, who was standing on the landing outside her bedroom. Lucan told the child that everything would be alright and that she should go back to her room. He then laid his wife on her bed and went to get a flannel from the bathroom to clean her wounds. The duchess seized her chance and ran down the stairs and out of the front door. She ran along the street to the Plumbers Arms, bursting in the door of the pub screaming blue murder.

The pub landlord comforted the duchess and tended to her injuries while calling the police and an ambulance. Wounded and hysterical, but now safe, she had escaped death and her body ending up at the bottom of the English Channel by the most extraordinary of circumstances.

The police were quickly on the scene at Lower Belgrave Street. Two officers forced open the front door and made an inspection of the house. Downstairs in the basement it was dark and the lights were not working so one of the officers went to get a torch while the other officer went upstairs where he found three children asleep. The officers, now able to see by torchlight, found that a light bulb had been removed and was lying on a padded chair. They replaced the bulb and now the light yielded some gruesome discoveries. In the hall they discovered a length of lead piping wrapped in surgical tape covered with blood and bone. Leading down into the kitchen they noticed blood on the walls and floor and then they almost walked into a large canvas mailbag soaked in blood. The top of the bag was folded over but the fastening cord was still loose. Lifting the flap they discovered a shocking sight. Inside was the body of a young woman, her head smashed in.

For Lucan the game was well and truly up. He had done a runner and disappeared into the November night, sparking the police to launch a red alert for his detention. Within an hour a virtual small army of police had arrived at 46 Lower Belgrave Street, searching every room in the house, witnessing the murder scene and checking the back garden, the walls and the outside basement area.

The first senior officer on the scene was Sergeant Graham Forsyth of the CID. He set in motion a search of Lucan's mews cottage in Eaton Row, but there was no evidence to suggest that he had gone there.

At around 10.30pm Lucan's mother arrived at Lower Belgrave Street telling Sergeant Forsyth that her son had phoned her asking that she collect the children. The Dowager Countess of Lucan went on to tell the officer that her son had related a story that he had been passing the house when he had witnessed a struggle taking place in the basement between his wife and a man. He said that he had entered the house but the intruder had escaped, and his wife, Veronica, had then accused him of murder. The scene in the basement had been 'shocking,' her son had said, 'with blood and mess everywhere.' Forsyth questioned the countess as to where Lucan was living and what sort of car he owned. She told him that he rented a flat in Elizabeth Street and owned a

Chapter Seven

blue Mercedes. The Sergeant then allowed Lucan's mother to collect the children and arranged for a policeman to accompany them back to her home in St Johns Wood and stay with the countess in the event that Lucan might contact his mother again.

Forsyth, realising the enormity of this case, which would almost certainly create headline news rang his immediate superior, Detective Chief Inspector David Gerring.

Gerring who had been in bed, dressed immediately and set off for Belgravia. The detective told his wife that he would be back in a few hours. He would not see his wife or home for the next four days. On the drive into London, Gerring collected his immediate boss, Detective Chief Superintendent Roy Ranson. As the two men sped over Vauxhall Bridge they could have had no idea that they were about to head-up the biggest and most publicised murder mystery of recent times, a case that would have a profound affect on their lives and careers and despite all their efforts they would never apprehend the main suspect.

However, Scotland Yard could not have chosen two better men for the task ahead. Both had earned commendations for their handling of sensitive cases. Ranson, the more reflective and steely of the two, had investigated the missing tax papers of Harold Wilson. Gerring was more of the tough no-nonsense type. He had earned the nickname 'Buster,' for his efforts in breaking up the seriously villainous Richardson gang in 1968. Soon after he was promoted to the head of CID for the Belgravia area and had investigated the shooting attempt on Princess Anne.

They were a formidable partnership and went about their work like a couple of bloodhounds, the scent of Lucan never far from their nostrils. They were prepared to work day and night until they found their man – dead or alive.

Once at Lower Belgravia Street, Ranson and Gerring immediately took charge as the lead investigators. The two officers were briefed by Sergeant Forsyth and once they had examined the crime scene made their way to Lucan's splendid five-bedroom apartment in Elizabeth Street. His blue Mercedes was parked outside. The two officers forced open the front door of Lucan's flat and made a search of the premises. In the bedroom the earls clothes were neatly laid out on the bed ready to change into evening dinner wear. Nearby, were his car keys, cheque book and driving licence. Inside a bedside drawer Ranson found his address book and passport. Ranson would later say that the flat seemed to be silently waiting for its owner to return home.

From Elizabeth Street, they made their way to St George's Hospital where they interviewed Lady Lucan who had just been attended with sixty stitches to head wounds. Despite the ordeal she was lucid and calm as she described to the detectives that she had surprised her husband leaving the darkened basement kitchen and he had then launched a vicious attack, hitting the duchess over the head and then trying to strangle her. She went on to say that it was herself that was the intended victim as the nanny would normally have been away that night but had changed her usual night off. She stated that she and Sandra Rivett were of a similar build and that in the dark he had mistakenly killed the nanny instead of herself.

Both men agreed that Lady Lucan was a highly lucid and convincing witness and never wavered from the original statement she gave to the detectives.

By the time Ranson and Gerring returned to Belgravia the house had been sealed-off but word had spread of a socialite murder and there was now a hoard of journalists along with television and radio crews milling outside the house.

Chapter Seven

A team of forensic officers had arrived but their task was pretty much impossible, as so many policemen had moved freely around the house stepping in blood and leaving finger-prints on doors, furniture and windows. Also there had been so much blood in the basement that transference of vital forensic material in rooms, stairs and the garden had been inevitable.

I would learn that this unfortunate, but unavoidable break-down of vital forensic evidence would have huge implications on the case and give rise to all sorts of inconsistencies as to what actually happened on the night of the murder and would be seized upon by theorists and Lucan supporters who wished to pick holes in the police investigation and discredit the evidence given by Lady Lucan.

In most cases, murder scenes are sealed off and a forensic team with head to toe protective clothing gather vital evi-dence of blood, fibres, skin and hair that has not been acciden-tally transferred or contaminated. For understandable reasons this was not possible on that fateful night. When the first two officers had entered the house and established that a ghastly murder had taken place they called for back up. Many more officers arrived, and knowing there were three young children in the house, conducted a thorough search to establish the killer was not still on the premises. They had to do this immediately. It was not possible to seal off the crime scene for the forensic people, they had a duty to make sure the children were safe.

The following day saw an explosion of press headlines. The lunchtime edition of the *Evening Standard* bellowed the story:

'BELGRAVIA MURDER: EARL SOUGHT. BODY IN SACK – COUNTESS RUNS OUT SCREAMING.'

The police believed that Lucan had a boat moored somewhere on the south coast and that after murdering his wife, Lady Veronica Bingham, the plan had been to clean up the murder scene, pack his wife in the mailbag, and then dispose of her weighted-down body out into the murky waters of the English Channel.

In the hours, days and weeks following the brutal attack on Sandra, the police were able to piece together a series of events following the murder. The one missing piece of the jigsaw was the earl himself.

After his wife had ran screaming to the Plumbers Arms, Lucan had apparently driven away in an old Ford Corsair that he had borrowed from his friend, Michael Stoop, a fellow Clermont Club member. He then made a phone call from somewhere to his mother saying that something terrible had happened and would she get a taxi and hurry round to the house in Belgravia and collect the children. The police were unable to trace where this call came from other than it was from a private subscriber and not a telephone box. Lucan then drove to Grants Hill House, in Uckfield, Sussex, the grand residence of his good friends the Maxwell-Scott's. He arrived there shortly after 11pm and was ushered into the house by Susie Maxwell-Scott who told him that her husband, and Lucan's friend Ian, was staying in town at the Clermont having drank too much and not wanting to risk driving home.

Susie made coffee and gave Lucan a large brandy. She later told the police that he looked dishevelled and was very distraught. As he calmed down somewhat with the brandy he opened up to Susie telling her that something horrific had happened. Lucan told her that he had been passing the house in Lower Belgrave Street, and from the pavement had seen into the basement where an attack was taking place. He rushed in through the front door but the attacker had taken flight and escaped. He had only caught sight of the back of the assailant he apparently told her.

Whether Susie Maxwell-Scott believed this story or whether it was a true account of what he actually said to her was anyone's guess. Lucan then telephoned his mother who was safe back at her home in St. Johns Wood with the children. She told him the children were safe and fast asleep and told him to take care of himself. She then asked her son if he would like to speak to a policeman who was with her. He declined saying he would call the police in the morning.

Lucan then asked Susie Maxwell-Scott for some paper and envelopes and proceeded to write two letters to his firm friend, Bill Shand Kydd, the husband of Veronica's sister, Christina.

Dear Bill,

The most ghastly circumstances arose tonight which I briefly described to my mother. When I interrupted the fight at Lower Belgrave St. and the man left Veronica accused me of having hired him. I took her upstairs and sent Frances up to bed and tried to clean her up. She lay doggo for a bit and when I was in the bathroom left the house. The circumstantial evidence against me is strong in that V will say it was all my doing. I will also lie doggo for a bit but I am only concerned for the children. If you can manage it I want them to live with you - Coutts (Trustees) St Martins Lane (Mr Wall) will handle school fees. V. has demonstrated her hatred for me in the past and would do anything to see me accused. For George and Frances to go through life knowing their father had stood in the dock for attempted murder would be too much. When they are old enough to understand, explain to them the dream of paranoia, and look after them.

Yours ever

John

Having sealed this letter Lucan then wrote a second letter to
Bill Shand Kydd:

FINANCIAL MATTERS
There is a sale coming up at Christies Nov 27th
which will satisfy bank overdrafts. Please agree
reserves with Tom Craig.
Proceeds to go to: Lloyds: 6 Pall Mall, Coutts, 59,
Strand, Nat West, Bloomsbury Branch, who also
hold an Eq. and Law Life Policy.
The other creditors can get lost for the time being.
Lucky

According to Susie Maxwell-Scott's version of events Lucan
left her house shortly after 1.00am telling her that he had to
get back to sort things out. He had asked Susie for something
to help him sleep, and she had given him four valium pills.
Susie Maxwell-Scott was the last known person to see Lord
Lucan before his stealthy disappearing act. Whether she
gave a true account of this visit by Lucan on the night of the
murder has always been open to speculation.

From Uckfield it would appear the earl drove to Newhaven,
on the coast, and parked the borrowed Ford Corsair in Norman
Road.

From here, Richard John Bingham, Seventh Earl of Lucan,
vanished into thin air, never to be seen again.

The day after the murder, Friday 8 November, Detective
Chief Superintendent Roy Ranson and Detective Chief
Inspector David Gerring set up an incident room at Gerald
Road Police Station. Search warrants were organised and
photos of the wanted earl were distributed to forces around
the country. The two officers returned to the cottage in Eaton
Row and Lucan's five-bedroom apartment in Elizabeth Street
and took away his diary and address book containing all his

friends and contacts. Lucan's blue Mercedes was towed away to be checked over and the forensic people carried out further examinations at Lower Belgrave Street, the mews cottage and Lucan's flat.

Ranson and Gerring visited the earl's exclusive clubs and restaurants and set up discreet watches on those closely associated with him.

At the Clermont Club, Billy Edgson, the doorman, told the detectives that Lucan had pulled up outside the club in his blue Mercedes at around 8.45pm the previous evening – the night of the murder – and that they had exchanged a few words before he drove off saying he would be back later. At the reception desk they learned that the earl had booked a table for 11pm that night.

Billy Edgson's statement that he had seen Lucan shortly before 9pm created a conundrum and another chink in the police case against the earl that his supporters would jump on. If Edgson saw Lucan at around 8.45pm then it would have been pretty difficult for him to get to Lower Belgrave Street in time to prepare for a murder which apparently took place between 8.45pm and 9pm.

On the Saturday the 9th, the police got their first real breakthrough. Bill Shand Kydd, went to Gerald Road Police Station and handed over the two letters he had received by post from Lucan.

The letters bore an Uckfield postmark and soon Ranson and Gerring were on there way to the Maxwell-Scott's country pile, Grants Hill House, in Sussex.

The Maxwell-Scott's were very good friends of Lord Lucan. The couple lived in splendid isolation and considerable comfort with their seven children and German Shepherd dogs. Susie was a barrister and her husband Ian was a Clermont director and cousin of the Duke of Norfolk.

Susie Maxwell-Scott confirmed that Lucan had visited her on the night of the murder and that he had written some letters and made a telephone call to his mother.

'Why did you not telephone the police?' Gerring asked pointedly.

'He told me that he was going to sort things out,' she said, and then added, 'I saw no need to do anything.'

This laissez-faire attitude infuriated Ranson and Gerring, which was just a foretaste of things to come as it would not be the first time they would encounter such aloofness from Lucan's inner circle of well heeled, privately educated elite who, it seemed, were prepared to close ranks to protect their friend.

It must have been in the detectives mind to arrest her on the spot but she was a barrister and would kick up an almighty fuss and, besides, the two detectives had a much bigger agenda and a bigger fish to fry. They could always come back and charge her at a future date should they so decide.

On the Sunday, four days after the murder, the police got the break they had been praying for. Lucan's borrowed car had been found in Norman Road, Newhaven. Ranson and Gerring were at home catching up on sleep – the first rest they had managed to grab since the murder.

When informed of the discovery they hotfooted it to Newhaven.

On inspection of the Ford Corsair it was found that both the drivers seat and passenger seat were bloodstained, as well as the dashboard and steering wheel. A neighbour told the police that he had looked out of his window at 5am and the car was not there but when he next looked at 8am the car was parked opposite his house. Susie Maxwell-Scott had told the police that Lucan left her house shortly after 1.00am,

Chapter Seven

which begs the question where did the earl go in those hours after leaving Uckfield?

But it was in the boot of the Corsair that the detectives would discover a most incriminating object that would seal Lucan's guilt beyond any doubt. Lying between two bottles of vodka was a cosh, a length of lead pipe bound with surgical tape. A bludgeon that was identical to the blood stained weapon found at the murder scene.

CHAPTER EIGHT

Having found Lucan's borrowed car in Newhaven the police now concentrated their efforts on that area of the south coast. Officers were drafted in from London to search the Sussex Downs. Police from Eastbourne and Brighton, along with tracker dogs, joined the London police in a methodical combing of the hills and forests that straddled behind, and either side of the busy Ferry Town.

Detective David Gerring, headed a team of officers to interview Sealink ferry staff and searches were carried out in the marina and on fishing trawlers moored at the quayside. They also questioned staff of pubs, guesthouses and hotels in the town. Immigration staff were quizzed as to whether a man resembling Lucan had tried to obtain a 48-hour passport on the morning following the murder.

Detective Roy Ranson, was conjuring with the idea that Lucan might have committed suicide by throwing himself overboard from a ferry halfway across the Channel – ferries for the French coast departed daily from Newhaven. But that was no more than a hunch and so a team of frogmen was organised to plumb the River Ouse, the marina and harbour.

The army also helped in the search with around a hundred soldiers combing thick gorse and undergrowth, which covered vast areas of the uplands. A group of volunteer professional pot-holers checked caves and inlets along the coast.

As the manhunt intensified Gerring set off to France with an interpreter to interview hoteliers and staff at the seaports of Dieppe, Cherbourg and St Malo. Alerts had also been sent to airports and seaports to be on the lookout for a tall, slim Englishman, possibly travelling on a false passport.

Interpol in Paris had been flashed a message which read: 'Wanted for murder and attempted murder: Richard John Bingham, Seventh Earl of Lucan. Please arrest.' Meanwhile, Ranson had extended the search along the coast as far as Eastbourne and Peacehaven, but now with the help of a new piece of sophisticated equipment acquired from Plessy that was used in the Bond film, *You Only Live Twice*. This was an auto-gyro with an array of cameras using X-ray, infra-red and ultra-violet light that could hover in the air and detect decomposing matter on the ground, even penetrating through forests and thick cover. The gyro did find something but it was not the earls body, but that of the skeletal remains of a judge who had disappeared three years earlier.

As the days went by in Newhaven, the two lead detectives were in no mood to give up the hunt. Ranson felt sure that this area held the clue to Lucan's escape or suicide. More police were drafted in to forage the hills and woodlands and frogmen and deep-sea divers extended their search of the coast, the River Ouse and the harbour.

While the manhunt was painstakingly proceeding on the south coast, the lead detectives were being kept up to date with information that was coming in by the day from the London police.

On the Monday following the murder, Michael Stoop, who had loaned Lucan his old Ford Corsair, telephoned Gerald Road Police Station to say that he had received a letter from the earl.

The letter read:

My Dear Michael,

I have had a traumatic night of unbelievable coincidence. However I won't bore you with anything or involve you except to say that when you come across my children, which I hope you will, please tell them that you knew me and that all I cared about was them. The fact that a crooked solicitor and a rotten psychiatrist destroyed me between them will be of no importance to the children. I gave Bill Shand-Kydd an account of what actually happened but judging by my last effort in court no-one, yet alone a 67 year old judge - would believe - and I no longer care except that my children should be protected.

Yours ever, John

According to Michael Stoop, the duty officer had told him to hand the letter in at the police station when he was next passing – a fact disputed by the police.

Stoop, produced the letter at 3am the following morning, presumably when he had strolled out of the St James's Club. When asked for the envelope he said that he had not realised its importance and had thrown it away at the club where it had been delivered minus a postage stamp.

The police went immediately to the St James's Club in search of the envelope and its all important postmark. They were too late, the rubbish had been collected and taken away.

Whether this was a deliberate act by Michael Stoop to insti-
gate a delay and keep the envelope out of police hands was a
matter of dispute between him and the police. Nevertheless,
the police had the distinct feeling that Lucan's friends were
being less than co-operative, and that their ulterior motive was
to help one of their own, no matter what crime he may have
committed.

On the day after the murder, John Aspinall had called what
can only be described as a 'knights of the round table' lunch
meeting at his house in Lyall Street, Mayfair.

Bill Shand Kydd was there along with Dominick Elwes,
Charles Benson, Michael Stoop, Daniel Meinertzhagen and
Stephen Raphael. Jimmy Goldsmith would almost certainly
have attended if he had not been in Dublin on business.

The police, aware of this meeting, saw this as just another
attempt by the so-called Clermont Set to close ranks and for-
mulate a plan of action to help their friend – A fellow knight
and one of their elite inner circle.

Detective Chief Superintendent Roy Ranson would later
write: 'The Lucan Clan were aloof and unapproachable,
regarding themselves as better than other people.' His deputy,
David Gerring, was less polite calling them the 'Eton Mafia.'
In the following years he would state: 'These people had a
weird idea that they were somehow superior beings. That they
were above the law.'

In James Ruddick's excellent book on the Lucan story, he
recounts how the police came up against a wall of aristocratic
ambivalence. Foot policemen carrying out interviews of the
well-heeled, leisured aristocracy, were relating how some of
these people held a totally blasé view about the murder of
Sandra Rivett. One woman was reported to have said: 'What
a shame, nannies are so hard to come by these days,' and
another toff had joked about Lucan: 'It's not as though he's

done something really bad, like vote Labour.' The police were also receiving numerous hoax calls saying that Lucan was in this or that casino and giving the police the run-around. Detective Roy Ranson called these hoax calls, 'The horse-play of the upper classes.'

Ranson was also being deeply frustrated by those he wished to interview who would say something like: 'Terribly sorry, old boy, can't see you for a few weeks, I'm off to Austria to do some skiing.'

There was no doubt that the police were having a hard time dealing with a class of wealthy Mayfair types who probably thought that the police should be concentrated in the East End of London, dealing with gangs and drug barons rather than encroach into the sacred areas of Mayfair and Belgravia and their exclusive world of dining and gambling at Crockfords, Brooks, St James's and the Clermont Club.

But not all of Lucan's allies adopted disrespect towards the police. Bill Shand Kydd had been more than co-operative and had made it clear that Lucan should give himself up and face the music, and Jimmy Goldsmith had been polite and straightforward when interviewed by the police.

On the twelfth of November, five days after the murder of Sandra Rivett, a warrant was issued by Bow Street Magistrates' Court for the arrest of Lord Lucan. Search warrants were distributed for houses and estates that were in any way connected with the missing earl. No fewer than twelve 'country estates' would be investigated.

In the following days searches were carried out in Scotland, Leicester and at Warwick Castle, whose presiding earl had married Lucan's second cousin.

At the same time Bill Shand Kydd made a public appeal on ITV's *News at Ten* for the earl to come forward, saying:

'Whatever the rights or wrongs John, contact me and we will get a solicitor and go to the police together.'

The Coroner's Office in London was pressing Scotland Yard for a date to hold an inquest into the death of Sandra Rivett, which was the last thing the police wanted. They were still hopeful of catching their man and were aware that should an inquest name Lucan as the murderer and he were later to be apprehended it would have a totally prejudicial bearing upon a future High Court trial. It was essential to catch Lucan and give him the opportunity of a fair hearing.

The Coroner's Office replied saying they were prepared to be patient given the unusual circumstances of the case and arranged a postponement until the following month. However, they stressed there should be a degree of urgency by the police due to the fallibility of witnesses memories.

After nearly two weeks the massive manhunt around Newhaven and the south coast was called off. The two lead detectives were left deeply frustrated; so many hopes had been dashed that this area would throw up the clues to Lucan's death or escape.

Perhaps the discovery of Lucan's car in a quiet street at the back of the Ferry Town was no more than a foil to give the police a false lead. If that had been the plan then it had worked brilliantly.

By the time Detective Roy Ranson and his deputy arrived at John Aspinall's sprawling estate and zoo, Howletts, in Kent, they were weary and in no mood to be treated with contempt by this gregarious socialite.

Aspinall told the detectives that the rumour circulating about Lucan having been fed to his Siberian tigers was absolute rubbish, sarcastically adding that his tigers followed a strict diet, which did not include human flesh. He then airily asked if the police, who were making a thorough search of the house and grounds, intended to pull up the floorboards of his living room.

Detective David Gerring, clashed bitterly with John Aspinall, reminding him in no uncertain terms that a murder had been committed and that anyone found to be helping the earl would be in big trouble. Aspinall countered jauntily by saying that: 'If Veronica had been his wife he would have throttled her years ago, and so would you.' he added.

On a further occasion the detectives visited John Aspinall's zoo the butler made them wait fifteen minutes before ushering the officers into a room where Aspinall was seated at a table with his mother and an African gorilla.

Aspinall was completely unafraid of the police and immune from media criticism about his continuing loyalty and support for Lucan. 'I formed the view he was secretly laughing at us,' David Gerring would later say.

Dealing with Aspinall's formidable mother, Lady Osborne, the granny of the present Tory Chancellor George Osborne was also fraught – she had not been nicknamed 'Al Capone with a handbag' for nothing – and the police met a cavalier attitude when attempting to interview her.

Aspinall's mother, having divorced whom he supposed to be his father, Robert Aspinall, a Maltese army surgeon with the Indian Medical Service, took up and married a sympathetic colonel. The couple moved from India to England and settled into village life in Sussex. She would have three more children with the colonel, but John, her love child, who was born in Delhi and moved with his mother to England would always remain her favourite. Some years after settling in England, Colonel Osborne inherited a baronetcy and overnight the one-time Mary Aspinall who had resolved so hard to distance herself from the dusty plains of Central India discovered to her delight that she was now Lady Osborne.

Chapter Eight

This must have amused John Aspinall immensely, for he would spend most of his working life courting the rich and titled, especially those with money to gamble at his poker and chemmy parties and later at his casino the Clermont Club.

The police knew that Lady Osborne was very close to Lord Lucan. It was said that he regarded her as his second mother and had sought her support and comfort as his marriage and finances slowly disintegrated. She, like him, was an inveterate gambler. After the Clermont was sold to Victor Lownes she still played at the club and would leave a chimp in a carrycot at reception while she went upstairs to gamble.

Dealing with the likes of Aspinall, his mother and Lucan's close associates who seemed to cock-a-snook at authority was heaping intense pressure on Ranson and Gerring to capture the runaway earl. The case had attracted huge media interest, set as it was, against the backdrop of the times. The murder of a working class nanny in posh Belgravia had struck an emotive chord with an already disaffected public.

It was impossible to study the Lord Lucan case without affording some time to learn about those who surrounded him, for they were so much part of the story.

The leading player in all this, was of course, John Aspinall. Unlike most of those who would later make up the Clermont Set, Aspinall had not come from a moneyed background. He was, as he would later learn, the penniless son of a penniless soldier.

His rise to wealth came about after a long and bumpy road in which fluctuating fortunes had come and then disappeared with depressing regularity.

His mother persuaded her new husband to pay for him to go to Rugby School, where he was a disinterested student who was eventually expelled. That was the last of any privilege that would be extended to him by his stepfather. After Rugby, he was on his own. Having done three years military service with the Royal Marines in which he neither achieved promotion or distinction he applied for a place at Oxford.

Amazingly, Jesus College accepted him, for no other reason it would seem, than he had played for Rugby's First XV.

At Oxford, his chosen subject, English Literature, soon took second place to the new passion in his life – gambling – a pastime he pursued with the utmost skill and vigour. Along with other students of a similar bent he gravitated to the legendary Maxie's in Walton Street, kept by a former vaudeville artiste. This was a serious gambling den where the more fortunate Oxford young bucks with rich parents to back up their IOUs, could gamble all day and night. It was at Maxie's that Aspinall would meet Jimmy Goldsmith and Ian Maxwell-Scott, both outrageous gamblers, and with whom he would forge lifelong friendships. Gamblers find each other and the seeds of what would later become the Clermont Set had been sown.

Aspinall trained himself to be a top-class player, for unlike most of his contemporaries in the smoke-filled rooms of Maxie's he did not have spare cash to lose, or wealthy parents to fall back on. He always displayed great self-control and concentration, but most importantly he was a teetotaller, which gave him a certain edge when other players began to flag under the influence of an endless supply of alcohol. After three years at university, both he and Maxwell-Scott decided to skip final examination day at Oxford, telling the invigilator that they were not feeling well. They then headed-off to Royal Ascot to watch the Gold Cup. For two dedicated gamblers who had little interest in studying for a degree, the choice between Finals and Ascot week was pretty clear cut.

Chapter Eight

After Oxford, Aspinall, and Maxwell-Scott, stumbled from one business venture to another, which always centred around gambling. With a loan from Ian's parents they set up as race-course bookies, which never took-off as this was a trade very much sewn up by the experienced layers who discouraged competition, and in any case, Ian could never resist gambling himself. They moved on to acting as shills in shady poker clubs in the West End and attempting to pull-off the occasional betting scam against the bookmakers. Money would come and go but most of the time they were broke and had to live off their wits until they could conjure-up the next round of funds.

On one of these occasions Aspinall sought out his father, hoping that he might oblige with a loan. His father refused. Aspinall asked why? To which Robert Aspinall replied: 'I am not your father.'

This was of course a huge shock to John who nevertheless took it in his stride and sought out his real father, a retired Lincolnshire Regiment major general, now living on an army pension in a flat in London. Aspinall went to the address and introduced himself to his father who invited his newly found offspring inside for a drink. Apparently it was a rather unemotional meeting of father and son.

Later Aspinall would relate this coming together and say: 'And do you know what – he didn't even offer me a fiver.' Aspinall knew that if he was ever going to achieve the fortune he craved it was likely to come from the only trade he really loved and understood – gambling. To this end, and on borrowed money, he set himself up at the Ritz hotel.

The story goes that when Aspinall tracked down his old ally Ian Maxwell-Scott to a smelly slum property in south London due for demolition, he found his friend crashed-out on the floor buried under sheets of the racing pages. 'Ian things are looking up.' Aspinall said. 'We've got a thousand pounds and we're going to stay at the Ritz.'

'Oh no, not the Ritz,' Maxwell-Scott replied. 'The food there is quite terrible.' Aspinall's poker parties at the Ritz were a great success. For all his shortcomings Maxwell-Scott possessed a vast knowledge of food and wine and only the best fare was on offer for their guests. Lobster and caviar were accompanied with the best clarets and vintage champagne.

Word spread about these lavish affairs and soon a new character would enter the life of John Aspinall. His name was Dominick Elwes, a successful portrait painter to the rich and titled including royalty. Elwes, was a happy-go-lucky playboy with a ready wit and an easy manner that attracted people to him. He was someone who could enliven any party with his good looks, charm and sense of fun. Aspinall took to him immediately. Along with his social contacts he was part of the mix the entrepreneur was always seeking in his quest for El Dorado, and Dominick would soon become the most ebullient of the five key-members that would make up the Clermont Set.

With Elwes introducing more classy punters to the Ritz soirées, Aspinall's network of elite, dedicated gamblers, which he had coveted from his Rugby days was ever expanding. Making and keeping the right sort of friends close to him was Aspinall's unique gift and he was unfazed when the Ritz eventually kicked him out for using their hotel as an illegal gambling venue. He had learned a great deal from the enterprise and had gained a special friend in Dominick Elwes.

After the Ritz parties there followed an aimless period before, and with financial backing, he set-up an off-course bookies at the back of Oxford Street, but his heart was not in the venture and he often left his mother to run the faltering business. He was still searching for that elusive niche in the market that his instincts told him was waiting to be discovered. He was aware that there were plenty of high rollers out there who wanted nothing more than to spend their leisure time sprinkling their abundant cash across a gaming table.

The answer he had been looking for came out of the blue. He and Dominick Elwes invited themselves to a gambling party in Mayfair. But the game was not poker, bridge or backgammon, it was baccarat chemin de fer, the game that had intoxicated gamblers throughout the centuries and which vast fortunes had been won and lost. For Aspinall the real beauty of the game, which he immediately realised, was the cagnotte, a percentage the bank would take for each game to cover so-called running costs and hosting the event. Aspinall had at last found the Holy Grail he had been seeking for so long and knew instinctively that he was the very man with the style, influence and connections to run these games better than anyone else.

And so he did. He was a perfectionist when it came to playing host. A fine house was rented in Brook Street, Mayfair. Ian Maxwell-Scott was in charge of the food and wine, Dominick was there with his infectious charm and bonhomie and a top class Italian croupier was engaged. The chemmy parties were a tremendous success and thanks to the cagnotte Aspinall was pocketing a fifth of every pound gambled. It was riches beyond even Aspinall's dreams and soon he was making up to £20,000 a night. He simply couldn't lose. The greater the stakes wagered the bigger his profits. What Aspinall had learned above all else on his bumpy road to riches and his climb up the mostly illegal greasy-pole of gaming was ambience. Gamblers could stomach losing and come back for more if that money disappeared in a certain style. Losses did not seem too bad when the best free wine and food was plentiful, the company was desirable and the evening was spent in sumptuous surroundings. Win or lose, punters had to feel that it had been an engaging affair – one to which they would return.

Understanding this was Aspinall's genius. Class and exclusiveness was the key – together with the players being matched with those of similar wealth or social standing. The Clermont Club was some years away but he was well on his way.

The one problem he now faced was to keep these chemmy affairs on the move. You could not stay too long in the one place and attract the police to uphold the shaky gaming laws. Running what could be considered a casino was illegal. Aspinall soon found a way round this. He had plenty of wealthy friends who were more than willing to loan out their houses in Mayfair, Knightsbridge, Belgravia and Chelsea and as word spread of these opulent affairs more wealthy high rollers appeared on the scene.

Around this time a new member of these floating chemmy parties presented himself. His name was Mark Birley. Mark had been a dedicated gambler from his days at Eton. He had recently married Lady Annabel Vane-Tempest-Stewart, the daughter of the Marquess of Londonderry. Mark was an astute businessman having cut his teeth at the advertising giant J.Walter Thomson where he had been a successful marketing man. Aspinall liked him enormously, realising they had much in common and the pair soon formed a strong friendship. When Aspinall opened the Clermont in 1962 with a subscription list of more than seven hundred members, Mark Birley leased the large downstairs area and turned this into one of the finest and most glamorous nightclubs in Town. Despite the clubs adherence to a strict dress code the venue became incredibly popular and was soon the favourite haunt of personalities and fashionable society.

Chapter Eight

Among those refused entry over the years for not being properly attired were Eric Clapton, George Harrison and Prince Andrew, which did no more than add appeal and exclusivity to this new and glamorous address.

Birley named his club Annabel's after his wife. As both Annabel's and the Clermont prospered Birley became increasingly immersed in the life and world of John Aspinall and the inner circle who surrounded him. With his astute business acumen he had calmly slipped into the role as the third member of the Clermont Set.

In the following years Birley and Aspinall had a falling-out and the staircase that linked both clubs, and which had been such a symbol of collaboration between the two owners and their venues was closed-off.

This had not been the only falling-out for Mark Birley, for despite the huge success of his nightclub and a seemingly happy marriage with three young children his wife Annabel, left him, falling into the arms of the predatory Jimmy Goldsmith.

Mark Birley, I discovered, was the first casualty to exit the Clermont Set under a cloud, but he would not be the last. It would get worse – much worse.

Of the Clermont Set, Jimmy Goldsmith, was by far the most shrewd and successful member. After Oxford he did his National Service with the Royal Artillery proving to be an excellent young officer. After his service he set his sights on making money with insatiable bravado, something he probably inherited from his intrepid father, Frank Goldsmith, Conservative MP for Stowmarket and a likeable and respected landowner.

When the First World War broke out Jimmy's father, Frank joined the Suffolk Yeomanry and fought for his country in Gallipoli and Palestine. However, at the end of the war he suffered from anti-German feelings relating to his German, Jewish roots. The hurt ran deep and he thereafter severed his ties from England and returned to France where he started a hotel business eventually building up a portfolio of over 40 grand hotels stretching from Paris to Monte Carlo.

When Germany invaded France at the beginning of the Second World War and at the age of sixty-one, he fled with his family back to England, the country he still loved and admired and duly tried to enlist in the British Army to fight the Nazis. Despite an appeal to his old friend Winston Churchill he was, unsurprisingly, turned down for active service due to his age. His two boys, Jimmy and Teddy, were sent to Canada while he and his wife retreated to Nassau to see out the war in comfort with their friends the Windsors and another grand hotel to manage, the Royal Victoria.

Jimmy Goldsmith was determined to be as dashing and entrepreneurial as his father but he would first endure a bitter taste of triumph and tragedy.

At the age of twenty-one he was introduced to a beautiful young girl by Dominick Elwes. Her name was Isabel, the daughter of Don Antenor Patino, a seriously wealthy Bolivian multi-millionaire who had no intentions of seeing his daughter take-up with a poor Jewish man who he regarded to be well below her class. But the young couple had fallen in love and despite all the efforts to keep them apart they eloped to Scotland and married.

Jimmy's first foray in to love and marriage ended barely five months later in Paris. Isabel, heavily pregnant died of a brain haemorrhage. The baby was saved by Caesarean section, a healthy, five-pound baby girl who Jimmy named Isabel, in memory of her mother and his first love.

How long it took Jimmy Goldsmith to get over this is not clear but in the following years he set about building up a business empire with voracious energy. He took many risks and nearly went bankrupt on many occasions, but would always bounce back with an even greater desire to win in the cut-throat world of capitalism. He won the British franchise for Alka-Seltzer and invested in low-cost generic drugs, which he imported into the UK. He gradually built-up a pharmaceutical industry investing in companies manufacturing a wide range of products.

In a partnership in the early 1960s Goldsmith founded the Mothercare retail chain. By the time Aspinall opened the Clermont Club, Jimmy, from humble beginnings, was already a multi-millionaire and by far the most wealthy and powerful member of the group.

Love him or hate him, Jimmy Goldsmith achieved much in his life, financier, industrialist, politician and later in life a leading environmentalist.

His marriage to Annabel produced three more children. The first child Jemima, became something of a celebrity with her beauty and marriage to Imran Khan, the famous Pakistani cricketer and politician. The second of two boys, Zac Goldsmith is Conservative MP for Richmond Park and former front runner to succeed Boris Johnson as Mayor of London.

And so to the fifth and final member of the Clermont Set – and Aspinall's favourite. He was a certain Lord Bingham, heir to the Sixth Earl of Lucan, a family descended from a long line of eighteenth-century Irish landowners. They had met at one of Aspinall's floating chemmy soirées and had hit it off instantly. Like Birley, Lord Bingham had picked up his serious gambling habit at Eton.

For Aspinall he was far more than just another addition to his growing coterie of rich, dedicated gamblers. Aspinall was impressed with this tall, strikingly good-looking aristocrat who had a certain reserved, almost shy demeanour. He had gained a reputation as a skilled bridge and backgammon player and demonstrated a detached, fearless manner at the baccarat table. That he had won a small fortune playing the game in France added to his appeal. He was very much an 'Aspinall' man.

When Aspinall spread his wealth among his friends with his African safari jaunts complete with private plane and the finest hospitality that money could buy, Lord Richard John Bingham was the first name on the guest list. The two seemed to find in each other something they both needed. For the young aristocrat, Aspinall had not only become a trusted friend but had afforded him the chance to spend his leisure time as he wished – playing baccarat. But it was more than just that, Aspinall had also introduced him to a society of wealthy, like-minded gamblers who would become close friends and form part of his social circle.

And so the Clermont Set was complete. People really do find each other. All privately educated, Downside, Eton, Rugby, and Oxford and the umbilical cord that had brought them all together was gambling. Aspinall and Goldsmith had become millionaires from nothing. It was – somewhat perversely – because they were gamblers that they had managed this. They had always been risk-takers. Losses and setbacks did not dissuade them or dampen their spirits as it might other aspiring businessmen. They simply brushed-off failures and started again. By the beginning of the sixties Aspinall had relieved enough cash from his wealthy gamblers that he was able to purchase number 44 Berkeley Square and shower a fortune on the Palladian building to restore the exquisite town house to its former glory. When the club, which Aspinall named the Clermont, opened its doors in 1962 its fabulous interior rivalled anything to be found in Deauville or Le Touquet.

Having won a landmark court case in 1958, Aspinall had, single-handedly, bought about major changes to the antiquated UK gaming laws. When the Clermont opened to such fanfare it was still only a shill – a gentlemen's club – but it was a beginning and a major relaxing of the law. Legalised casinos would follow but it would take a further six-years. John Victor Aspinall, had nevertheless, paved the way.

It had been worthwhile reading about Lucan's friends for I was attempting to paint a picture of the man I was studying and, bizarre as it might seem, possibly the very same person I planned to meet-up with again in Mallorca.

Having swotted-up on those that formed Aspinall's inner circle, I resumed my research into the murder of Sandra Rivett.

The papers had seized on the story of the Clermont Set, and now their readers were being shown glimpses into the world of the super rich who could afford to lose in a single night at the baccarat table more than a miner or milkman might earn in a year. And one of this elite – a peer-of-the-realm no less – had it seemed, battered a young woman to death at a house in Belgravia and escaped scot-free.

That he may have been helped to flee justice with the help and support of a powerful clan of wealthy insiders at an exclusive Mayfair casino made the scandal even more powerful and abhorrent. The story was no longer simply about Lord Lucan, but was increasingly focussing on the company that surrounded him. Many were believing that this was confirmation of a 'Them and Us' society that these Mayfair swells were above the law. Could it be that with their money and influence they were able to spirit a murderer out of the country to start life afresh in the sun?

The sense of injustice and resentment, whipped up by the press, was felt strongly by a disillusioned populace who were suffering amid the uncertainty and austerity prevailing throughout the UK at the time.

1974 was not a good year for the country. Apart from Abba singing *Waterloo*, and winning the Eurovision Song Contest in Brighton, reminding the British of a former great victory, there was little to cheer elsewhere.

The *Wall Street Journal* had branded Britain, 'The sick man of Europe.' A minority Labour Party were stuttering along having dismissed Ted Heath from office along with the three-day week and his failed mantra of 'Who governs Britain.' The message had come back from the voters, which simply said: 'Not you mate.'

Wilson's Labour Party had at least got the lights back on and had managed to pacify the unions for the time being, but inflation would hit nearly 20 per cent by the end of the year and public spending had increased to 35 per cent. The top rate of tax was increased to 83 per cent.

In February, an IRA coach bombing killed twelve on the M62.

In March, ten miners died in a methane gas explosion at Golborne Colliery near Wigan, Lancashire, Later that month the government re-established direct rule over Northern Ireland after declaring a state of emergency.

June and July, saw further bombs explode outside Westminster Hall and the White Tower inside the Tower of London.

Throughout July, England football supporters endured the ignominy of watching an economically resurgent West Germany win the World Cup. A tournament missing England as they did not even manage to qualify.

In August, Courtline and its subsidiaries went bust leaving 100,000 holidaymakers stranded abroad.

October saw another IRA bomb kill five in a pub in Guildford, Surrey. Harold Wilson won the second election of the year, but with only a three-seat majority. The SNP had their best ever showing winning eleven seats.

In November, twenty-one people were killed in a single night from two more pub bombs in Birmingham.

As I sifted through so much material relating to the murder at 46 Lower Belgrave Street, it was evident that this crime could not be disassociated with the social and political aspects that centred on the times.

Indeed, there were powerful individuals at places like the Clermont Club who really did believe they were somehow above the law, immune to the troubles of the age and that it was only themselves who could come to the rescue of the country should the unions or communist factions threaten the social order of a land that only they knew how should be governed.

Heading this crazy right-wing group was Colonel David Stirling, founder of the SAS. He had plenty of support at the Clermont with among others Greville Howard who had worked as an aide to Enoch Powell and Michael Stoop, with his fine war record and the man who had loaned Lucan his car. There were many others at the Clermont and other Mayfair clubs who were ready to join Stirling's *de facto* army who would protect the country against a communist takeover or a general strike.

What all these grandiose prima donna's seemed to have in common was a hatred of Harold Wilson and his government. They believed Wilson had communist leanings and was a KGB plant along with his friend Lord Kagan who was implicated with a Russian officer at the Soviet Embassy. This paranoia of the Labour Party stretched to Tony Benn who they absolutely despised, seeing him as a class traitor.

Despite the lordly right wing mutterings behind smoke-filled gaming rooms in Mayfair, Harold Wilson had won the General Election in October, and now a certain message needed to be relayed to the public. Discreet memos were being passed down from MI5 and the Home Office to Scotland Yard.

Chief investigators, Ranson and Gerring had been made aware by the top brass within Scotland Yard that it was essential they catch Lucan at any cost. Not just for the murder of Sandra Rivett, but to send a clear message to the society that surrounded him – You are not above the law, nor are you running the country.

The searches of houses and estates from Scotland to Kent had drawn a blank. Meanwhile, so-called sightings of Lucan kept pouring in, but they were no more than a waste of police time. However, in December, Detectives Ranson and Gerring thought that they had hit lucky. Reports were coming in from Australia that the police had arrested Lord Lucan. It was not to be; once photographs had been sent to the Australian police it was clear that the man they were holding was not the missing earl.

But it was a wonderful catch all the same. The man they had nabbed was none other than John Stonehouse, the Labour MP and Postmaster General, who had faked his death by leaving his clothes on a Miami Beach and disappearing to be presumed drowned.

He was deported back to the UK and given a seven-year prison sentence for fraud. But the main man could not to be found and the police were no nearer finding the disappearing earl than they had been at any time since the night of the murder. As each day and week passed the chances of finding him were becoming more remote.

Richard John Bingham, Seventh Earl of Lucan, had flown the nest.

CHAPTER NINE

I had got stuck into my research of the Lucan case but it was a
lot harder than I could possibly have imagined. I found myself
sifting through some forty years of stories, claims and counter
claims, new revelatory press articles, and one time silent
family members and associates of the earl who were suddenly
popping out of the woodwork and espousing their views to
the media about his guilt or otherwise, and whether he might
be alive or dead.

Although I could vaguely remember the case way back in
the seventies, I had not realised the enormity of interest and
publicity about the story that had seemingly gone on forever
and that even after four decades had simply refused to go away.

Ploughing through all this material was absorbing but also
somewhat confusing. Not many observers, apart from the
police, could quite agree as to how events had unfolded on the
night of 7 November 1974, and what happened afterwards.

Speculation and theories kept surfacing with intriguing
regularity in the press, magazines and the television year after
year.

Chapter Nine

I was coming to the end of my enforced rest at home and my course of antibiotics, but I had used the time well and was not going to be hurried back to Mallorca. The journalist Paul King would have to wait until I was armed with all the facts and ready to conjure up the boldness to meet up again with that dapper, and maybe most elusive runaway in British criminal history – Mr. Sidney Ainsworth.

I knew deep down that I should have handed this over to Paul King with the proviso that whatever the truth he would refrain from getting Sidney into any trouble. It was his line of work. He was qualified to investigate this – I was not. Nevertheless, I would try and hold my nerve and stick with my plan. So long as I could keep my identity a secret I should be safe, and could walk away at any time.

The books and articles I had downloaded about Lord Lucan had proved very interesting and was the best way for me to really get a grip on this tale.

In 1994, on the twentieth anniversary of the Lucan disappearing act there erupted a frenzy of renewed interest in the mystery.

Three books were published as well as a Channel 4 *True Stories* documentary and the BBC and Granada chipped in with their offerings on the riddle.

Two of the publications were by the Scotland Yard detectives who were in charge of the murder inquiry, and competition between the two books was intense.

Retired Detective, Chief Superintendent Roy Ranson, led the investigation. His book –*Looking For Lucan* was scheduled to tie-in with the Channel 4 documentary. Ranson's book was also the subject of a battle for serialisation rights. When the *Daily Mail* published extracts, the *Daily Express* ran a 'spoiler' – Its own serialisation based on –*Lucan Lives* a book by

Ranson's deputy, former Detective, Chief Inspector David Gerring.

While Ranson and Gerring at least agree that Lucan is guilty, the Granada Production –*The Trial of Lord Lucan* took on the novel approach of recruiting a jury to decide Lucan's guilt or otherwise. (After two hours of deliberation they were unable to reach a decision and were split right down the middle).

Ranson's book describes in methodical detail the murder scene, and the evidence that was collected, as well as details concerning the Coroner's Inquest which led to a major change in how such inquests would be handled in the future. In later accounts of the investigation it became clear that he and his deputy, David Gerring, did not always see eye-to-eye and sometimes reached different conclusions about the case.

Ranson, despite giving the initial impression that he believed Lucan had committed suicide, suddenly announced a complete volte-face come the twentieth anniversary of the enigma, stating his belief that the earl was alive and living in Africa.

With a crew from Channel 4's production team *True Stories* Ranson set out to Botswana in search of one of the world's most elusive fugitives. They visited Gaborone, the bustling capital just fifteen miles from the border with South Africa. Here, armed with pictures of Lucan that had been artificially touched up to age him they interviewed anyone and everyone, especially those who liked a gamble at the main casino. They spent three weeks in Botswana also visiting the Tuli Block, which is home to a number of privately owned game farms offering safari tourism.

It was known that Lucan had holidayed in Africa with John Aspinall on one of the entrepreneur's safari jaunts and so there was a connection with the continent.

However, Ranson and the TV team returned home empty handed and none the wiser than when they had set out. It had all been somewhat frivolous, searching out a story that had no real substance or research to back up claims that Lucan had ever fled to Botswana. Ranson's son, writing in the *Daily Mirror* some years later revealed that his father had kept a photograph of Lucan in his wallet right up until the day he died.

The third book to appear on the twentieth anniversary of the murder of Sandra Rivett was a work by the journalist James Ruddick. This book was the best of the three by a country mile. The book was carefully compiled over a number of years and was superbly written and researched. In his title – *Lord Lucan. The Truth About The Century's Most Celebrated Murder Mystery* Ruddick looked afresh at the whole drama, seeking out interviews with a host of the major players and gaining an insight into the thinking and theories that had persisted for so long.

He interviewed Detective Roy Ranson as well as his deputy, David Gerring who was by now running a pub in Kent. Gerring was able to throw light on the thorny problem of how different blood groups found at the murder scene had turned up in unexpected places, giving rise to much controversy about how the forensic evidence was managed. Gerring also confirmed his gut feeling that he had held from the beginning of the investigation, that Lucan, probably with the help of the 'Clermont Set' – described by him as the 'Clermont Mafia' – had escaped justice and ended up abroad to see out his days.

But the most revealing of interviews that Ruddick managed to pull-off was a series of discussions with Lady Lucan who was by now living in somewhat reduced circumstances at the mews cottage in Eaton Row that she and Lucan had owned and which was perched behind what was once their former grander residence in Lower Belgrave Street.

James Ruddick handled these interviews with great care and sensitivity over a period of months, building up a feeling of trust and friendship with Lady Lucan. She was articulate and precise in her recollections of what took place on the night of her intended murder. Amazingly, there was no bitterness in her demeanour and she had got on with life despite family disputes and the many unkind articles that continually turned up in the tabloid press.

Tellingly, she remarked that it was not the men at the Clermont casino that had resented her presence at the club but rather the women. Her husband, she conceded, was the most handsome of that set but had never been unfaithful, despite being enshrined within that circle of extravagant, self-indulgent promiscuousness. His vice was gambling and he had eyes only for the Chemmy Nine.

The other major event around this time was that Lucan's son, George Bingham, on behalf of the family, had asked Scotland Yard to declare his father dead. This, I read, was a very complex situation. For one reason should the police agree to his request and Lucan was to turn up, it would cause legal confusion and problems at a future trial. Also there was the issue with the Inland Revenue. If the earl was declared dead, then death duties would come into play on the dwindling Lucan family trust. It was not until October 1999 that the High Court eventually acceded to the family's request, thus allowing them to finalise details relating to his estate and gain full probate. However, a death certificate was not issued at the time.

In the same year, George Bingham, sought permission to take his father's place in the House of Lords, but The Lord Chancellor, Lord Irvine of Lairg, was unable to issue Bingham with a writ of summons to the Lords without a death certificate for Lord Lucan.

But not every writer took the view that Lucan was guilty.

In Sally Moore's book – *Lucan. Not Guilty* She puts forward evidence supporting Lord Lucan's account of the events on the night of the murder. There were huge discrepancies with the forensic findings as to how different blood groups had been found where they should not have been. The forensic evidence threw up so many anomalies that Sally Moore could pinpoint many doubts about the police case.

According to Lucan's eldest daughter, Francis, the nanny went down to the basement at around 8.50pm to make tea. Billy Edgson, the doorman at the Clermont, gave a statement to the police that Lucan drove up outside the Club at 8.45pm in his blue Mercedes and had a brief chat with him saying that he would be back later. If Edgson's timing was correct then it would have been impossible for Lucan to have journeyed to Lower Belgrave Street in time to carry out the murder. It's a big possibility that Edgson statement was true, for let's face it, the job of a doorman is not overly pressed. They don't have an awful lot to do other than watch members come and go. Of course, pulling up outside the Clermont at that precise time, might have been a plan to give himself an alibi, and that a hired hitman was already in situ at Lower Belgrave Street. But that suggestion then beggars the question of why Lucan eventually made his way to the house? Surely, if that was his plan, he would have stayed well away from the crime scene.

The statements from Francis, and Billy Edgson, knocked a huge hole in the watertight case against the earl. There is little doubt that Sally Moore's book was carefully written and well researched over a number of years with the author seeking out interviews with family and friends of Lucan to substantiate her case.

Speaking to a newspaper in 1994 she commented: 'One of the injustices of the past twenty years is that the full truth about this case has not been able to emerge because of the stringent British libel laws. Masses of material had to be removed from my book for that reason. I would like to think that the whole truth will emerge – but I doubt it.' Sally Moore could also refer to those who knew Lucan well and who believed in his innocence. Bill Shand Kydd and his wife Christina, Veronica's sister, had stated how squeamish Lucan was, that the press portrayal of him as a cold-hearted gambling aristocrat was totally wrong and unfair. Lucan's sister, Jane, did not think he could have carried out such a brutal murder, a view held by his brother Hugh. There were many other close friends who came to his defence stating how kind and considerate he could be, that he was not the awful person personified by the media and the police.

With the foul up of the forensic evidence, the case against Lucan was not straightforward and left open a window of uncertainty. Christina, tellingly stated: 'If you've been married to someone for many years, how do you mistake them for someone else? The media had tried to say that (Veronica and Sandra) were similar, but they weren't.' What is also unclear is why Lucan did not murder his wife when he had the chance. Certainly he had attacked her and she had fought back for all she was worth, but Lucan was twice her size and it is almost certain he could have overcome her if he had really wanted to.

The best of the more recent publications I read was –*The Gamblers* by John Pearson, who had previously written a well received book about the Kray Twins and the East End of London's underworld. In his book Pearson cleverly paints the scene of Mayfair's high rollers, the super rich, the celebrities, the aristocrats and the eccentric wealthy who would come under the spell of John Aspinall and the Clermont Club.

This book, and the author's conclusions, were the basis of a feature length film by ITV Studios staring Rory Kinnear and Christopher Ecclestone. (Which I obtained and watched). What was so interesting about this title is that Pearson was able to interview Susie Maxwell-Scott, a firm friend of Lucan and the last person to see him before his disappearance. After a number of guarded discussions with Pearson she did open up somewhat with the view that he had escaped with the help of his friends, but certain people then took the view that Lucan was too much of a risk and a loose cannon to be kept alive, and that it would be better to do away with him. The time had come to call in the debt. At large, he would always be a risk to those who had helped him escape. Susie Maxwell-Scott threw in the view that he may have met his end in Switzerland.

Pearson reiterated the view that Lucan, armed with a cosh and a large US mailbag, intended to murder his wife, stuff her body in the sack and then hide the body in the boot of an old car he had borrowed from his friend Michael Stoop.

He would then establish an alibi for himself at the Clermont Club. When the time was right he would drive down to the south coast to where he had a boat waiting and, once out at sea, dump the weighted down corpse of his wife into the murky waters of the English Channel.

But this murderous plan had one massive flaw. The nanny had changed her usual night off and Lucan had failed to check that she had left the house. In the darkened basement Lucan had murdered the wrong woman.

This view was very much the conclusions of the police.

The other top class publication I read was –*A Different Class Of Murder* by the acclaimed biographer, Laura Thompson.

This was a beautifully scripted book full of historical information on the behaviour of past earls and the Lucan's that came before Richard John Bingham. While the book brilliantly describes the raffish aristocratic gamblers through the centuries, she touches on the feelings prevailing at the time of the Sandra Rivett murder and the disdain the public felt about this crime and the aristocracy in general. Laura Thompson takes the reader through the whole sorry picture of the crumbling marriage and lifestyle of the Seventh Earl.

This book was so incredibly detailed and researched that one wonders whether the author had a small army of people to help her put this work together. In the notes section alone there is something like a hundred press stories that were painstakingly sourced over a period of forty years. Added to this, the author could quote from a multitude of books and personal interviews with those that knew Lucky Lucan.

The author offers a number of scenarios as to what might have taken place on the night of 7 November 1974.

These take in the possibility that a burglary had been staged with a disastrous ending, with or without, Lucan's involvement. That the nanny, Sandra Rivett, may have been the intended target all along and that Lucky had innocently stumbled upon this brutal murder. The other prevailing hypothesis was that Lucan had hired a hitman to carry out the killing of his wife. One could presume that if this was the case then the hitman would have been told that the duchess would be alone in the house that night and would, therefore, have been unaware that he was attacking the wrong woman.

But of course the main suspect for the murder was Lucan himself. He had lost a bitter custody battle for his children. He was broke in more ways than one, and his wife, Veronica, stood between him and his beloved children and his former home with all its valuable contents.

You would have to think that one of those scenarios had to be the truth, or very near the truth.

Among one of the more audacious titles I cast my eye over was a book called – *The Final Truth*. This was a work by Duncan MacLaughlin, a retired Scotland Yard Detective, who had apparently tracked down Lucan in Goa, who was now going by the name of Barry Halpin, otherwise known as 'Jungle Barry' a hard drinking banjo player. Lucan had made his escape, according to the author, with the help of Graham Hill, the racing ace, in Hill's private plane. The story that Lord Lucan was 'Jungle Barry' had received prominent coverage in a number of newspapers.

More soberly, Lady Lucan was defiant, stating that Barry Halpin could not have been her husband, who was declared dead by the high court in 1999.

She told Sky News: 'It's unutterably boring. I could never imagine my husband looking so pathetic.'

Nevertheless, a lengthy extract of the publication was carried in the *Sunday Telegraph* and Mr MacLaughlin reported that he had been approached by other newspapers for the book and film rights. John Blake, the book's publisher said: 'I totally stand by the story. Lord Lucan may have taken Barry Halpin's identity when Barry died.' The *Sunday Telegraph* remained unabashed. A spokeswoman said the paper also stood by the article and said: 'It was pleased the story had stirred up such controversy.'

In a similar vein I read –*Lord Lucan. My Story* by the journalist William Coles. This tongue-in-cheek entertaining novel also sets the scene in Goa.

A memoir, apparently written by Lucan, resurfaces from the vaults of a firm of London solicitors and falls into the hands of the author who takes on the task of editing the manuscript. This work of fiction also goes for the hitman theory and that Lucan had a boat moored in Newhaven from where he would dispose of his wife's body out at sea.

The novel has John Aspinall and Jimmy Goldsmith spiriting their friend out of the country to India in a container ship and from there, onwards to Goa, where he lived out his life as a hopelessly addicted heroin addict. Reviewers generally agreed the book was highly entertaining and well written.

It was interesting that two totally independent authors had concluded that Lucky had finished his days in Goa in such wretched circumstances.

That Lucan intended to dump his wife in the English Channel was a view shared by most writers. Lucan had borrowed a car with a large boot and, it was rumoured, had made a couple of dummy runs to Newhaven where it was believed he kept a boat. He was a skilled sailor and the police and most of the media had deduced that no matter how the murder might be carried out it would be the earl himself who would dispose of his wife's body. He was the one with a boat.

What poetic justice it would have been if Lucan, as many believe, committed suicide by throwing himself from his boat in the Channel – the very end he had planned for his wife.

In June 2000 *The Telegraph* ran a story on the forthcoming book by Dame Murial Spark best known for her acclaimed work *The Prime of Miss Jean Brodie*.

Dame Murial was also keen to dip her toe into the Lucan riddle, but her fictional book was more on a humorous line of approach and laced with satire.

Aiding And Abetting takes the view that Lucky is alive, but this novel, perhaps because it came from the pen of a famous writer, bothered Lady Lucan no end.

Chapter Nine

She told *The Telegraph* that Dame Muriel's novel was absurd and warned the author to be aware of the legal issues surrounding the case.

'An idea like this is insensitive,' Lady Lucan said. 'It shows a lack of feeling for people who are still living with these events. I don't see how anyone can write anything about my husband without first approaching me and she hasn't done that. I am not only thinking about me but also my son. We have been suffering for 25 years. A quarter of a century is a long time to live with something like this and her book won't help. The proposition that he is somehow still alive is absurd and rather boring. My husband was a heavy drinker who would have surely been dead now even if he hadn't disappeared. People do have to be careful what they write, even in a work of fiction. The suggestion that he was somehow helped to stay on the run by friends like Sir James Goldsmith is nonsense. He wouldn't have risked his family and fortune for my husband.'

The Telegraph report went on to say:

Lady Lucan has worked tirelessly to combat what she feels are half-truths surrounding her husband's disappearance. Earlier this year she closed down an Internet site called lordlucan.com, claiming that it infringed her son's intellectual property rights because he might one day be entitled to take his father's title.

Her concerns are shared by the family of Sandra Rivett. Fred Rivett, Sandra's brother-in-law, said: 'I'm of the view that Lucan is dead. It is irritating when people rake over the past in this way for their own ends. It's not a pleasant thing to do.'

Why Lady Lucan should have taken such umbrage to Murial Spark's fantasy story is strange, as the book is probably the most innocent of all the publications, and whilst lampooning aristocratic buffoonery, the narrative is firmly on her side.

There had been so much speculation about Lucky Lucan over the years that the story had taken on some sort of mythical status. I was amazed to uncover just how much had been written about the missing earl.

That a privileged peer of the realm, who had enjoyed all the good things in life, Eton and an exclusive education, holidays in exotic locations, racehorses and speed boats together with a luxury house in Belgravia could murder a working-class young woman, probably on low wages, and get away scot-free was an unpleasant conundrum. It's the not knowing that has kept the story running for forty years. If Lucan's body had been washed up on a beach in Newhaven a day or so after the murder there would not have been twenty books about the Seventh Earl, or a thousand newspaper stories, or press serialisations of forthcoming novels, or a host of TV programmes and a feature length film.

It was also daunting to discover how few writers could agree with the series of events that led to the murder of Sandra Rivett. For every question answered there was another unanswered. The more I delved into the case the more ambiguous it appeared. The raft of facts and theories were never totally convincing and always came up short in trying to make the story fit together.

Over the past forty years the British media has fed eagerly on the Lucan story and the possible whereabouts of the vanishing earl. The improbable death of the sadly expendable nanny, Sandra Rivett, has receded to almost a side issue set against the frenzy of stories as to where the earl might be holing-up if he had got away, and who might have helped him escape.

Chapter Nine

He has supposedly been spotted in almost every country in the world. People returning from vacations and claiming they had come across the wanted earl had turned into something of a parlour game.

A year after the murder Lucan was said to be in Mozambique. In a *Guardian* article I came across, Richard Ingrams, (of *Private Eye*) wrote: 'It has always been my hunch that Lucan is alive and is lurking in this part of the Dark Continent. I also uncovered many other so-called sightings and rumours that the earl was living in this part of the world.

In February 2012, the *Daily Mail* ran a story on a recent BBC report.

The story ran:

Is this the proof Lucan started a new life in Africa? There have been 'sightings' in Goa and Down Under. Now a new witness claims she knows the truth. A witness claims she arranged plane tickets for Lucan's eldest two children to fly to Kenya and Gabon where their father would observe them.

Of all the countless theories surrounding the disappearance of disgraced peer Lord Lucan following the murder of his children's nanny almost 40 years ago, the image conjured up by the latest claim is the most compelling.

It would suggest that the fugitive peer did flee to West Africa and – most extraordinarily – that his children were flown out there so he could see them.

This story came from a woman named as Shirley Robey who stated that she arranged tickets for the children. When asked if she realised when she made the bookings if she knew Lucan was living in secret in Africa. She replied: 'I believed that was the case.'

In the same week as the BBC story, the *Daily Telegraph* reported:

The wife of Lord Lucan has claimed she would have helped her husband get away with murder – had he not injured her so badly that she couldn't assist him. 'I would have helped him if it was possible,' She told *The Telegraph*. 'I wouldn't have given him money, I would have said, go away I will handle it from here.'

However, Countess Lucan said she was too badly injured to help her husband and instead had to seek help to have her injuries treated.

Had he not attacked her, the Countess said she would have told him to leave, denied seeing him and protected him.

Countess Lucan also confessed she still had feelings for her husband, even though he beat her with a lead pipe, leaving her with a scar across her head.

'I remember the happy times,' she said. She added that even though it was so many years ago that he disappeared, Lord Lucan is still a part of her life and a part of herself.

In February 2013, Hugh Bingham, Lord Lucan's brother, told a journalist from the BBC's *Inside Out* programme – That the fugitive aristocrat died in 2004 and is buried in Africa. Hugh Bingham apparently made the startling disclosure in an 'unguarded moment' when the cameras stopped rolling after an interview at his Johannesburg home. 'I know this as a fact.' he was reported to have said.

My research had thrown up stories that Lucan has been sighted in Iceland, South America, France, New Zealand, Australia, Italy, Germany, Canada, Greece, Norway, The Bahamas, Madagascar, The Philippines, Hong Kong, Japan and many other places!

After reading so much material and a seemingly endless raft of rumours, sightings and suppositions it was time for me to swot up on facts – I needed some basic facts.

Chapter Nine

I would soon be returning to Mallorca to see a certain elderly gentleman who spends his afternoons at the Café Plaza sipping brandy. This mysterious chap has taken me into his confidence, asking me to believe that he is Lord Lucan, the fugitive wanted for murder who has been in hiding for the last forty-one years. Of course his story is fantastic and inconceivable but despite that he has gone out of his way to identify himself in a very convincing manner and the unbelievable has taken on a whiff of believability. Before meeting up with him again I was determined to know everything there was to know about the man he is claiming to be and the dreadful crime surrounding that person.

The Coroners Court was not interested in sightings, theories, the views of armchair detectives, novelists or publicity seekers. The court was only interested in looking at hard evidence to establish how, and why, a 29-year old woman was murdered in such a brutal manner and who was responsible.

Chapter Ten

Scotland Yard were never keen on a Coroners Inquest into the death of Sandra Rivett although they knew that sooner or later there had to be one. Seven months after the disappearing act by Lord Lucan they still clung to the hope that he would turn up somewhere.

Their objection to an inquest was that should a jury find him guilty and he was thereafter to be apprehended then it would be a near impossibility for him to receive a fair trial in a High Court. How could a jury be found that would be impartial given what had already been decided and prodigiously publicised?

Scotland Yard had delayed an inquest for as long as they were able but on Monday 16 June, 1975 at Westminster Coroner's Court, Dr Gavin Thurston, deputy coroner to the Royal Household, began proceedings.

Dr Thurston had been carefully chosen for this much awaited case, which had attracted huge media interest.

His qualifications were impeccable with many years experience to handle what was certain to be a high profile, and possibly explosive inquiry – a case, which would test his patience and legal skills to the limit. As it transpired, it would also turn out to be a landmark case and lead to a change in the law.

He had conducted the inquest into the death of Judy Garland and the suicide of Brian Epstein, manager of the Beatles. He had also presided over the apparent suicide of the boxer Freddy Mills.

The only blot on Dr Thurston's otherwise perfect CV was that he had dismissed the possibility of murder too quickly in the Freddy Mills inquiry, which would later be challenged. Freddy Mills was world light-heavyweight champion between 1948–50. On retiring he ran a nightclub in Soho but had surrounded himself with crooks, most notably the Kray twins and, it was rumoured, had mafia connections. Like Lucan, he had money problems and had been desperately trying to sell his club. He was found dead in his car outside his nightclub having seemingly shot himself through the eye.

I did a quick google search to learn more about the coroner, Dr Gavin Thurston. I came across a small obituary for him in the British Medical Journal (he died in 1980, aged 69). Here, he was described in glowing terms for his firmness and dignity in all the cases he had presided over. It was said that he had handled more famous cases than any other coroner and noted that the murder of Lord Lucan's nanny required particular patience and application.

Before the Lucan case he had conducted inquests into the deaths of Adlai Stevenson, the former US presidential candidate and UN Ambassador who dropped dead while walking in Grosvenor Square, Mama Cass, of The Mamas & the Papas, Stephen Ward who was caught up in the Profumo affair and Jimmy Hendrix.

After the Sandra Rivett inquest, he was the coroner who presided over the assassination of the MP Airey Neave, the first British officer to successfully escape from Oflag 1V-C at Colditz Castle, whose legs were blown off in a car-bomb attack by the INLA at the House of Commons. Following that case he was in charge of the inquest into the death of the tragically self destructive Keith Moon.

But it would be the Sandra Rivett inquiry that would be his toughest case due to the fact that the main protagonist was nowhere to be found. After months of delay the inquest would just have to go ahead no matter what might have become of him.

The scene on the first day of proceedings was very much to set the tone and atmosphere of this inquiry, as the different camps huddled themselves together like little armies ready to defend their corner.

The earl's family and supporters were not going to acknowledge his wife, neither did they extend any sort of benevolence towards Sandra Rivett's family which, given the circumstances, would have been a reasonable common courtesy. Not a single member of the 'Lucan set' offered any words of comfort to the Rivett's.

The press had been busy since the murder of Sandra, highlighting the cosy privileged world of Lucan's friends and their arrogant behaviour towards the officers investigating the murder of a working class nanny who had found herself innocently caught up between feuding aristocrats in posh Belgravia.

Now this group would have to run the gauntlet of the press and their cameras positioned daily outside Horseferry Road Coroner's Court and come under the gaze of journalists crammed three deep inside. The spotlight was now well and truly directed on some of Lucan's inner circle for the first time. There could be no hiding behind the doors of stately piles in the country or inside the enclaves of exclusive Mayfair clubs.

Lucky's elite circle were friendless as far as the rest of the country were concerned but this circle were not to be dismissed easily. They had long imagined a status and class for themselves, and would stick together showing little signs of regret or shame when giving evidence at the inquiry.

The journalist Peter Birkett, in a *Daily Mail* article wrote:

'The demeanour of the Lucan set portrayed a splash of colour to a depressing chronicle of tragedy, and that they regarded the inquest as an occasion for a public display of solidarity.'

He went on: 'The leading personality of their set is wanted on a murder charge. Therefore, it is particularly important that they put on the right show; that they dress correctly; that they behave with brave confidence; that every move they make should reflect their loyalty to the missing man and the importance for them of Lord Lucan's sense of honour. So it comes down to a question of style. And if their style is not to the taste of the rest that is a matter of indifference. Proud, unbending and exclusive, they do not seem worried by what the world thinks of them.'

The inquest would highlight the fact that an aristocrat, planning to dispose of a problem wife was never the whole story – nor would it ever be. For Lucan's family, friends and acolytes nothing would ever be the same again.

Once positions had been established in the courtroom it became clear that Lady Lucan had been completely ostracised by her once good friends and family. It was as though this whole drama, which was about to unfold, was all her fault. She is, noted a reporter 'a woman deeply alone.'

But she did have one very good friend in Sergeant Forsyth, who had played a major role in the investigation. Forsyth had witnessed the unsympathetic treatment she had received from Lucan's allies and the closed ranks of the Mayfair gambling community who had sought to put the blame on her. Sergeant Forsyth took it upon himself to see that at least one person would befriend the beleaguered woman and protect her throughout this ordeal.

He would collect the countess in the morning and escort her into the courtroom. At lunch he would take her somewhere quiet, and at the end of the days proceedings drive her safely back to Belgravia.

An inquest, I was to learn, was not the same as a High Court trial. The two are very different and an inquest is conducted in accordance with various rules, which are far removed from a trial.

Witnesses can, if they so wish, be legally represented in court but cannot be discredited or subjected to aggressive or hard-line questioning in cross-examination, which is a privilege of a High Court trial alone.

The various camps in the Sandra Rivett inquest were all legally represented. The police retained the services of the lawyer Brian Watling, and their position was clear. They had not wanted an inquest because they were still hunting the missing earl and wished him to appear before a High Court. But as they could not find him, and were aware they could not delay an inquest forever, it would be desirable if the conclusions of the Coroners Court upheld their unbending belief in Lucan's guilt.

The Rivett family were represented by David Webster, whose main aim was to see that the family of Sandra should be informed as to what exactly happened on the night of 7 November and get some sort of closure as to how and why she was killed.

Lady Lucan had the lawyer Brian Coles on her side and it would be his job to see that she was not intimidated, that it was not the countess who was on trial and that all courtesies should be extended to his client given the injuries she had sustained after being attacked by her husband. Her lawyer would impress on the court that Lady Lucan was an innocent party and that she had already suffered greatly.

The absent Lord Lucan was represented by Michael Eastham, whose services had been paid for by the earl's mother, the Dowager Countess. His job was a near impossibility given that outside Lucky's circle he was a friendless figure. The nanny had been murdered and he had scarpered. Eastham's wish was to pick holes in Lady Lucan's version of events that took place on the night of the murder. To do this he needed to cross-examine her, but as he was soon to learn, the countess could not be subjected to certain questions and he would be reminded that she was protected from having to say anything that might discredit her as she was not on trial.

Dr Gavin Thurston opened the proceeding of the Sandra Rivett inquest with a carefully worded speech to the jury:

'There has been much pre-publicity regarding this inquest which has made this case rather unusual. The events surrounding the death of Sandra Rivett has provoked much public interest and has been a burning topic of controversy right across the country. You, the jury, may already have formed opinions and prejudices about the characters involved from reading the newspapers or watching television reports. However, you must now put any views you might have formed to one side. The job of the jury at this inquest is to address only the facts that will be laid before you. Whatever verdict you reach must be based solely on the evidence you hear in this courtroom.

The responsibility of a jury at an inquest is different from that of a High Court jury in that you have to determine who had actually died, when they had died, and, if possible, how. In certain rare cases a jury at an inquest has the right to name a person whom they consider responsible for murder – if murder is suspected.

Of course this could be a problem if a jury was to name someone as guilty who was later to turn up before being given the opportunity of a High Court trial. Obviously such a situation would affect and prejudice any later proceedings.

In view of this I have deliberately delayed this inquiry in the hope that Lord Lucan would show up. That would have rendered this inquest unnecessary. Under those circumstances Lord Lucan would have been charged and tried. If he had been found guilty, then the Coroner's Court could freely record that he had murdered Mrs Rivett; if he were acquitted, then the Coroner's Court would simply record that Sandra had been killed by 'A Person' and the police would have gone on looking for that 'Person.'

Ultimately, it is for you, the jury, to decide. Lord Lucan has been given every opportunity to come forward. He has not done so. He has therefore left others to make conclusions in his absence. If you decide on the evidence laid before you that you could name someone whom you thought responsible for the death of Sandra Rivett, then you have the right to do so. You have got to decide on the evidence whether you can name that person.'

The first witness to be questioned was Roger Rivett, Sandra's estranged husband. He spoke generally about their relationship, when he had last seen Sandra and confirmed that she was rather small in stature. Five foot, two inches, he confirmed.

The coroner then spoke to one of the first officers that had attended the house on the night of the murder who explained what he had witnessed and gave a broad description of the layout of the building. He told the court that a light bulb had been removed from the basement kitchen and had been left lying on a padded chair.

He explained that it was not possible to see into the basement from street level without a light on and even then any view would be very restrictive.

This was an important statement as Lord Lucan had told his mother in a telephone conversation shortly after the murder that he had been walking past number 46 when he had witnessed a fight taking place in the basement. An assertion he would later repeat to Susie Maxwell-Scott some hours later at her house in Uckfield, and in letters sent to Bill Shand Kydd.

His story of seeing an assault taking place from the pavement outside the house would be shot to pieces at the inquest as it would be categorically stated by the police that to see into the basement from outside was a virtual impossibility. (Something I would soon confirm for myself).

Next to take the stand was Lady Lucan, and the coroner immediately asked that a chair be brought for her. Once seated she almost disappeared behind the oak panelling. She wore bible black with a white turban to cover her head wound. She looked a demure figure as the June sunlight streaming in from the overhead glass dome captured her in all her loneliness and vulnerability. It must have struck many observers in the courtroom how such a small and seemingly frail woman managed to stave off and survive such a brutal attack by her husband. Nevertheless, she came across as strong willed and prepared to answer questions without fear as to what others might think of her. She was also confident enough to cast an occasional glance around the courtroom and look her detractors full in the eye.

That Lady Lucan was in the witness box was controversial in itself. There was the law relating to marriage and giving evidence against a husband. She could easily have been excused from giving evidence, but the coroner had decided that she should take the stand. That this happened seemed odd, presumably she would have agreed to be a witness and her lawyer would have had to agree with this also. One wonders if her council had come to some understanding with the coroner that if she were to willingly testify then she should not be pressurised in any way by Lord Lucan's lawyer as to what she had said.

It was also agreed that if she took the stand she could only say what happened to her when she was attacked, but could not mention anything that would incriminate her husband with the murder of the nanny. As this was an inquest and not a High Court trial a fine line had to be observed as to what witnesses could say.

She was in the dock for two hours. She told the coroner about her relationship with the earl. Their early marriage and that he was a professional gambler, the bitter court case for custody of the children and various aspects of their life after her husband had moved out of the family home.

The coroner moved on to ask her about the nanny, Sandra Rivett, and the timing of events on the night of 7 November. He also asked her why the nanny had changed her usual night off and whether she and Sandra were of a similar build.

The coroner then asked who had attacked her.

'It was my husband,' she answered.

The countess then described the attack in detail saying that he had battered her about the head and thrust gloved fingers down her throat and tried to strangle her and gouge out her eye. She had managed to grapple with him and had grabbed his testicles at which point he desisted with the fight.

Lady Lucan then told the court of her escape from the house and her dash down Lower Belgrave Street to the Plumbers Arms pub where she was looked after until an ambulance arrived to take her to St George's Hospital.

'Have you seen your husband since that time?' the coroner asked.

Veronica shook her head. 'No I haven't.'

Dr Thurston then asked very solemnly: 'You have no doubt that it was your husband who attacked you?'

'No doubt at all,' she replied firmly.

Dr Thurston then asked her if there had been anyone else present, did anyone brush past her? Did she hear any sounds?

'I saw nobody else at the time or at any time during the evening,' she reiterated.

'Is there anything in your evidence you wish to alter?' the coroner asked.

'No there is nothing.'

Michael Eastham representing Lord Lucan steamed straight in with his cross-examination of Veronica. 'You entertained feelings of hatred towards your husband, didn't you?' he asked pointedly.

Immediately the coroner intervened. Such aggressive questioning would not be allowed. Mr Eastham protested, pointing out that he was there to prevent the jury from reaching a verdict that might bring a stigma to Lord Lucan's name. I need to question Lady Lucan's testimony as to whether her account is honest or a fabrication, he told the coroner.

After a lengthy delay in private with all four lawyers present the coroner came down in favour of Lady Lucan. She was not to be subjected to any questioning that might discredit her – she was not on trial.

Mr Eastham was furious, how could he represent his absent client without questioning the testimony of his wife? His task was impossible without discrediting Veronica and her version of events. Mr Coles, acting for Lady Lucan stated that there were clearly laid down criteria under which witnesses could be cross-examined at an inquest. It would be an intolerable infringement of Veronica's rights if she were subjected to verbal attack or innuendo in the witness box. The lawyer for the police agreed, as did the solicitor for the Rivett family.

To appease Mr Eastham somewhat, the coroner told him that he would have plenty of ammunition come the forensic evidence and that he should concentrate his efforts on the scientific elements of the case.

It was agreed by the coroner and the other lawyers that he could not discredit Lady Lucan, or the testimony she had given under the strict rules of an inquest.

When proceedings resumed and the jury had returned to their places, the coroner asked Mr Eastham if he had any more questions for Lady Lucan in the light of his ruling.

A clearly frustrated Mr Eastham replied: 'In the light of your ruling I don't think I can assist the jury at all and I have no further questions for the lady.' Lady Lucan rose slowly and departed the witness box.

Reading about this inquest you couldn't help but think it was unfair to the earl's supporters. The coroner, while wanting to be just, may have unwittingly allowed himself to be swayed. Most in the courtroom, the media and the public were sympathetic to the battered and now ostracised countess who it seemed was being afforded a kindness and protection that made it impossible for anyone to put forward the view that Lord Lucan might be innocent. – that his wife could give evidence for nearly two hours and not be challenged was a courtesy that was not to be extended to some other witnesses who were in support of the runaway earl.

Lord Lucan's lawyer must have known he was up against it. The picture of Lucky's frail, but convincing proud wife, had hardened opinions against his client to the point of no return.

In all, the coroner, Dr Gavin Thurston called on 33 witnesses to give evidence at the inquest. The police spent many hours in the witness box relating what they had discovered on the night of the murder and their subsequent efforts to apprehend Lord Lucan.

Experts from the Police laboratory gave evidence relating to the lead piping found at the murder scene and the second piece of piping found in the boot of the Ford Corsair, discovered in Newhaven. They also spoke at length about the fingerprints taken from number 46 Lower Belgrave Street, Lucan's flat and the Ford Corsair. Unfortunately, no positive prints for Lord Lucan were attainable. All the prints in the basement at number 46 had come from the police, the children or from Mrs Rivett.

The pathologist, Professor Keith Simpson, outlined to the court the injuries Sandra had received when he had conducted his post-mortem. There were no signs of any sexual attack, he said, and death had taken place before she had been placed in the mailsack, which was covered in blood.

There were four major injuries to the head and minor injuries to her face, neck and shoulders. The injuries would have caused deep bruising to the brain and had caused her to inhale a large quantity of blood through her mouth and nose. He told the coroner that an unconscious person cannot clear the airways of blood by coughing and that death had been caused by blunt head injuries and inhalation of blood.

When shown a photograph of the lead piping which was found at the scene, the professor agreed that it was highly likely to have caused the injuries to both Sandra Rivett and Lady Lucan.

The landlord of The Plumbers Arms was called as a witness. He described how Lady Lucan had entered his pub covered head to toe in blood. He claimed that she shouted 'Help me, help me, I've just escaped from being murdered,' and, 'My children, my children, he's murdered my nanny.'

By the third day of the inquest it was the turn of the earl's supporters to give evidence and, hopefully, present an alternative view.

The first witness was Lucan's mother, the Dowager Countess. The coroner asked her a series of questions relating to the two phone calls she had received from her son on the night of the murder, when she had last seen him, and what his financial situation was like.

The coroner then asked the dowager how her son had seen a fight taking place in the basement of number 46, which he had related to her in his first phone call.

'He told me he was passing,' the dowager said. 'I know he frequently went past the house. It was very near his own flat.'

The coroner seemed satisfied with her answers but Brian Watling for the police was not. In a very pointed manner he kicked off by saying. 'Did the Dowager Countess of Lucan know that anyone giving a false statement to the police was liable to be prosecuted?' The dowager looked taken-aback but said she knew that was so.

Mr Watling then grilled her incessantly on slight differences about her statement given to the police on the night of 7 November and what she was saying now. The questioning was pretty aggressive and was at complete odds with the niceties afforded to her son's wife, Veronica. At the end of the lawyer's severe cross-examination of the dowager he waved a hand at the jury with the curt remark. 'You have seen this woman for yourself. I need go no further.'

You would have thought that the coroner might have intervened with this rough questioning of Lucan's poor mother but he decided not to.

The next to take the stand was Susie Maxwell-Scott, the last known person to see Lord Lucan before his disappearance.

She was a trained lawyer and the daughter of a QC and was not going to be ambushed like the last witness. She told the coroner that she had known Lord Lucan for many years and that he was a kind and charming man who was devoted to his children to a far greater extent than most men.

Susie Maxwell-Scott reiterated the story that the earl had told her shortly after the murder when he had arrived at her house: 'He told me that he had been walking past the house when he had seen a man attacking his wife in the basement.' She went on: 'He said that he had let himself in through the front door and had gone down to the basement where he slipped in a pool of blood. He said the man had made off. He went to his wife who was covered in blood and hysterical, she then accused him of hiring a man to kill her.'

Susie Maxwell-Scott was in the witness box for two hours and stayed cool and calm throughout, never letting the lawyer Brian Watling get the better of her, telling him at one point that, unlike the police, she did not have notes to fall back on and had to rely on her memory as to what took place and what was said. She also confirmed that the earl had written two letters to Bill Shand Kydd, which she had posted on his behalf the following day.

At the end of Mr Watling's cross-examination the coroner asked:

'Did you offer to let him stay the night?'

'I tried to persuade him to stay the night but he said he must get back and clear things up.'

She came across as an excellent witness but whether she was telling the whole truth about her very dear friend would always be a topic for speculation.

Bill Shand Kydd gave a statement to the court regarding the letters he had received from the earl, which he had handed over to the police immediately.

After giving much evidence he asked the coroner if he could be excused from the remainder of the day's proceedings as he had an important business meeting.

That afternoon he was photographed at Royal Ascot in the Royal Enclosure. Embarrassingly for him his picture appeared on the front page of the following day's *Daily Mirror*.

Dr Margaret Pereira the Senior Scientific Officer in the Biology Division at New Scotland Yard entered the witness box to take up the thorny issue of the blood samples she had taken at number 46 and how some samples did not tie-in with Lady Lucan's version of events.

Lady Lucan was blood group A (found in about 42 per cent of the population). Sandra Rivett was blood group B (found in about 8 per cent).

Fittingly, most of the blood in the basement was that of Sandra's and most of the blood on the stairs and landing leading away from the basement was that of Veronica's where she stated she had been assaulted by her husband.

So far so good. But there were problems, which Lord Lucan's lawyer seized upon. He questioned the Scientific Officer: 'How was a spot of blood which was Sandra's group B blood, found on Veronica's shoe, when she had told the court that she had never ventured into the basement? And how could it be,' the lawyer went on, 'that there was also a trace of Veronica's blood group on the mailbag containing

Chapter Ten

Sandra's body. How did it get there?' Dr Pereira put forward the view that there could have been accidental transference. The anomalies with the blood samples could never be totally resolved to the liking of everyone, but as Dr Pereira pointed out, there had been so many police officers on the scene that unwanted transference and contamination was highly likely.

In other evidence I came across, Detective Gerring told a journalist many years later: 'Some forty officers had moved around the house, some with police dogs, and it would have been a miracle if there had not been accidental transference of blood.'

On the fourth day of the inquest and having heard from over thirty witnesses Dr Gavin Thurston brought proceedings to a close.

In his summing up he went over all the salient aspects of the case. He then told the jury. 'If you are satisfied with the evidence you have heard that there was an attack by another person then your verdict will have to be murder. And you have got to decide whether you can name the person responsible.'

Finally he told the foreman of the jury that he would accept a majority verdict so long as there were no more than two dissenters.

As the court emptied, the throng outside the court became even larger with journalists and TV crews eagerly awaiting the verdict. Amongst the crowd were some in top hat and tails waiting for the news before heading off to the races.

One of these wags quipped to a reporter, 'Damned inconsiderate of the coroner to arrange this inquest to coincide with Royal Ascot.'

The crowd milling outside Horseferry Road Coroners Court did not have to wait long for the jury to return to their places. They had been out for just thirty-one minutes.

Dr Thurston asked the foreman if they had come to a majority decision.

'Yes,' he said. 'It is murder by Lord Lucan.'

The Sandra Rivett inquest was never supposed to have been a trial but that is what it had turned into.

The family and friends of Lord Lucan vented their anger and disillusionment as they emerged from the court and into the June sunshine.

The Reverend William Gibbs, Lucan's brother-in-law, probably spoke for all of Lucky's supporters when he said: 'This is not British justice. To me it is frightening and amazing that a man can be named in court as a murderer without being given the chance to defend himself. I know, and the family know, that Lord Lucan is innocent. This is not justice and must therefore be ignored.'

After Lady Lucan had been driven away, her solicitor read out a statement on her behalf. 'Lady Lucan was neither pleased nor displeased with the verdict. She was only concerned with establishing the facts,' it went on. 'Her husband's interests had been represented in court and the jury had made up their minds. She now hoped to resume a normal family life.'

If Lord Lucan were to suddenly turn up – still a possibility in the summer of 1975 – It would be a virtual impossibility for him to receive a fair trial in a High Court.

The law had to change. And it did. Soon after the historic Rivett inquest, Coroner's Courts were no longer permitted to name a person as guilty.

Wherever the vanishing earl might be he was still making huge waves.

Chapter Eleven

Back in March while on holiday in Mallorca I had stopped at a café on my way into Palma. There, I had encountered, quite by chance, a dapper elderly Englishman who wiled away his afternoons at the Café Plaza sipping brandy and puffing on cigarillos.

He approached my table and asked if he might talk with me. He was most pleasant and I felt at ease chatting with him, our conversation being mostly about London and the sporting scene back in England.

He told me his name was Sidney Ainsworth and that he was resident in Mallorca, and that it was here, in the sleepy town of Molinar, that he intended to see out his days. Sidney dressed very smartly, which along with his somewhat upper-class accent, rendered him an air of quiet sophistication. You would have taken bets on it that he had been privately educated.

On taking my leave of him, he asked most politely, if I would post a letter for him when I retuned home. I wasn't keen on this but as there was nothing obviously untoward about the man I agreed. The letter was addressed to a publishing house in London.

On my next visit to Mallorca I ran into Sidney again at the Café Plaza. We chatted for a while and once again he asked if I would post a document for him from London. It was of course, clear to me, that he did not wish anyone to know where he was living – that he did not wish his mail to bear a Mallorcan postmark.

Needless to say, I was suspicious, but Sidney came across as such a charming character that I found it hard to refuse what seemed a simple favour to someone far from home and who seemed lonely. He was most grateful and wanted to pay me for my trouble but I refused to take any money from him.

However, knowing where I was staying, he sent a letter to my hotel containing five hundred euros and a note to the effect that I might like to open the envelope and read his document and, if I so desired, to take the matter further. He asked only that I keep his whereabouts a secret. He said that I was his last big gamble.

It was all most strange. My initial thoughts were that despite his style and somewhat posh ambiance he had got himself into some financial mess and decided to up-sticks, move to Spain, and see out his day's in some sort of forced seclusion.

He was getting older, and now with failing health, it seemed he had something to say to a publishing company in Bedford Square and wished to take me into his confidence.

I read Sidney's incredible document on my flight home and so began the weirdest adventure of my life. It was all quite daft of course, but having met Sidney and read his story I was intrigued. I was hooked by curiosity, even though I was certain there had to be a clever twist somewhere along the line. I did not tell my family or friends about Sidney for fear that I would be laughed at or accused of being stupidly naive. It was my little mystery journey and I would keep my cards close to my chest and try to discover what it was all about and, the rest, as they say, is history.

Sidney's document, in itself, was interesting, but meant little as anyone with some time on their hands could have put a story like that together with just a little research and some imagination.

What gave Sidney a huge whiff of scary authenticity was the letter I had posted for him after our first encounter. That letter was to a long lost friend of Lord Lucan and an old Clermont member, Colin Hedley-Davies. In his letter Sidney had gone out of his way to identify himself and prove that he was the person he was saying he was.

Mr. Hedley-Davies was duly checked out by a clever, fact seeking journalist, Paul King, who confirmed that this elderly gentleman had indeed known Lucky very well and that the letter he had received had to be genuine. Hedley-Davies told the journalist that only Lucky could have written that letter as it related stories only the two of them could possibly have known about.

Of course, it was all totally ridiculous and bizarre, but having met Sidney, I had to admit there was something compelling about him. There was no hint of deviousness in his manner. He came across as being highly educated and there was no indication that he was being influenced by another party.

Despite how crazy it appeared, sometimes in life you just have to follow your instincts. And that is what I had been doing. If the story was a fake it would not matter, better that, than always wonder about the truth.

What was also most odd is that Sidney allowed me to know who he was purporting to be. I was a stranger and it was an almighty gamble on his part to take me into his confidence in such a way. I could have given his story to the newspapers or reported him to the police. He could never have been sure what action I might take. I had often pondered this gamble of his but also thought that maybe it was not such a big risk after all. If I had 'shopped' him he could quite easily have said that he did not know me and had never given me any documents to post on his behalf. He could take it further and say that it was me trying some clever scam and trying to use an old English pensioner as some sort of foil for my own ends.

But for the time being, and as Sherlock Holmes might say: 'the game's afoot.' Whether he was Lord Lucan or a clever imposter was still to be discovered but between myself and a journalist we were definitely going to find out. My forced stay at home with illness had been well spent. I had read many books about the vanishing earl and had poured over a thousand-and-one press stories. I felt something of an expert about the murder of Sandra Rivett and what took place on the night of 7 November 1974 at number 46 Lower Belgrave Street.

In a silly daydream I imagined going on Mastermind and facing John Humphrys.

J.H. 'Your name is?'

'Adam Baker.'

J.H. 'And your occupation?'

'Retired typesetter.'

J.H. 'And your chosen specialist subject?'

'The life of Lord Lucan.'

J.H. 'The life of Lord Lucan. Adam Baker, you have two minutes. Your time starts now: What was said to be Lord Lucan's favourite meat dish?'

'Lamb chops.'

J.H. '(yes.) Lord Lucan attended which prep school in London?'

'Arnold House'

Chapter Eleven

J.H. '(correct.) What was the name of the coroner at the Sandra Rivett inquest?'

'Dr Gavin Thurston.'

J.H. '(yes.) Lord Lucan borrowed a car from Michael Stoop in 1974 that was later (the buzzer goes) – I've started so I'll finish – later found in Newhaven. What was the make of the car?'

'It was a Ford Corsair.'

J.H. 'It was a Ford Corsair. You passed on just one. The name of Lord Lucan's Doberman Pinscher was Otto. Adam Baker, you have scored 17 points.'

Breaking away from my little fantasy I decided to recap on all that I had learned about the runaway earl before booking a flight and heading off to see that mysterious old rogue, Sidney Ainsworth, at the Café Plaza.

So many writers and commentators had come up with opposing theories as to what might have taken place on the night of the murder, and who was responsible.

There had been claims and counter claims that had rumbled on for the last forty years. The author Sally Moore had made a brave attempt to paint an innocent picture of Lucan in her book, but the police case against him was hugely compelling. That he was involved in the murder, solely or otherwise, seemed impossible to contradict.

I poured over a lot of the notes I had made during my week of study about the case and decided that instead of thinking too much about what others had been postulating I would play detective myself and see if I could arrive at some conclusion as to Lucan's guilt or otherwise.

I wrote down what was in Lord Lucan's favour if one wanted to make out a case for his innocence. This is what I came up with.

For Him:

All of his family and friends spoke well of him. That he was a good man who loved and cared deeply for his children. That he was not a violent person and was, in fact, quite squeamish. This fact is very much in his favour as the attack on Sandra Rivett was most brutal and hardly the act of a squeamish person and someone, who it was said, hated the sight of blood.

The doorman at the Clermont gave evidence that Lucan had pulled up in his car outside the club at around 8.45pm. If this is correct then it would have been most difficult for him to then commit a murder at Lower Belgrave Street, which to all intents and purposes, took place at around 9pm. If the doorman's account is correct it blows a huge hole in the police case against Lucky. His wife stated she had been attacked on the stairs and landing and did not enter the basement, yet mysteriously some of her blood group was found on the sack in the basement containing Sandra's body.

Christina Shand Kydd, made an interesting point: 'If you've been married to someone for many years,' she ventured, 'how do you mistake them for someone else? The media had tried to say that Veronica and Sandra were similar, but they weren't.'

This statement by the sister of Lady Lucan, went right to the heart of the enigma. Even in the semi-darkness it seemed unreal that Lucky could mistake the nanny for his wife. He had been married to Veronica for twelve years. The man would surely have been aware of how she moved, her build, her very being. One quick, and mistaken, blow to the head in that dark basement might be acceptable to believe, but the attack on Sandra was a sustained assault. That Lucan would not have realised he was bludgeoning the wrong woman does not ring true – something is very odd here – this does not add up. I find it hard to believe that he could attack the wrong person.

His main accuser was his wife, and it is fair to say there was no love lost between the pair of them. It might be assumed that the countess harboured thoughts that her husband was out to kill her and was all too ready to point the finger at him.

Lord Lucan said that he was innocent. He told Susie Maxwell-Scott, the last known person to see him, that he interrupted an attack on his wife and that she then accused him of murdering the nanny. Lucky also stated this line of innocence to his mother and in a letter to Bill Shand Kydd and a further letter to his friend Michael Stoop.

Lord Lucan was telling people that he was innocent. In his favour it would seem he had quite a bit going for him.

It was now time to look at the other side of the story. What was not in his favour?

Against him:

Why did he feel it necessary to borrow a car from his friend Michael Stoop when he had a perfectly good car of his own? There could only be one reason, and that's because he knew his own blue Mercedes would be most conspicuous in, or near, Lower Belgrave Street.

In his dark and depressing moods at the Clermont Club he told close allies that he intended to kill his wife. He was determined, no matter what it might take, to win back custody of his children from a wife he believed was unsuitable to look after them.

In the weeks leading up to the murder he desperately tried to borrow money from wherever, or whoever, he could. He was facing financial ruin.

Why did he attack his wife if, as he had stated verbally and in letters, he had stumbled upon a murder being committed by another person?

And how was it, that if he had seen a murder taking place at 46 Lower Belgrave Street, that this just happened to be at the precise time he was passing the house? That is too much of a coincidence to be taken seriously.

He had stated that when he passed the house he could see into the basement area and had witnessed a violent act being perpetrated. That could not be the truth. It was clearly established that from pavement level you could not see into the basement. If he was prepared to lie about that, then how could one believe anything else he had said?

If he was innocent and another person was the murderer then why run away? That is definitely not the act of an innocent person.

And how could it be that when his borrowed car was found some days later in Newhaven an identical cosh, the same as that found at the murder scene, was discovered in the boot of his car?

That he was involved, one way or another, in the murder of Sandra Rivett seemed basically irrefutable. After all my research on the case I had reached the decision that he was guilty as hell. It was impossible not to arrive at any other conclusion.

Perhaps a certain Sidney Ainsworth, resident in Molinar, Mallorca, could tell more? However, I still harboured doubts as to his true identity and so had formulated a series of questions to test his story.

But there was one question I would put to him that had intrigued me more than any other issue that I had read about.

Why two murder weapons? Why two coshes?

The murder weapon, a piece of lead pipe wrapped in surgical tape, was recovered at the scene of the murder and another identical bludgeon – which had not been used – was found in the boot of Lord Lucan's borrowed car.

There were many elements relating to the murder of the nanny that did not fit together but this damning evidence was most peculiar and totally unintelligible.

It made no sense at all, and the police and most writers, being unable to explain this aspect of the case, had simply brushed the anomaly under the carpet.

Is it likely that a person intent on murdering someone with a cosh would go to the trouble of making a second cosh? The answer is a resounding No. No. No.

If someone was going to shoot a victim it's possible, but hugely unthinkable, that they might take a second gun in the most unlikely event of the first gun jamming or somehow failing to go off – But a cosh?

Only one serious writer that I had come across had attempted to explain this most inconvenient conundrum. In James Ruddick's book, he had put forward the theory that Lucan had hired a hitman and had decided himself what the murder weapon should be. He had made a length of lead pipe and then realised that it might be too long as the basement ceiling was low and someone over six-foot tall would have difficulty wielding the pipe above head height. According to this writer's theory, Lucan then made a shorter version of the lead cosh.

Well done to Mr Ruddick for at least trying to offer an hypothesis, something that virtually every other commentator had shied away from.

But this writer must have been biting his lip with his stab at trying to explain the unexplainable. If Lucky thought a shorter pipe would be better, then why not just cut a bit off the end of the longer pipe?

The police could not, and did not, offer an explanation and the latest heavyweight publication on the murder mystery published in 2014, covered four theories and 52 pages of how the murder might have been planned and carried out without once confronting the thorny issue of why there was one murder weapon found at the scene and another identical bludgeon discovered in the boot of the borrowed car.

For anyone trying to discover what lay behind the murder of the nanny this aspect alone should, surely, be taken very seriously. And that was my intention. I had discovered an element in the case that had seemingly gone over the heads of others who had strangely failed to realise how significant this could be.

I had booked a flight to Mallorca, but had a couple of days to spare. After a week stuck in my flat nursing a chest infection and pouring over a mass of material about the Lucan investigation I needed to get out and about and take in some fresh air.

I would spend a day in Newhaven, the town so central to the vanishing earl's disappearance and where the police and army spent two weeks searching for him.

Newhaven was one of the few coastal towns in East Sussex I had never visited. On the website the town advertised only one decent hotel and that was fully booked. I started looking for somewhere nearby and was finding myself searching all the way back to Brighton before finding what looked a good hotel in Rottingdean, the home of the famous girls school, Roedean.

I arrived at the White Horse Hotel, Rottingdean, in the early afternoon having hailed a cab from Brighton Pier. The hotel was fine but the weather was foul with strong gusting winds and rain blowing in from the sea.

The following day the storm had blown itself out to reveal a clear blue sky. After a hearty breakfast I set off on the coastal path to Newhaven. The first couple of miles were pleasant but the path soon filtered away and I found myself walking besides busy coastal roads. I decided to abandon the walk and take a bus into Newhaven. As the bus neared the town, the sweeping landscape of the South Downs came into view. I imagined the scene some forty years earlier as the police with tracker dogs and sticks combed those uplands and woods searching in vain for the body of Lord Lucan.

Once in the town I found a library and scanned the shelf containing books and leaflets on local interest. I wanted a map to find out where Norman Road was located. There was plenty of literature about Newhaven and its history but no maps. At the reception desk I was lucky and a kindly lady found me a map, the last one they had.

Norman Road was a ten-minute walk away, all uphill. The road where Lucky's borrowed car was found was similar to most of the roads in Newhaven. An upmarket Coronation Street but with the houses higher and mirroring each other either side of a narrow road. A single yellow line ran down one side of the road and I wondered if that had been a feature forty years ago when the Ford Corsair was abandoned here on that cold November morning.

I made my way back downhill to the marina, which lay on the western side of the River Ouse. There were about fifty small boats moored up in neat little rows. It struck me how easy it would have been if Lucky had access to a boat here to slip out of the marina into the wide mouth of the Ouse and disappear into the darkness and the beckoning French coast. I stayed awhile and pondered if that might have been the escape route all those years ago.

On the other side of the Ouse was the eastern part of the town with its busy ferry terminal – another possible passage to freedom for Lord Lucan.

Newhaven is not the loveliest town on the south coast, finding itself sandwiched between its more glamorous neighbours Brighton and Eastbourne. I decided that I had seen enough of the place and made tracks back to the centre and the train station.

As I walked along a towpath next to the river, the town council had made a brave attempt to liven up the area by hanging colourful draping flags from lampposts extolling the virtues and history of the town. I learned that until 1884 the only way to cross the river was by ferry or by fording it at low tide. (I made a mental note to look-up what fording meant). A little further on, one of these banners caught my eye and made me smile. It stated in a chorus of different coloured letters: "Did you know that when Lord Lucan vanished in 1974 following a murder his car was found in Norman Road, Newhaven?"

I concluded the town needed every bit of local interest it could muster.

It had been a good exercise to have a look around Newhaven as so many theories centred on this part of the coast as to the earl's possible escape or suicide, albeit that there was no real evidence that he had ever set foot here. It was only on the word of his friend Susie Maxwell-Scott, the last person to see him, that he had left her house around 1.15am. It was possible that he had stayed overnight at Uckfield while his friends in London came up with a plan to help their aristocrat friend with a safe house until he could be spirited out of the country. Someone else could have driven the car to Newhaven and left it there to give the police a false lead.

Newhaven rail station turned out to be a small branch line and London travellers were informed they should change at Lewes. From Lewes I caught a good connection back to Victoria. It had been an interesting little bit of sleuthing but it was to get better.

I popped into the Ladbrokes betting shop situated deep inside the bowels of Victoria Station. There was a good race coming up at Sandown but I had about ten-minutes to kill before the off.

I decided to go for a quick cigarette, but outside the shop, I realised that to weave my way out of this huge crowded station, have a smoke and get back in time for the race would be cutting it fine. Then, to my surprise, I noticed a side exit almost where I was standing. Outside I dodged a couple of taxi drivers almost coming to blows in an argument about queue jumping. A little further along this incredibly traffic-choked thoroughfare a street-sign opposite caught my eye.

I dodged my way across the road and checked the sign. I was amazed at my luck and the coincidence. I had, by pure chance, stumbled upon Lower Belgrave Street. I wandered along this rather up-market street and there – on the other side was the Plumbers Arms pub. It was a warm early evening and it looked as though there were more people outside the pub than inside, mostly office types who had grabbed an early escape from work and were having a few drinks before heading home to the suburbs.

How nice, I reflected, that the pub had kept the same name for the last forty years and had not transformed itself into a glorified gastro pub with a new trendy name.

I crossed the road and counted down the house numbers. The properties, whilst very nice and substantial, were not as grand as I had imagined. As I passed the houses I took note of the basement areas that they all shared in common. The police were absolutely correct. At pavement level you could not see into the basement rooms as Lucan had proclaimed. His story was a lie.

Number 46 was the same as all the others, but here the owners had installed a nice flower box on the ground floor windowsill full of bright summer blooms, a kaleidoscope of new life and colour splendidly dismissing any dark memories that might still linger in the bowels of that house.

Seeing the basement area for myself was a strange experience for I had read so much about the dreadful event that took place behind that downstairs window on the night of 7 November 1974.

The cornerstone of Lord Lucan's claims of innocence was that from this vantage point he had witnessed an assault taking place in the basement. It was a story that could so easily be disproved and, had quite rightly, branded him a liar from the outset.

His poorly thought out story, the wrong person being murdered, not one, but two crude murder weapons, it was all so tragically shambolic that crime writers have been scratching their heads for decades trying to make sense of it all.

I moved along the street and took the first right and found Eaton Row. The mews was a dead-end and I felt a little uneasy strolling along here. Unless this is where you lived or were making a delivery you would not have any business in this quiet and rather private mews.

There was number five, the mews cottage where Lady Lucan now lives – alone, and it is said, in reduced circumstances. The frontage of the house was dominated by a large square window where filthy net curtains hung shielding her from prying eyes.

Behind those nets, which had not been taken down and washed in years, lived the reclusive and, defiant to the end, countess. From her backyard she would be able to see her former five-storey grand home. A constant and almost cruel reminder of a former life. That house, so dominant from her back window was once hers. It was where she and her new dashing husband, Lord Bingham, moved to immediately after a celebrity marriage and where the couple raised three beautiful children. A place holding memories of so many good years, holidays in Monte Carlo and the Algarve, winter skiing in Switzerland and Austria, dining at the best restaurants in Knightsbridge and horse riding weekends with friends at country estates. A world of style and privilege.

Now that former life was no more than a distant memory, lost in a crumbling marriage that turned to bitterness and revenge and which ultimately ended in tragedy.

The countess had escaped being murdered but she had lost virtually everything else into the bargain.

I resisted a silly urge to knock on her door and say something like: 'I'm awfully sorry to bother you Veronica, it's just that I think I know where your husband is.'

She would almost certainly slam the door in my face and threaten to call the police. – and I wouldn't blame her.

Twenty years ago the journalist James Ruddick had taken a chance, and without any prior attempt to make an appointment, had knocked on her door. He must have caught her in a good mood for she agreed to speak to him and the pair went on to form a close relationship whereby she gave him much interesting information for his forthcoming book.

I walked out of the mews, casting a final glance at those filthy net curtains and wondered about the small lady hidden away behind those nets who harboured such a harrowing story to tell.

I headed for the tube station. I had to get home and pack a few things ready for my trip to Mallorca where I intended to meet up again with Mr Sidney Ainsworth and determine whether by some remote chance he really was Veronica's long lost husband.

The man was very believable, but of course it was hugely improbable. It can't be true, I kept telling myself – It simply can't be.

Chapter Twelve

It was a hot and humid day in Mallorca and having packed a new mobile phone in my rucksack I set off from the El Cid hotel in the early afternoon for the four kilometre walk to the quiet little town of Molinar.

Before leaving London I had replied to another text message from Paul King asking how I was, and did I have any news for him. The enquiry as to my health was nice, but was probably secondary to his desire to get some information on what might be the biggest scoop and biggest payday of his journalistic career.

As I walked along the coast I rehearsed in my mind how to handle what could turn out to be my very last encounter with the mysterious Sidney Ainsworth if he failed in any way to answer some important questions I intended to put to him.

Arriving at the Café Plaza I was surprised to see how busy it was. All the outside tables were taken and there was no sign of Sidney. I perched myself on a bar stool and ordered a beer.

Where was he I wondered? Had he been and gone? I finished my beer and ordered another one and as I did so, and

Chapter Twelve

to my delight, I saw Sidney hobbling across the square. For a moment I did not register that it was him for there was something different about the way he looked. I could see he was dressed very smartly but he was wearing white trainers, which did not go at all with his dark blue slacks and lightweight summer jacket. He was also walking with the aid of a stick. He approached the café very slowly, pausing only to share a few friendly words with one of the waitresses. As he made his way to the bar I waved and caught his eye. I pointed at a spare stool next to mine, whereby he smiled broadly, raised his stick in the air and gingerly made his way over to me. We shuffled our stools so that we could face each other and for a few seconds simply eyed each other silently and cautiously.

Sidney took off his panama hat and laid it on the bar. I noticed he had a bruise on his forehead and a certain blue-like darkness could be seen under his eyes. Despite this I had to admit he was still quite a striking individual for his age with those sharp inquisitive grey eyes and that lined leather-tanned face.

'How are you Adam?' he said softly, leaning forward and grasping my hand. 'I'm so pleased to see you again my dear boy.'

I waited while the waitress poured him a large El Toro brandy.

'I'm fine Sidney,' I answered.

He took a sip of brandy and then cast his eyes around the busy café as though uneasy about something.

'Are you alone Adam?' he said turning his gaze back to me.

'Of course I am,' I replied firmly.

Sidney lit one of his small cigars and then considered me for a while as the smoke drifted between us.

'Did you read my manuscript?' he asked very quietly and carefully.

'Indeed I did Sidney,' I said. 'I was shocked and truly astonished and that's why I have come back to see you.'

He leaned towards me, wary eyes darting left and right ensuring nobody was in hearing distance. 'So you know who I am then?' he said, his voice just a whisper, his eyes examining me.

I took a sip of beer and looked at him hard. 'No, I don't Sidney,' I said matter-of-factly, 'I only know who you are claiming to be.'

Sidney rocked back on his stool showing a rebuffed but cool expression. He then deliberately changed the course of the conversation. He tapped his walking stick against the sole of one of his trainers. 'What do you think of these Adam?' he said in a slight mocking tone. 'I feel somewhat foolish wearing them but I had a little stumble. My landlord,' he said – and then broke off from what he was about to say. 'Have I mentioned to you my landlord?' he enquired in that slow velvet voice of his. 'He is so good to me, nothing is too much trouble for him. Lovely man. He heard that I had taken a fall and so he kindly purchased these sports shoes for me from a shop in Palma.'

Sidney's face held a wan smile. 'I never thought I would wear such modern things but they are so comfortable and I find I am more steady on my feet with them.'

Perhaps Sidney was right, I thought, that we should talk of other things for a little while, there was no need for me to rush this meeting.

I pointed to the bruise on his forehead. 'Did you get that from the fall?' I asked. He wiped a finger gently across his forehead.

'Yes,' he murmured. 'It's my silly fault, I should be more careful. Anyway Adam,' he said easily, 'I really am pleased to see you. I was never sure if you would return here – whether I would ever meet up with you again.'

Chapter Twelve

Sidney took a sip of brandy and eyed me thoughtfully. 'Other than my friends who originally helped me you are the first person I have opened up to. I hope you will forgive me for taking you into my confidence in such a selfish and dangerous way.'

'Why me Sidney?' I asked gently, 'It's not as though you know me. You took a big gamble on a stranger, Oh, and bye the way,' I added somewhat flatly, 'I intend to keep addressing you as Sidney.'

He smiled weakly and tapped his stick on the floor. 'That is perfectly fine by me Adam, best it should always remain like that. I do not want to get you into any sort of trouble dear boy. I have been most presumptuous in hoping that you might help me and I will fully understand should you wish to disregard this old man you see before you. To go on your way, to forget you had ever met me. I think I have put you in danger and I feel sorry I have done that.'

For a moment he stared in the direction of the sea, his mind somewhat preoccupied. Then he turned back to me. 'Perhaps you would allow me to explain why I took such a big chance with you.' His conversation was, as always, slow and deliberate, his words carefully chosen. He waited for some customers to pay their bill over the counter before continuing.

'Time was marching on for me Adam. I knew that sooner or later I would have to take a gamble on someone if I wanted my story to be told. The friends who kindly helped me in the past are no longer around. I cannot return to England or, for that matter, to any other place as my passport,' he paused for a few seconds and threw a throwaway hand before going on, 'my passport, if I can call it that, has long since expired. So here I must stay. Here is where I am marooned which suits me fine as this is a lovely safe place for me to see out my days.'

He lit another cigarillo and thoughtfully watched a pall of smoke rise before continuing. 'When we first met and I asked if you would post that letter for me I offered you some money which you refused to take and your obvious honesty impressed me. We talked happily about that casino case I had been following in the papers, which you knew about and like me you were interested in horse racing. But unlike me, it seemed you could enjoy having a bet and it had not developed into a problem, which it had been in my sorry life. Anyway, Adam, I enjoyed talking with you immensely and promised myself that should I meet you again I would stick my neck out and take a chance that you might help me. Over the years I have spoken to many people who have passed by here but nobody fitted the person I was looking for until you came along. Of course it was a huge gamble, but I had made up my mind that I would take one last punt, the biggest and maybe the last of my life. I would take a chance on you.'

A waitress buzzing nearby stopped and shared a little joke with Sidney about his new trainers. It was clear that the staff at the Café Plaza held him in great affection. He was a regular here and probably their best customer no matter what time of year.

But who was he really I was still asking myself? Was he attempting to pull off the most audacious impersonation act of all time – and if so why? If that was the case then how the devil had he contrived to identify himself to an old Clermont member, one of the few people still alive who knew Lord Lucan well and could confirm his story. If he was a fraud then all this was more than just clever, it was nothing short of bloody brilliant.

These thoughts were flashing through my mind as I kept an eye out for a table to become free as where we were sitting was far from ideal with staff and customers brushing past us.

Chapter Twelve

I saw a couple and their young kiddies with toy scooters vacating a table in a nice secluded spot. I picked up my beer and Sidney's brandy and moved fleet-footed to claim it. Sidney followed slowly with his walking stick held out in front of him like some sort of water divining rod. We made ourselves comfortable, arranging our chairs to gain some shade being offered by a few magnificent palm trees that acted like giant umbrellas against the glare of the sun.

I took a sip of beer and smiled thoughtfully at Sidney, still not sure what to think or what to make of him. It was very confusing and otherworldly. I could not relate this polite soft-spoken character to the criminal that I had read so much about – a man accused of killing a young nanny in Belgravia all those years ago.

'I have to tell you where I am with this story of yours Sidney,' I said, keeping my voice low and restrained, although now we were in a nice quiet spot and a fair bit away from other tables and the hustle and bustle of the bar area.

'As I said,' I continued. 'I did read your document and as you might imagine I was pretty horrified but also suspicious. Against my better judgement I decided to follow-up your story once it had been posted to that publishing house and so I phoned Warren not knowing what to expect.'

Sidney moved a little uneasily in his chair, his eyes focussing on me intently.

'Anyway,' I went on in a considered manner. 'I met this chap Warren, and we discussed the letter you had to sent to his father, and we also talked about your manuscript. Warren was not the nicest person I had ever come across and made it clear to me that he was unable to help you, that his publishing company could in no way handle such a risky and problematical story.'

Sidney remained silent, stroking his beard and eyeing me keenly, his face giving nothing away.

'However,' I said, still keeping my voice low, 'he confided in me that your letter to his father was spot on, that his dad had confirmed it could only have come from one person.'

I noticed Sidney's eyes brighten and glitter somewhat.

'As it was possible your manuscript might be genuine, Warren handed all the papers over to a freelance journalist associate of his named Paul King.'

Sidney suddenly shook his head and looked very agitated.

'You haven't told anyone where I am have you Adam?' he asked urgently.

'No no, Sidney,' I said firmly, immediately calming him down. 'I have not told a soul where you live so you need not be concerned in that respect.'

Sidney gave me a relieved smile and thanked me softly. He settled back in his chair and lit another cigar. I caught the eye of a waitress and ordered some more drinks.

'All the same Sidney,' I said, 'I did meet up with this Paul King and he impressed me immensely. He told me that he had travelled down to Surrey and spoke to your friend Colin about that letter and he is satisfied that you have identified yourself to the best of your ability. He thinks he might be able to help you get your story into print. The sticking point is this Sidney. Your letter and manuscript is most compelling and interesting, but in itself is not enough proof for Paul King to be able to persuade a newspaper to buy the story. To that end, he wants to interview you, to satisfy himself that you are who you say you are.'

Sidney hunched forward tapping his walking cane on the floor, his face suddenly full of anxiety. 'I don't trust journalists Adam, please don't bring him here. I would sooner forget all about this and burn the rest of my papers than allow a newspaperman to know where I am. I'm sorry, I will not go that far.'

Chapter Twelve

He leaned across the table and stubbed out his cigar shaking his head in a show of frustration. He had spoken with unusual speed and certitude, and his face had drained of some colour.

'Tell me this Sidney,' I said softly, trying to get the conversation back on track. 'Would you undergo an interview and give your fingerprints if I could assure you that your whereabouts would remain a secret, that nobody could have any idea where you are living?'

Sidney leaned back clutching his stick in both hands. 'Of course I would Adam, he said quietly and confidently. 'I am willing to undergo any sort of scrutiny to prove who I am so long as I can finish my days here in Molinar, alone and in peace. That's all I ask. I want my story to be told but I will never allow myself to be arrested after all these years and endure a trial that would drag up so much hatred, not just against me but my family and children. I cannot allow that to happen.'

We took a little pause from talking as the waitress replenished our drinks and cleaned our table.

Sidney hunched over his brandy. 'I'm a bad man Adam, I know that, but the media and the courts were intent on a public crucifixion, a show trial. For all the wrong I had done the retribution directed to those associated with me was not right. That's why I have stayed in hiding all these years. The police were not just after me but also my family and friends.'

He reached into his jacket pocket and produced a small pill bottle that he rattled to the side of his face. 'I have carried these with me for what seems a lifetime and they are never far from my grasp. The label states they are for a heart condition but they are not.' He smiled grimly and put the bottle back in his pocket. 'Aspers sourced them for me many, many years back, and luckily I have never had recourse to swallow a couple and say goodbye to it all. I have somehow survived these last forty years but it has been unimaginably fraught. I have always been looking over my shoulder, always aware that a knock on my door might be the police. Along with that I have carried with me so much shame and guilt. Not a day goes by when I do not think about poor Sandra, about my family and more especially my children who I could never see growing up and doing well for themselves despite all the grief I had brought to bear on them.'

Sidney took out a handkerchief from his top pocket and dabbed beads of sweat from his head, carefully avoiding that nasty bruise.

'How did you fall?' I asked, thinking a change of subject was in order.

'I really don't know what happened Adam.' he said with a tight, self-depreciating smile. 'I wasn't drunk or anything like that, I just keeled over.'

'Sidney, I need to ask you something,' I said, in a careful tone. 'I have been reading up on the Lord Lucan case and have tried to make sense of a huge amount of information from various sources, but there is one part of the case that has baffled and intrigued me no end, something I can't comprehend or work out.'

Sidney leaned forward and gazed at me fixedly, ready for the question.

I was now going to ask him the 64,000 dollar question, not just to hear what he might say but more importantly to get his reaction. I looked him steadily in the eyes and asked almost in a whisper. 'Why two murder weapons?'

Sidney suddenly stared at me aghast, his eyes seemed to bulge slightly. He made to respond raising a hand towards me, but as he went to speak he started to cough. He quickly reached for his handkerchief and covered his mouth. It was as though he had swallowed something that had gone down the wrong way. He rose slowly and stumbled towards a palm tree, which he leaned against while coughing furiously. I was about to go to over to him and pat him on the back or something, but I waited and after a little while he turned and made his way slowly back to our table. Once seated he raised a hand in a gesture of apology and then wiped moisture from his forehead and wet reddened eyes.

'Are you alright Sidney?' I said with a note of genuine concern.

'I'm most sorry,' he murmured, his voice still croaky. He released a last little cough and seemed to recover his composure.

'You took me by surprise Adam.' he said, his voice slowly calming. 'If you would like to know why there were two pipes, about Terry and why…'

I quickly interrupted him. 'Terry?' I asked, confused.

Sidney smiled apologetically and shrugged. 'How stupid of me,' he said, almost talking to himself. 'Of course you would not know about Terry, nobody would. I was getting miles ahead of myself.'

Sidney had recovered from his coughing fit, so much so that he lit another cigarillo and then having sent a puff of smoke into the air took a good sip of brandy.

He inclined towards me and spoke with quiet passion. 'Adam, the story is all there, every damned word, all typed on my trusted Olivetti. You were the first person I trusted to read the beginning of my story and I would be happy for you to read the rest. Part two is finished and but for a few words, part three and the final part of my life's story will be completed.

Everything is explained in all its ugly detail. I have left nothing out. Better my story does not die with me but the truth is told. I have thought about doing this for many years and feel the time is now right to come clean and get all this off my chest. It's the one decent act I can do before I die. Then the guessing and wild speculation that has gone on for the last forty years can come to an end. The police and the media had got it all wrong. That's why it's right for me to relate the real events while I can.

And let me tell you this Adam,' he said, shaking his head sadly, 'When people read my story they will know the silly conclusions they arrived at were way off the mark.'

Sidney rocked a little in his chair and considered me for a moment. Then he took off his watch and handed it to me in silence. It was a heavy, chunky Rolex. I turned it over and read the inscription on the back: 'BE LUCKY J.A.'

'Very nice,' I said, as I handed it back. 'I take it the J.A. is John Aspinall?'

Sidney nodded. 'Aspers gave it to me a lifetime ago. It would be my insurance he told me. I believe it's very rare. Only about a dozen were ever made. Aspers told me that if I was ever in money trouble then I would always have this watch as a guarantee to raise some money but never to part with it permanently.' Sidney tapped the face of the watch, his face set hard with the memory. 'Aspinall was a good and most generous friend to me. Fortunately, I have never had to pawn or sell the watch. I believe it has increased in value over the years. It would be nice if I could leave the watch to one of my children but I guess that might not be possible.'

Sidney arched his eyebrows at me as though having a sudden idea. 'Adam,' he said thoughtfully, 'If anything should happen to me, please take the watch, I would very much like you to have it. I believe it's very valuable.'

'Thank you Sidney,' I responded warmly, 'That's a most kind and generous offer, but you must hold on to it. I'm sure it means a lot to you.'

Sidney gazed at me for a few seconds, his face betraying a mixture of decades old emotions. Then he asked softly.

Chapter Twelve

'I must ask you an important question Adam.' He paused and took a deep breath. 'Do you believe who I am?'

He had taken me somewhat by surprise. I thought for a few moments and then held his eyes. 'I'm not sure Sidney, I'm not sure what to think. All this seems so unreal, so incredible.'

He moved his chair a little closer to the table. 'Allow me to tell you a story Adam,' he said, his tone engaging. 'In my letter to Colin Hedley-Davies, I mentioned a girl called Nicole and I would like to tell you the story behind that.'

I nodded and gestured for him to continue.

Sidney rested his cane between his legs and settled himself. 'Colin and I were very good friends and regulars at the Clermont Club, although Colin was not a gambler like myself, his passion was bridge, which was also a favourite card game of mine. We played regularly at the Clermont and the Portland Club.'

Sidney lit one of his cigarillos and spoke as if to the thin trickle of smoke that drifted away into the warm air, only occasionally turning to meet my eyes. 'We became friendly with Nicole, a young girl who worked at the Portland Club. Colin and I were very fond of her. She was French but spoke perfect English. Nicole was not only very pretty but was an excellent worker. She remembered everyone's name, where they liked to sit and what their favourite drinks were. We would often chat with her and as time went by she let it be known to us that she would love to work at the Clermont and learn about the gaming industry. She asked us ever so discretely if we could put a word in for her. We said we would, but that it might not be easy, as the Clermont did not train their own dealers or inspectors. Aspers recruited his people ready trained from the casinos in Paris and Deuville. Nevertheless, we did manage to get Nicole a job at the Clermont once we told Aspers what a wonderful girl she was and that it would be worth the effort in giving her a foot up on the ladder and teaching her to be a dealer. On our recommendation they took her on and all went well. She took to the job like a duck to water and the players and staff loved her. She was also making good money, double what she had been earning at the Portland.'

Sidney paused for a few seconds as though turning the events over in his mind before continuing in a calm, reminiscent tone.

'As I say, all went well for the first few months, but then suddenly there was a slight visible change in her demeanour, as though something was troubling her. I think only Colin and myself noticed this as we had come to know her so well and were keen to see her make a success of her new job.

While dining at the Criterion one evening I saw Nicole at a far table with two men I recognised as recent members of the Clermont. She did not see me and eventually they all left together. In the following weeks I became aware that whenever Nicole was dealing roulette these same two men would be gambling at her table. Whenever the opportunity presented itself I would stand behind her table and watch her dealing at a discreet distance. She was cheating – 'palming' high value chips. These, no doubt, she would later pass on to her two male accomplices.

One evening Colin and I waited outside the club for Nicole to finish her shift. As she approached us she looked happy but her smile quickly vanished. She knew immediately why we were waiting to see her. She stopped in front of us and began to sob. We told her that we had no intention of getting her into trouble. If Aspers knew she had been cheating at his casino he would not have called the police but would have made sure she was disgraced and her name blackened all over town.

We told her what she must do and nothing more would be said. The next day she dropped a note into the Clermont explaining that her mother had been taken ill in France and regrettably she had to return home. The club were sad to lose her, she had, all agreed, been a wonderful addition to the staff. We never saw her again.'

Sidney turned to me and let out a resigned sigh.

'I doubt that Colin has ever related this story to a living soul and you are the first person to have heard this little tale from my lips. We would have both kept this story to ourselves for the last forty-odd years. So you see Adam,' he said, his eyes showing a sudden intensity. 'Though it shames me to admit it, and despite closing my mind and running away from the past, I am the person who I say I am.'

Sidney turned sorrowful eyes over my face.

'My name is Richard John Bingham – and what's more, I can prove it.'

I told myself to stay calm and think carefully of how I would now proceed with this meeting. 'Sidney, you told me that you would undergo an interview and give your fingerprints if you could be assured that nobody would know of your where-abouts, is that correct?'

Sidney tapped his cane against the table and nodded solemnly. 'Of course I will,' he said with an easy assured tone.

'Very well then,' I said evenly. 'This is the plan.' I rummaged in my rucksack and handed Sidney a mobile phone.

He held the phone as though it might blow-up in his hand. He shook his head doubtfully which I was expecting. 'Have you used one of these?' I asked.

'I know of them of course, everyone seems to have them,' he said dubiously. 'But I have never had the slightest reason to own one.'

I took a gulp of beer and stretched out my legs. 'The idea Sidney, is that Paul King interviews you over the telephone.'

I spoke firmly, trying to muster enthusiasm in my voice. 'I will ask him to use my mobile and at the end of the interview I will take my mobile back from him. That way there can be no chance that he could do a trace on the call. I don't think he would try to do that, or if it would be possible anyway, but we will take no chances. Your whereabouts will remain a secret.'

Sidney was clutching the mobile with both hands and looking very bemused. 'I don't know how these work Adam.' He laid the mobile on the table and smiled sadly.

'It's not easy to teach an old dog new tricks you know.'

I delved into my rucksack and handed him a charger unit, an adapter and a small user-guide booklet.

'Just familiarise yourself with the basics Sidney,' I said, trying to sound encouraging. 'But don't worry too much, just get the feel of the thing. Tomorrow I will call by your apartment at twelve noon, if that's fine by you, and we will go over everything and have a little rehearsal. All I would ask you to do for now is put the mobile on charge before you go to bed tonight. I think you will find that quite straightforward.' I pointed at the little booklet. 'It's all in there.' Sidney nodded, still looking very doubtful and sheepish.

I finished my beer and let out a tired sigh. 'It's been a long day Sidney, what with my early flight. I think we should break off now and make a fresh start tomorrow.'

Sidney showed a contented smile. 'That sounds a good idea Adam,' he said brightly. 'Thank you for all you are doing for me. I feel guilty that I have burdened you with so much. If my story is worth anything then I hope you will take whatever you wish, that you are rewarded for the work and the risk you are taking on my behalf. I do not want anything myself, just that my story is told and that you remain safe and come out of this on top.'

Chapter Twelve

Sidney went quiet, deep in his own thoughts, gazing past me at nothing in particular.

I studied him, assembling in my mind all the strange aspects of this amazing story. That letter he had sent identifying himself, which was almost certainly genuine. His somewhat noble bearing still clinging to him, a leftover of a former life. The charming and totally believable story about the French girl which can easily be double-checked. The clear willingness to be interviewed and give his fingerprints. And that Rolex watch with its inscription. It all fitted together. The parts of the jigsaw had been gradually, and scarily locking into place.

As ridiculous as it appeared, I was looking at Lord Lucan. Surely, it had to be. Nobody could possibly conjure all this up were it not true. Could they?

I suddenly felt very tired and uneasy about the situation I found myself in. I could feel my heart fluttering and beads of sweet running down my cheeks. The palms of my hands had suddenly become wet and clammy.

But, there again, it was a very hot day.

CHAPTER THIRTEEN

I knocked on Sidney's door shortly before noon. I felt more relaxed after a good nights sleep and ready to continue with this escapade after the previous days travel exertions, and the heady responsibility I felt whilst listening to his utterly compelling story about the person he was proclaiming to be. There had been many questions I had planned to ask him but having spent some more time with Sidney, further probing seemed unnecessary. The man and his story was irresistible. I was totally taken in.

I heard shuffling behind the door and guessed that Sidney was looking at me through the little spy-hole set in the door. A chain clattered and the door slowly opened.

Sidney smiled nervously, quickly checked there was nobody else in the corridor and beckoned me inside. I followed him into the small lounge. He gently eased himself into one of the two armchairs set against the window and gestured for me to take a seat opposite him. His new mobile was on the floor connected to a wall socket and I was pleased to see that he had worked out how to charge the device.

Chapter Thirteen

I pointed at the mobile. 'Well done Sidney,' I said encouragingly, 'I'm pleased to see that you have the phone on charge. You will need to do that every few days.'

I noticed the small user manual resting on the arm of his chair. I picked it up. 'Did you manage to have a look at this?' I asked.

Sidney nodded with a puzzled expression. 'I will have a go Adam,' he said grimly, 'but its years since I used any sort of phone. You will have to bear with me I'm afraid.'

'Don't worry,' I said. 'We will have a little test run. I'm sure you will pick up the basics pretty quickly. After all,' I added, 'every kid on the block has a mobile these days.'

He let out a slightly nervous laugh. 'I'll do my best Adam, but you only have to look at my old typewriter to see how up-to-date I am with new technology.'

I glanced over at his Olivetti with reams of paper stacked neatly by its side. A typed sheet rested in the carriage. What a story might be there I wondered.

I showed him where to locate my mobile number, which I had stored in the memory, how to turn the device on and off, and how to make and end a call. He listened attentively and it was pleasing to see that he seemed relaxed. While going through all this with him I tried not to sound condescending, reminding myself that if he really was genuine, this man was Eton educated, albeit that mobile's were not around in those days.

I went through the instructions a second time and then asked if he was ready to make a test call to my mobile. He seemed happy with the idea. I went out into the corridor and waited for Sidney to phone. It went well other than his voice was not clear and seemed to be far away. I returned to the room and saw Sidney staring down at the device in some confusion. I explained to him that he must hold the mobile to his ear at all times, just as if it were a normal telephone receiver. We tried again and now everything was fine. He seemed pleased with himself.

'Not so mysterious as I had imagined,' he said cheerfully.

'We'll go through it all again in a little while Sidney,' I said. 'But as I mentioned to you, the journalist also needs your fingerprints. I'm not sure how precise they have to be but are you willing to give this a try?'

Sidney opened his hands towards me. 'Of course Adam, I am more than willing to do everything within reason to convince this journalist chap.' He paused and then asked mildly. 'What did you say his name was?'

'Paul King,' I said. 'I believe he is trustworthy and definitely your best bet if you ever want to get your story told.'

'Ah, Paul King.' Sidney muttered to himself.

From my rucksack I produced a small ink pad and some A4 sheets. I had practiced doing my own prints and the results had been far from perfect but the simple fact that Sidney had not objected one iota to giving his fingerprints said everything.

I pulled a small table up to his armchair and asked him to do one digit at a time, touching the ink pad very slightly and then placing his finger on the paper. It was all a bit messy and probably a waste of time and the first few sheets I crumpled-up and threw into a waste bin at the side of Sidney's desk. After about half an hour of trial and error we had got some reasonable prints and once these had dried I placed the sheets in an envelope. I apologised to Sidney, saying that I found doing this somewhat embarrassing. He laughed and seemed unconcerned.

'Let's go down to the café Sidney,' I said. 'We'll have a drink and a chat and another little test run with your mobile.'

Sidney eased himself slowly from his armchair. 'Adam,' he said, while adjusting his balance and reaching for his stick.

'You have been spending money on my behalf. You must let me pay you dear boy, you must be out of pocket with all this.'

'We can talk about money down at the café,' I said. 'It's no big deal at the moment.'

Sidney collected his mobile and door keys, still muttering that he wanted to pay me. After we had both washed ink from our hands in the bathroom we made our way to the Café Plaza. The walk down the stairs and across the square to the café took some time as Sidney was still unsteady on his feet. His recent fall had obviously shaken him as he moved with a certain degree of fragility. At the café we found a nice secluded table, settled ourselves and ordered some drinks. We chatted about nothing in particular for a while before I asked if he was ready to run through using his mobile in a little rehearsal for what he might have to endure when being interviewed by the journalist Paul King. This time, I would ring him, and once again I went through the instructions for receiving and ending a call. I needn't have worried for I was pleasantly surprised how perfectly at ease he was with his new mobile. I walked towards the beach front and phoned him. He answered with a subdued, nervous hello.

I asked him a series of simple questions. What date was his birthday? How long had he lived in Molinar? and such things. I was pleased with how well this went. He answered in his normal deliberate manner, but with a fair degree of confidence.

I could see him at a distance as the café was gradually filling up and the tables being taken by a mainly local clientele. Anyone casting an eye in his direction would not think twice about him. Just an old boy having a chat on a mobile, maybe to one of his children or grandchildren. This little play-acting seemed so dreamlike. The sun was shining and the café had a pleasant buzzing atmosphere. Nobody here could know what lay behind all this. That the dapper old chap on his mobile was rehearsing for an interview that would determine whether he was one of the most wanted criminals in British legal history. I still found it hard to come to terms with the weirdness of the situation. But there was still one more hurdle to negotiate, the biggest of them all. The telephone interview with Paul King would have to be decisive if I were to involve myself any further in this freaky affair.

I returned to our table having taken a couple of cheeky and secretive photos of Sidney on my mobile. I congratulated him warmly on how quickly and confidently he had risen to the test.

He smiled and thanked me but still looked abashed and unsure. I now needed to iron out some details with him. I lit a cigarette and relaxed back in my chair, beer in hand.

'Sidney, I need to go through a few things with you.' I said softly. He inclined forward resting his stick between his legs and held my eyes.

'When this journalist interviews you it's possible he might try and trick you. He's a very shrewd guy and has spent his career weeding out the truth of a story. Don't be tempted to go head-to-head with him. Just give him short answers to his questions, don't try and elaborate on anything.'

Sidney nodded silently.

'If he should ask you something you cannot answer,' I continued in an even voice, 'simply say you don't know. Keep calm and just concentrate on giving him answers that you are sure about and don't let him try and fluster you. I will be there when this interview takes place and will speak to you when it's over. Lets hope it goes well.'

Sidney straightened his back and lit a cigarillo. 'Do you have children Adam?' he asked out of the blue.

'A daughter,' I said. 'She is a vet, has her own practice in Brighton. My wife and I are separated but we are on good terms. We all get together quite frequently.'

'That's nice,' Sidney said delicately. 'What has hurt me more than anything in all these lonely years is not seeing my children. I only wanted the best for them, that's what this sorry story is all about.' He shook his head wearily gazing at the ground.

I looked around the café, the place was doing a good trade and now every table was taken. A waitress buzzed by and I ordered some more drinks.

'Sidney,' I said mildly, 'If your story is taken by a newspaper you need to work out what you want to do with any money that might be coming your way. You cannot channel anything to your children, and I would sooner not get involved in the cash side of things.'

Sidney shrugged and leaned on his stick. 'I don't want anything for myself Adam, I have enough cash to last me out.' Sidney suddenly looked concerned and showed a slight edge of panic in his voice. 'If a newspaper should take my story how can I be sure that I will remain safe? That they will not try and seek me out?'

'That's where this journalist earns his money,' I said keenly. 'It will be his job to sell the story having never met you and with no knowledge of where you might be. He will say that the manuscript, fingerprints and various evidence came into his possession by way of a go-between who wanted to remain anonymous. He will simply say that he trusts the person who passed the story on to him, that he has checked the authenticity of the document, but has no idea as to the identity of the go-between or where that person can be found. Paul King tells me that he has never betrayed a confidant, that he has often obtained information from contacts who wish to remain secret. I trust him to keep us all safe and unknown, including Loudon House Publishing who you initially contacted. The bottom line Sidney, is that you will have to trust this journalist if you want your story to find its way into the public domain.'

Sidney nodded solemnly. 'I have come this far thanks to your efforts Adam. As I mentioned, should there be money for my story then I hope you look after yourself first and foremost. You have been taking a big risk in helping me.'

Our drinks arrived and we sat in silence for a while. I planned in my head what to do next. It was now down to an interview that would have to be carried out over the airwaves and I wasn't sure how Paul King would take that, but I could see no other way forward. Sidney was determined not to meet him face to face. This idea of using a mobile was the best I could come up with.

'Sidney, I'm flying back home later today,' I said casually. 'I would like you to phone me, 2pm your time, for the next few days. I need to speak to Paul King and set up this interview. Do you still want me to go ahead and arrange this?'

He held my eyes and spoke carefully. 'This journalist wants proof, I understand that now. So yes, I know who I am, and so I'm happy to answer questions about myself so long as I cannot be traced. That has always been my only concern.'

'Very well then,' I said. 'We'll go for it. In the meantime Sidney you should decide what you want to do about the money side of things should this journalist manage to sell your story. He tells me it won't be a fortune because of the uncertainty involved. All the same, if you pass this interview you should give the matter some real thought.'

Sidney nodded gravely. 'I will think about it Adam, and thank you. But I have to admit that I'm feeling nervous about this. That I am taking a risk.'

'If it's any comfort to you Sidney, we are all taking a risk.'

Chapter Thirteen

I made to get some euros for the bill, but as usual Sidney would have none of it.

'I'm staying for a little longer Adam,' he said most politely. 'I'll settle up when I leave. I need to think things over.' He looked tired and I could tell that he was unsettled.

I picked up my rucksack and reminded him to ring me at 2pm the following day. At Palma airport I was pleased to see that my flight back to London was on time.

I sent a text to Paul King asking if he could meet me for lunch the following day at the Pizza House in Goodge Street.

I was still asking myself how, and why, I had immersed myself in such a treacherous enterprise? But I had, and would stick with it for a little longer. My curiosity in this amazing story was still winning me over. I had to find out. I had to find out if by some miracle Sidney Ainsworth really could be Lucky Lucan.

CHAPTER FOURTEEN

Paul was waiting for me, seated by a window table when I arrived at the Pizza House. We shook hands and shared a few pleasantries. He asked if I was fully recovered from my chest infection. I told him I was fine and had met up again with Sidney and would bring him up to date. We put matters aside for the moment and studied the menu. We both went for the veal and ordered a couple of beers. When the waiter had departed with our order Paul studied me for a moment before asking brightly. 'Well what news Adam? Time is marching on, and I'm well ahead of the game at my end.'

I told Paul that I had some good news and some bad news.

He raised his eyebrows at me. 'Go on then Adam,' he said uneasily, 'let's have the bad news first.'

I waited a few moments while the waiter poured some bottled beer into our glasses.

'It's like this Paul,' I said carefully, 'Sidney is frightened out of his wits that his whereabouts might be discovered.' I took a deep breath. 'Whether he is our real man or not I don't know, but he refuses to meet you.'

Paul shook his head wearily. 'Before you go any further Adam,' he said breaking in quickly, 'let me explain the difficult position I'm in. I've found a proprietor who is interested in the story so long as I'm willing to put my reputation on the line that the story is genuine. On top of that I have to deal with this newspapers lawyer who is a pain in the backside. As it stands I'm being asked to trust you, who, if you'll forgive the pun, I don't know from Adam, and a person somewhere in Europe who claims to be Lord Lucan, who I have never met and who refuses to meet me.' Paul brushed his hair back away from his glasses and narrowed his eyes at me. 'My problem is that I only have your word that this Sidney character really exists.' He waved a hand dismissively. 'I'm sorry, but I can't work like that.'

'Okay Paul,' I said softly, looking at him steadily. 'I can't be absolutely sure this man is genuine, but the situation is this. If he is real, you and I have to appreciate the stand Sidney is taking. He won't take the slightest chance of being found. He is paranoid about that, and if he really is Lucky, so he should be. The man carries a couple of pills with him that he's intimated are cyanide. Any hint of being arrested he will take his life rather than be apprehended. That's the sort of guy we are dealing with. His collaboration in this was made very clear to me. He tells me he's managed to stay on the run for forty years and is not going to take any risks at this time in his life.'

I paused for a few seconds and raised my hands up at Paul. 'As for myself, I want to take you into my trust. I'm nervous about all this and have immersed myself in what may well turn out to be a deadly game. I have never been after money or publicity but have allowed myself to be swept along by curiosity. Now I could be harbouring a wanted criminal. Believe me, I would be happy to pass everything over to you.

I know it's your line of business and, unlike me, you have not got close to Sidney and taken on some sort of misplaced sympathy for the old boy. I have got too close to this man.' I took a sip of beer, and waited for a moment.

'You told me you would never betray an informer who wanted to stay safe. Is that correct?' I asked meaningfully.

Paul nodded. 'Definitely,' he replied with intent. 'I give you my word that your involvement in this will not be passed on to anyone else.'

'In that case,' I said, inclining towards him. 'I would like to work with you. I'm over my head with this. I'm not qualified to handle something so dangerous and I definitely don't like the position I've found myself in. If he really is Lucan and this went wrong I could end up in prison.' I produced a battered old business card from my wallet and handed it to Paul. 'My name is Adam Baker.' I pointed at the card Paul was studying. 'That's where I live, my phone and e-mail details,' I said evenly. 'You can check me out, I'm on the electoral roll. Also when we next meet I will show you my passport.'

Paul smiled warmly and we happily shook hands across the table.

'Thank you Mr. Adam Baker,' he said with a small laugh. 'You can trust me I assure you, and it really is essential we work together. Now we know each other we must both trust and protect ourselves. As you say this is dangerous and I need to know that you will safeguard me also. I want to work with you in a partnership of mutual trust. Together, I believe we can crack this nut.'

'I'm happy with that,' I said readily. 'If you wish more proof about me I will be happy to take you to my home, show you my utility bills, the deeds to my flat, whatever you wish.'

'Just your passport will be enough,' he remarked easily, as our meals arrived. We ate in silence but for a few words that had nothing to do with the main agenda. When the waiter had cleared our table we ordered another couple of beers and both relaxed back in our chairs ready to talk freely.

'So what's the good news Adam?' the journalist asked keenly.

'Well Paul,' I said, 'it's like this. He's more than willing for you to interview him, to ask whatever you like within reason. But he does not trust journalists and so won't meet you in person and give away his whereabouts.'

Paul leaned towards me sporting a wry smile.

'So how am I supposed to interview him then?'

'By mobile,' I said matter-of-factly.

We broke off talking for a few moments while the waiter delivered our beers. Paul took off his glasses and began cleaning them, weighing up what I had just said.

'That's a pity,' he said softly. 'Did you tell him that he could trust me? That I have never broken a confidence in all my career?'

'I did,' I replied, noting the disappointment in his tone. 'He told me that he would sooner burn his manuscript than meet you. So you see, I have tried my damnedest.'

Paul stared dreamily out of the window for a while. Outside, Goodge Street was getting busier with workers streaming out of offices for the lunch break. Then he turned to me. 'This makes it problematical for me,' he said slowly. 'How will I know he's alone, that he is not being prompted by someone next to him?'

'He's alone Paul,' I said flatly. 'You'll have to take my word on that. In any case you would know immediately if anyone else was helping him. His answers would not be spontaneous. I have had to teach him how to use a mobile and doing it this way is the only thing I could come up with. What other option did I have?'

'Okay Adam,' Paul said after some thought. 'I can appreci-ate the predicament and congratulate you for your efforts. As I said, I've been busy at my end and have plenty of probing questions ready for him. I've done my research and if he's not our man I'll soon find out. So Adam, tell me a little more of your meeting so that I can build up a picture of him.'

'Well, like you Paul, I've been doing some intensive research of my own. What do you know about the actual murder?' I asked.

Paul shrugged. 'I'm no expert on that side of it, my research has centred on the man himself. What I remember of the case is that he intended to kill his wife and dispose of her body out at sea. Apparently he bashed the nanny to death by mistake and then scarpered.'

'That's roughly the accepted story,' I said quietly. 'But did you know there were two murder weapons? Two identical coshes?'

Paul looked at me quizzically, and raised his eyebrows. 'Why two coshes?' he asked keenly. 'What was the explanation?'

'That's the puzzling part,' I said, warming to the story. 'It seemed that nobody was interested in tackling what was a real conundrum. The police offered no explanation and most of those who wrote about the case simply swept the matter under the carpet.'

Paul's eyes locked on mine. 'Don't tell me,' he said excit-edly. 'You asked Sidney the question?'

'I did,' I said crisply.

'Brilliant. What did he say?'

'Well, he went to answer me but it was as though I had touched a nerve. He went into a coughing fit. I was worried about him for a while, but when he had recovered he told me that everything I wished to know was in the second part of his story, that I could be the first to read it.'

Chapter Fourteen

'Have you got the document? Did you read it?' Paul asked, barely able to contain himself.

'No,' I said, 'I left it with him.'

Paul looked at me as though I was tragically simple-minded. 'He offered you the story and you didn't take it?'

'I can get it at any time,' I said smartly. 'It's his story and he has not received a penny for it, or any indication as to whether his tale can be published. It seemed inappropriate to take the document until he has passed your test and we can tell him if a newspaper will be brave enough to take on his story. Anyway,' I added soberly. 'We don't know for sure if it's him yet. Let's get your interview underway and pin this down before we jump the gun.'

Paul smiled at me with a hint of conspiracy. 'Now that you've met him again Adam, what's your gut feeling about the man?'

I thought carefully for a moment before answering. 'I can't be absolutely sure because it's too much of an astonishing tale to take on board. Who would believe that Lucky Lucan could still be alive and wanted to come clean? It's all very surreal and scary. But the way he talks, his mannerisms, everything about him seems right. He showed me his wristwatch, a big chunky Rolex. The inscription on the back had the letters J.A.'

'John Aspinall?' Paul interjected keenly.

'Yes. Sidney told me that Aspinall had given it to him years ago, that it was special and only a certain amount of them were ever made.'

Paul rubbed his hands together, a glint in his eyes. 'If Aspinall gave it to him you can bet your bottom dollar it wasn't cheap.'

'I'm no expert on watches,' I said. 'But that watch could now be worth a small fortune. He said that if anything should happen to him he would like me to have it.'

'Nice touch, but it could be a fake,' Paul offered with a hint of mischief.

I checked the time. It was nearly one o'clock. I placed my mobile on the table.

'I've told Sidney to ring me at this time each day,' I said quietly. 'When he phones what would you like me to say about this interview? When do you want to arrange it?'

'Let's not hang around, I'm ready,' Paul said forcefully – 'Tomorrow?'

'Okay,' I said. I picked up my mobile and told Paul that I was going outside for a cigarette and hoped Sidney would phone me as instructed. I turned down a side street by the restaurant, lit a cigarette and waited for my mobile to ring. Right on time the phone buzzed and vibrated. The line from Mallorca was clear. I exchanged a little small talk with Sidney before asking him if he was ready to undergo the interview at the same time the following day. He said he was happy to do so. I made my way back into the restaurant still talking to him. Paul was watching me fixedly. I sat down and bought the conversation to an end, telling Sidney not to worry, that he should stay calm when he spoke to the journalist. To remember all I had told him.

'We're on,' I said evenly.

We did not talk for a moment as the waiter tidied our table and asked if we would like a dessert. We both declined and instead ordered a couple of coffees.

'Well done Adam,' Paul said cheerily. 'Tomorrow it is then.'

'There was something else Sidney told me that might interest you Paul,' I said in a low voice. 'And it's something you might be able to double check with Warren's dad. Sidney spoke of that letter he sent identifying himself. In there somewhere is mention of a girl named Nicole.'

Chapter Fourteen

Paul gazed at me reflectively, calling on his memory. 'Yes, I remember,' he said quietly.

'Well, Sidney explained to me what that was all about. It seemed he and Colin got the girl a job at the Clermont, but after a few months they discovered she was cheating. They confronted her away from the club and basically told her that if she were to leave nothing further would be mentioned. She left immediately and the pair of them kept this embarrassing tale to themselves.'

Paul's face brightened. 'That's a great story. I can check that with Colin. I have his telephone number and he said that I could keep in touch with him. I also need to remind him how dangerous this is turning out to be, to keep all this between himself and Warren.'

After finishing our coffees Paul grabbed the bill and insisted on paying. We shook hands warmly. It had been a good meeting we both agreed. If Sidney really was the elusive Lord Lucan we were soon to find out.

'Till tomorrow,' I said.

Chapter Fifteen

Today was the day this bizarre adventure would prove to be real or come to an abrupt end. I arrived at Paul King's terraced house in Fulham half-an-hour before the intended time of the interview as we needed to go over some details. I had a heavy feeling of trepidation as Paul ushered me into his office. Paul made us coffee and once settled behind his desk he rubbed his hands gleefully in a gesture of expectation. He was looking forward to this I soon realised. He was thinking that he might soon be talking to the elusive Lord Lucan. We chatted amicably about how this crucial and determining interview should be conducted.

'You must remember,' I said quietly, 'this man is over eighty and has only just learned how to use a mobile phone. There is no point in trying to pressurise him.' I spoke with a polite hint of firmness.

Paul shot me a slight affronted look. 'I have no intention of doing that,' he said crisply. He opened a desk draw and produced an A4 sheet with lines of neat type and tick boxes on the right of the paper. He was well prepared.

'Also,' I said. 'I don't think you should ask him any pertinent questions as to the murder crime. I reckon that would be unfair.'

Paul removed his glasses and eyed me carefully biting the temple tip of his specs.

'We haven't paid for information like that,' I added, trying not to sound curt.

Paul nodded and shrugged his shoulders. 'You are absolutely right Adam.' He ran his finger down the paper and crossed out a couple of questions.

'Anything else?' he asked.

'Yes,' I said, drawing on my thoughts. 'I have told Sidney to stay calm when he speaks to you, to answer concisely and not to try and elaborate on details. I told him that if he can't answer a question to simply say so,' I paused, then added. 'If he comes through this, then you should try and persuade him to meet you. I would like that.'

Paul rubbed his hands and smiled wolfishly. 'I phoned Colin Hedley-Davies about that letter,' he said brightly. 'He confirmed the story about the French girl Nicole. He told me that nobody other himself and Lucan would have had any knowledge as to why she left the Clermont Club so suddenly. It was a secret the two of them kept to themselves. Before I ended the call there was a long pause and then he muttered in a somewhat chilling tone: 'Good God, the man's still alive.' So the proof that Sidney really is Lucan is stacking up.'

'He's not put a foot wrong so far,' I muttered uneasily.

'Oh by the way,' I said producing an envelope. 'Here are his fingerprints. Not very professional I'm afraid, but the best I could manage. Sidney made no objection.'

Paul eyed the sheet of black prints. 'They will do Adam. Well done. It's a long shot in any case and that he was willing to give them says everything. I have a friend within the bowels of Scotland Yard. As this case has never been officially closed there is still forensics knocking around. My information is that many prints were taken at the murder scene and at Lucan's flat and some could not be accounted for.'

'Also this is my passport,' I said, sliding the document over the desk. Paul scanned it quickly and returned it to me.

'You're fine Adam,' he said easily. 'I'm delighted to be working with you.'

I looked at my watch. 'Just a few minutes to go,' I said cautiously. 'It's nearly one o'clock.' I placed the mobile on the desk and we waited in silence. The arranged time came and went. I kept checking my watch and gazing at the silent mobile. It was now ten minutes past one. Sidney had not phoned. Paul showed his concern by running his fingers down his cheeks and tapping his knuckles on the desk. I could feel my face heat up.

And then, just as I was about to give up and phone Sidney myself, my mobile vibrated with a ring-tone that made me sit up with a jolt.

Sidney spoke in his slow careful way. He apologised for not phoning on time, giving some explanation about his medication. I went through a little encouraging small talk with him. How was the weather there? How was he feeling? I told him Paul King was with me and was he prepared to speak with him? He told me he was ready but I could detect a note of nervousness in his voice.

'I'm now going to put you on to Paul King,' I said softly. 'Good luck Sidney.' I handed my mobile to Paul.

'Hello there Sidney.' The journalist said warmly, a voice betraying what might be coming later. Paul went through a few pleasantries in a soft supportive voice before asking Sidney if he was ready to answer a series of questions. There followed a few seconds silence as Paul's pen hovered over the prepared A4 paper. I got up from my chair and went to the back of the room. I wanted to be adrift of the interview. My hands had become clammy. It was now all or nothing, the clever journalist versus Sidney Ainsworth, the man who claims to be Lord Lucan. We were all set.

'May I begin?' Paul asked pleasantly.

The first few questions seemed rather easy, by design, I guessed.

'Where did you get married? What was the address of the first flat you rented in London? Do you have a scar on your body?'

Paul carefully ticked the boxes. Then it seemed he was throwing in an easy question followed by something obscure. There were pauses creeping in as the journalist probed for clarification. I had told Sidney not to get into a dialogue like this. Now I could see from my standpoint that some crosses were scattered with some ticks. I paced up and down the room preferring to listen to this drama from a distance. I could just about see that Paul's pen was parked at the bottom of the page. At last the interview was coming to an end. But then, he turned the sheet over, and I could see there was something like another twenty questions. I thought this was going too far and moved towards the desk, my face showing disapproval. Paul raised a hand that gestured me to stay back. He was in full flow and continued with a stream of questions with renewed vigour.

'You changed trainers in 1968. Why?

Why did you hire a car and drive to Wales in 1971?

How did you come by the scar you have?

What did Marcia Tucker give you as a leaving present in 1945? What was the name of the only two-year old horse you owned?'

The ticks kept coming. Then Paul started asking questions about bank accounts and money in Swiss banks; now the conversation between the two of them seemed to be breaking down. Sidney was obviously not coming up with the right answers and the tone in Paul's voice was more pointed. Now it was a lawyer's voice dissecting what was said and scheming to discredit the answers. There was a long discussion about these accounts and various debts and loans before Paul cut Sidney short from whatever he was saying.

'Let's move on,' the journalist said assertively.

I could see that his pen was about half way down the page. From there on it was all pretty quick.

'What was the make of your first car?

What gift did you receive when leaving the Guards?'

And then, apart from one question, it was ticks all the way down to the last question.

'How many winners did Bill Shand Kydd ride for you?'

I had no idea what the answer might have been, but it was obviously correct, for it was another impressive tick. It had been a ruthless interview even for a young person but Sidney was old and frail and I was wondering how he was feeling. But now, to my surprise, the pair of them were chatting away like old friends. Thank you for talking to me Paul was saying and how good it would be if they could meet up at some time. You can trust me to help you, Paul crooned down the line. Then came some goodbyes before Paul handed me my mobile.

I had a few words with Sidney who sounded drained. He asked in a very slow and tired voice how it had gone. I said I would ring him the following day at our arranged time. I sat down at Paul's desk and let out a low whistle. Paul was gazing at me intensely. Then, without warning, he suddenly brought his fist down hard on the desk scattering pens and paper. I was startled and stared at him in bemusement.

Chapter Fifteen

Paul's eyes glittered fiercely. 'He got everything right,' he blared, throwing his arms in the air.

We sat and smiled at each other for a few seconds. It had always been a hell of a long shot; we had known that from the outset. But Sidney's story had been more than compelling and that he had never asked for money gave the enterprise a definite note of credence and a tale certainly worth following up. I reached for my coffee, which had gone cold.

'What was all that about bank accounts?' I asked.

Paul gave me a sly grin. 'Oh that was nothing. I was playing silly games. Trying to get him rattled. Even so he made a good fist of answering some impossible questions.'

'What did he say about meeting you?'

'He was most charming and polite. Said that he would like to think it over.'

Paul swept his hair back roughly as was his wont. 'Now that we have come so far Adam, what more can you tell me about him? We must work together on this.'

'Like you I don't want to betray a confidence,' I said. 'I think It's right that I stick to my promise to keep him secret until such time as he agrees to meet you. But I can show you what he looks like,' I added brightly. I called up the photos on my mobile and showed them to Paul. He zoomed in on the pictures and studied them for some moments with an inquisitive grin.

'So that's Sidney,' he said with a chuckle. 'I must say he certainly looks the part.' He slid my phone back to me and spoke lowly. 'We must keep all this to ourselves Adam. At the end of the day you have never met me, and I don't know you. I take it you have not spoken to anyone about this other than myself and Warren?'

'That's right,' I said comfortably. 'I always took the view that if I talked to others about this I would be laughed at, that

I would be discouraged from doing some sleuthing of my own and weeding out the truth. This has been my secret journey and I'm hoping that it will soon be over and I can get my own life back on track.'

'Well, you've done well Adam. You might have helped crack an enduring mystery that has gone on for over forty years. It could be we are the first to know that Lord Lucan did indeed escape and is still alive. If we can pull this off it will be the biggest story in decades. But we're not quite there yet. I'm still waiting on the results of his handwriting and then maybe his fingerprints will nail this beyond a shadow of doubt. You are right to keep Sidney's whereabouts to yourself. I really admire you for that. You are not prepared to betray a confidence, which is how I work and behave. That's why I'm so happy to be on board with you.'

'I think it's time to talk about what his story might be worth,' I said cautiously, not wanting to sound pushy about money.

Paul settled back in his chair, folding his arms across his chest. 'I've been busy in that respect,' he said, his tone business like. 'There is much to discuss with you. I have been speaking to an editor and his proprietor. On my guarantee this story is genuine and that the manuscript is not circulating elsewhere they are prepared to pay £250,000 in cash for the full rights. My problem though, is dealing with the newspapers lawyer that I told you about. The man is a real nightmare who knows nothing about journalism, only about putting legal barriers in my way. I will probably have to go direct to the proprietor and bypass him.'

Paul rapped his pen on the desk in a small gesture of concern. 'Also we need to remind ourselves that if Sidney really is Lord Lucan he is a wanted murderer. If we were honest citizens we would have gone to the police right away. But we have not done that and have no intentions of doing so.

Apart from the money, we are taking the view that it's better his tale is told. If the police tried to arrest him his story might die with him and that would benefit nobody.'

Paul made a mocking chuckle. 'That's very much the journalist in me talking – but I think it's true all the same. However, the real conundrum is this: Their lawyer is, quite rightly, trying to protect the newspaper from crossing the line between what is legal and what is not. He also has a responsibility to see that his bosses do not pay a lot of money for a hoax story.'

Paul cleaned his glasses and looked at me carefully.

'Remember what I told you about the Hitler Diaries?' I nodded, this was all very messy I thought.

Paul continued in a steady voice. 'The catch 22, is this. If the newspapers lawyer believes the story to be genuine then he has a professional obligation to go to the police. So you see Adam the obstacles I have to negotiate. It's tough; this story is fraught with danger, an absolute minefield. The big trump card I am holding is that I have met the proprietor a couple of times and he likes me, so much so, that he gave me a contact mobile number for him. That, I can tell you, is really quite something.'

'Who is he?' I asked.

Paul smiled and shook his head. 'Believe me Adam, you don't want to know. He's very wealthy and likes to keep himself very much in the background.'

I decided to stay quiet and just listen.

'Anyway, I have the ear of this proprietor who has always been a maverick. I'm going to speak with him. Ask him to get the lawyer off my back. Tell him the story is well worth the fee and ask that he arrange to release the cash. I will throw in the line that we have to move quickly before any other paper gets wind of the story.'

I made a small laugh. 'Very good,' I said. 'You are some character.'

Paul settled his arms on the desk and held my eyes. 'You understand that if I can pull this off we will be dealing with hard cash. There must be no paper trail back to my informer – which of course is you, and to a lesser extent, Warren and his father. Adam, you must be very careful. You cannot walk into a bank and open an account with a load of cash. In fact there are lots of things that cause suspicion if you try to use large amounts of ready money. You will have to behave with the utmost caution and common sense.'

'I understand that,' I said quietly. 'Truth is, I would sooner not get involved with Sidney's money. I would be happy for someone else to have that responsibility.'

'I can't help you there I'm afraid,' he said matter-of-factly. 'You'll have to sort that out with Sidney.'

Paul settled back in his chair and interlocked his fingers. 'I need to go over the money side of things with you,' he said, somewhat pensively. 'I hope I don't come across as being greedy but I do think I'm entitled to a substantial fee if I am able to sell this story. I would like fifty per cent, which is £125,000. Warren wants 10%, which is £25,000 – not unreasonable considering the story came from him in the first place. That leaves £100,000 for yourself and Sidney to divide up as you think fit. You may be thinking that my cut is too much so let me explain my input and why I'm asking for that percentage.'

Paul staightened his shoulders and tapped a pen against his chest. 'I will be the one taking all the risks. When you, Warren and Sidney take your cash, you are then totally in the clear. Nobody will know who you are, or that you received any money. But that's not the happy position for me. I asked the newspaper to deal with me as an anonymous person but they were not prepared to do that. If the police lean on them they want to be able to explain how they came by the manuscript. All of which means that if the story gets printed the police will pull me in for questioning. I will tell them that I had an informant, someone I would meet in the park. This person would handover documents and I would handover cash. Sorry, I would say to the police, I don't even know this man's name. I will tell the cops that I verified the story with various evidence that was handed to me and with a stringent telephone interview with the person claiming to be Lucan using the informants mobile phone – but I have no idea where this person might be.'

Paul waved a hand and said indifferently. 'I'm a freelance journalist and perfectly at liberty to pay someone for a story and sell it to a newspaper. The police would question me about the money. I would say that it nearly all went to my informant and that only a small percentage was kept by me to cover my time and expenses. They would not believe me of course – but so what – they could do nothing.'

I shuffled in my chair. 'I appreciate your position Paul,' I said mildly while continuing to listen to what felt like a heartfelt lecture.

'The police do the same thing,' he went on. 'They pay snides all the time to get information they would never otherwise obtain. I'm doing nothing different to what they do. But as I say, I'm taking the risks, it will be me alone in the firing line. I think fifty per cent is reasonable in the circumstances. But the police are the least of my concerns.' he continued perfunctorily. 'I'm laying my career on the line here. I think I can sell this story backed up by my good name and reputation in the business – something I have worked hard at for the last twenty years. If this story went belly up my career would be in tatters. Nobody would trust me again. Without wanting to beat my own drum I don't think any other journalist could have got the ear of this particular proprietor as I have done and simply on my good word get him keen to buy this story. A story which is heaped with problems.'

Paul looked at me thoughtfully waiting for my response. I stared at the ceiling and ran all this through my head. I couldn't argue with the case he was making. He would be the one being leaned on, covering for myself and Warren – not to mention a certain old boy in Mallorca. Also, I believed him when he said he was probably the only journalist able to sell such a dangerous story. It was in my mind to bargain with him but as I had never been chasing money I thought of a different line of approach.

'Okay Paul,' I said after a good think. 'It would be only fair to run this by Sidney, but if he is happy – how about this? The story is in three parts. What say you pay the £100,000 in three instalments? You already have part one. When I get part two and you are happy with it you handover £60,000, and then the balance when you receive part three.' Paul smiled willingly and we shook hands over his desk.

'When can you get part two?' he asked eagerly.

'When can you get the money?' I replied saucily.

Paul took off his glasses and wiped his eyes. 'I think I will bypass the newspapers lawyer and go straight to the proprietor. But it's not easy to arrange large amounts of cash. You'll have to give me a few days to sort things out.'

I made to leave. It had been a fraught and overpowering afternoon. 'Let's stay in touch,' I said willingly.'

I made for home and ready to book an immediate flight to Mallorca.

Chapter Sixteen

Here and there I could escape the footpath on my journey into Molinar and walk along the beach. The soft sand underfoot, the smell of the sea and dodging the occasional rogue wave that tried to wash over your shoes was invigorating, but these little excursions were short lived before encountering rocky outcrops that jutted out into the sea. Then it was a scramble back up to the concrete footpath to continue the walk alongside the cycle lanes that weaved their way into Palma.

On the rocks some fisherman could be seen sitting idly alongside their rods, some with umbrellas shielding their exposed position against the fierce September sun.

I had telephoned Sidney the previous day asking that he meet me for lunch at the Café Plaza, our usual rendezvous. I told him that we had much to discuss. I was still thinking of him and referring to him as Sidney, the charming old boy that I had met by chance some five months earlier, although now it was looking more and more likely that he was telling the truth as to his real identity – which was a terrifying thought.

I would deal with him as two separate people, which in a way, is what he was. The real man he was claiming to be I would put out of my mind as it was too much for me to comprehend. He would remain Sidney Ainsworth, the dapper chap that I felt comfortable with and not some criminal aristocrat of forty years past.

I came to the busy café and could see Sidney sitting at the bar. I approached him with a smile and offered my hand. His handshake was firm as he cast flitting meerkat-like eyes over my shoulders to check that I was alone.

Sidney wore a bright short-sleeved shirt tucked neatly in at the waist. On the bar rested his panama hat alongside a large brown manila envelope. I ordered some drinks and took in Sidney's face. He looked a little weary. The nasty bruise on his forehead had settled but his face showed an aged greyish tinge fighting with those suntanned features.

As all the outside tables were occupied we decided to go inside the café where we could talk privately. Sidney shuffled along in his bright sports shoes tapping his walking stick before him. He held tight to that large envelope, the contents of which might surely put an end to so many years of speculation and mystery.

We settled at a window table and Sidney laid his hat and the document in front of him.

'Is that part two of your story?' I asked discreetly.

Sidney nodded. 'It's all there Adam,' he said heavily, sliding the document towards me. 'Nearly all off my chest now. Part three is finished really. The last page has been resting in my typewriter for ages. I've been putting off typing the last few words.'

Sidney's weak smile played tug-of-war with his sad eyes.

'Silly of me really,' he said deliberately. 'I feel those last ending words will be the last of me also. That I will have signed myself off for good.'

'You passed the interview with flying colours,' I interjected quickly to lighten the mood and conversation.

Sidney smiled stroking his beard. 'Goodness knows where that journalist dug up all that information. He seemed to know more about me than I was aware of myself.'

'Paul thinks he can sell your manuscript,' I said tapping the manila envelope. 'I need to speak to you about how much your story is worth and what might be due to you.'

Sidney shrugged and waved a hand. 'It's more important to me that my story is told. I have known for a long time what I must do. That I should come clean. I might as well now. At my age and in my health.'

I spent some time going through the details of how Paul King wanted the money to be divided and relating to Sidney the problems in selling such an explosive story. Sidney agreed the journalist deserved his percentage and was pretty uncon- cerned with whatever money would be due to him. We chatted comfortably for a while before Sidney asked that we go back outside the café as he wished to smoke a cigarillo.

The tables out in the open were still all occupied but we managed to weave our way between them to a small outside wall where we perched ourselves in the shade of some palm trees. I handed Sidney his brandy, which I had carried for him and then held up his document.

'Do you want me to go ahead and hand this over to Paul King?' I asked softly.

'Yes please do that,' Sidney said without hesitation, and then added. 'Make sure you are properly recompensed Adam, for everything you have done for me. For all the risks you are taking. Please make sure you keep safe. I am very concerned for you, that I have involved you in a such a nasty business. The document you have explains everything Adam. I am beyond redemption of course, but you will read just how wrong the police and the media were about my intentions. They all failed to understand the obvious.'

I placed the manila envelope in my rucksack. I would, as I had done with part one of his story, read the papers on my flight home. It would be good to stick to some sort of convention in this surreal escapade.

'You must think about the money, Sidney,' I said, knowing how unpalatable that sounded. Deep down I knew it was wrong for anyone to receive cash for a story detailing murder and lives ruined. But I could not change that, and an investigative journalist was not going to take all these risks for nothing. Money was, unfortunately, a big part of this extraordinary and sad affair. Sidney lit a small cigar and watched a pale of smoke disappear into the warm air.

'How about donating to charities?' I offered.

He suddenly held my eyes with an enquiring look. 'What a lovely idea Adam. Hmm Yes,' he added, drawing on his thoughts. 'I could do some good – Yes,' he repeated again. 'Tell my story and give something back into the bargain.'

'Have a think about it Sidney,' I said. I finished my beer and grabbed my rucksack.

'I'm flying back to London tonight. Make sure you keep your mobile on charge. I will phone you every other day at 2pm your time.'

Sidney rose with me and shook my hand. 'Thank you again Adam for all your help. I'm so pleased with my last big gamble, that I took a chance with you. My life has been full of tragically bad gambles.'

'Well let's see how events unfold,' I offered encouragingly. 'Oh by the way Sidney,' I said, suddenly remembering something I had been meaning to ask. 'How many winners did Bill Shand Kydd ride for you?'

Sidney made a little chuckle before coughing into his handkerchief. His eyes had become watery.

Chapter Sixteen

'That was the easiest question of all Adam – The answer was none.'

I had booked extra legroom on the flight back to London. Having stored my rucksack in the overhead locker I laid Sidney's document on my lap. I felt strangely calm considering I was to be the first to read what might prove to be one of the most explosive and revelatory stories of the last forty years.

Once the plane had climbed and levelled out I undid the clasp on the manila envelope and extracted a ream of neatly typed A4 sheets.

I took a deep breath. Here goes, I said to myself.

Chapter Seventeen

THE STORY: PART TWO

MY NAME IS RICHARD JOHN BINGHAM, SEVENTH EARL OF LUCAN.

Part Two of my manuscript.

This part of my story was always going to be the most difficult and heart wrenching for me to relate.

I intend herewith to put on record the events leading up to the tragic murder of my children's nanny, Sandra Rivett, and what exactly happened on the night of 7 November 1974 at my house.

At the centre of this story is the complete breakdown of my marriage to Veronica and the war that continued between us regarding the custody of our children.

I have to tell this story without putting any blame whatsoever on my wife. That would be the easiest way for me to try and put the guilt elsewhere, which would be totally wrong and unfair.

I declare that the guilt is all mine. The failure of our marriage was not that my wife was a bad person or a bad mother she was nothing of the sort. Veronica was, and still is, a loyal and good person.

But let me start at the beginning:

I was enchanted with Veronica the moment I set eyes on her. She was petite with fine fair hair that flowed down and curled at her shoulders. She had lovely bright eyes and the sweetest of smiles. She came across as a little shy, which made her even more endearing. Her sister, Christina, who was more outgoing had married my dear friend, Bill Shand Kydd, a year earlier.

Veronica and I had what I believe is described as a whirlwind romance before marrying in November 1963, at Brompton Holy

Trinity. Our honeymoon was a grand affair taking the Orient Express from Paris to Istanbul.

My parents had been extremely generous in a marriage settlement for Veronica and me, which enabled us to rent a splendid house in Lower Belgrave Street. Veronica, with an interior designer friend set about redecorating and furnishing the house. Veronica was in her element restoring the house and her eye for style and detail was excellent.

Once the main living room had been decorated I hung the two paintings that Marcia Tucker had gifted me, in pride of place above the marble fireplace.

It was soon after getting the house into shape that my father died.

Despite the sadness of the occasion it was so nice that the all the family were together for his funeral and that we stayed with our mother for some time afterwards. We placed our fathers Military Cross in his coffin so we could tell ourselves that he went down with full military honours. He was a brilliant, marvellous man.

Now, of course, I acquired my father's titles: Earl of Lucan; Baron Lucan of Castlebar; Baron Lucan of Melcombe, and Baronet of Nova Scotia.

My new wife who just six months earlier had been plain Veronica Duncan became Lady Bingham when we married and was now Countess of Lucan.

A good chunk of the inheritance I received went towards the house and a new car. Life was pretty sweet for us at this time and I tried to encourage Veronica to play bridge and golf and have a try at fishing but these pursuits did not really interest her. She was a mother and a homemaker and that is what made her happy. Of course she knew of my love of gambling. Before we married I went out of my way to explain this part of my life to her. I did not want Veronica to have any false impression about the person I was or what being married to me would be like. She told me that she understood and would never try to dissuade me from a way of life that meant so much to me. Veronica was as good as her word. Never once did she complain about my gambling, although it must have hurt her to see me spend so much of my life at various clubs frittering away our inheritance.

Chapter Seventeen

By the time of our marriage my social life was very much in place and it was not something I was prepared to change. The Clermont had opened in 1962 and soon other clubs followed. I was a member of no fewer than five Mayfair clubs, all holding a certain attraction and an escape into another world that I craved. But the Clermont was my favourite second home, not just because of the grandness of the place, which John Aspinall had lovingly restored, and the chance to play any number of card games, but because this is where my friends were. Dear friends and like-minded gamblers who had become an integral part of my life.

Of course my lifestyle did not sit easily with those who did not know me. But I had never tried to pretend that I was any other person than a habitué of Mayfair clubs and a lifelong gambler.

Our first child, Frances, arrived a year after our betrothal and with the girl came the first cracks in our marriage. Veronica started to suffer from post-natal depression. Of course having a child should be the happiest time in a woman's life but sometimes it can go the other way and this illness is terribly debilitating.

Veronica suffered from tiredness and anxiety. We went to see various doctors and with the support of friends and family the symptoms improved. I tried to get Veronica interested in outdoor pursuits. We holidayed abroad and had weekend trips in the country with friends whenever she felt well enough.

Our second child, George, was born a couple of years after Francis. At this time we managed to secure the services of a very good nanny called Lilian. We would become most reliant on Lilian as Veronica lapsed into depression once more. This time we went through a round of new doctors and new treatments. We talked to counsellors and started a weekly consultation with a psychiatrist.

The following years, up until the arrival of our third child Camilla, in 1970 were a mixture of good times and not so good times. The horrible illness that my wife suffered from was never far from the surface.

For all that people may have thought of me, I was concerned and sympathetic towards my wife and what she was going through. I went out of my way to seek help for her from whatever sources I could find. Veronica was often confined to her bedroom, tired and downhearted, and living on a cocktail of drugs, anti-depressants, sedatives, lithium and moditen.

In 1967 I persuaded Veronica to spend some time at a clinic
that had been recommended to me. She agreed and we drove to
a private nursing home, The Priory, where they were expecting
us. When we arrived Veronica became agitated and refused to
get out of the car. I had tried but it was to no avail. We drove
home in silence.

Later on I would try again. This time to a clinic in Hampstead.
Veronica was at first agreeable to seek help there but after
being shown the facilities she refused to stay. We had a row
in front of the staff before she disappeared out of the front
entrance, making her own way back to our house. I had,
throughout our marriage, tried to help but it was fast becoming
an impossible situation. The medication Veronica was taking
was being increased year on year and if anything I had come to
realise this was not helping.

In darker times and not to cause upsetting scenes with our
children I would move into the mews cottage that was held in
trust and was situated just around the corner at the rear of
our home.

When things had settled I would return home and spend as
much time as I could with the children who were my great love
and for whose welfare I was continually concerned. Of course
our marriage problems were by now common knowledge
amongst our family and friends. Veronica who had always
complained of being lonely had asked that she accompany me
to the Clermont in the evenings when we would rely on our
nanny to look after our three children.

I could not refuse, but this arrangement just led to further
problems. Veronica had no desire to gamble and simply sat
downstairs drinking wine and looking unhappy before
eventually getting a taxi home. After a while this became
embarrassing for both of us, but she refused to give up this
ritual. Aspinall was not happy to see Veronica night after night
bringing an air of gloom to the club, but he never questioned
me on this, taking the view that it was something that I had
to resolve myself. The desperate relationship with my wife was
being paraded nightly at my club for all to witness.

Things came to a dramatic head early in 1973. For no reason
whatsoever, Veronica sacked our nanny on the spot. I was out
of my mind with fury. Lilian had been with us for many years
doing a brilliant job despite all the problems she faced in
our household. She had been loyal to us and the children and

was very much part of the family. I went to see Lilian and apologised profusely. She was a wonderful woman who later supported me in the child custody case. She, more than anyone else, knew the truth of the situation.

But for me, it was the last straw. I packed a suitcase and moved back into the mews cottage – this time for good. I could take no more.

From here onwards there were a succession of agency nannies, which of course, I had to pay for. Some of them lasting only a few days. With my wife's illness I was in a continual state of anxiety as to the care of the children. With one nanny after another coming and going I decided to take matters into my own hands. I rented a five-bedroomed house nearby in Elizabeth Street and employed a qualified nanny, Jordanka. I obtained an ex-parte court order that the children be handed into my care pending a full enquiry. With the help of a detective agency I took George and Camilla from a nanny who was walking with them in Green Park. Then I went to the school Frances attended, showed the headmistress my court papers and took Frances away.

I was so happy and relieved. The children were now with me and I intended bestow all my love on them and guard them. Each had their own bedroom and quickly settled into a new and better life at Elizabeth Street.

But of course this arrangement was only temporary. Veronica was hysterical when she learned I had the children. She sprung into action right away taking legal action to get the children returned to her. Some of Veronica's supporters said that my actions were outrageous and that I had in effect kidnapped the children.

The court case to settle the custody battle was set for 11 July. Before that date I was able to be with my children for three months and we were all wonderfully happy.

I felt comfortable with the case my QC, James Corbyn, would present to the court when the hearing opened. We had a mass of evidence relating to Veronica's psychiatric problems, which went back some ten years. Also we had many witnesses who would state that the children would be better off in my care including our nanny of many years Lilian Jenkins. Also backing me were two of the children's headmistresses along with friends and family who would give evidence on my behalf.

Even some of my detractors admitted that I was better equipped to raise the children.

My case was strong and my legal team were confident of winning what would be a titanic battle of wills between Veronica and me. Despite the strength of my position and the love and devoted care I could provide for my children I lost the case. It was the most devastating event of my life. Veronica had won and was handed custody of the children on the proviso that she employ a nanny to help her. The court case ended after nine days when my QC, advised me to concede defeat, and not stack up more legal fees on a cause I was doomed to lose.

Veronica had been very clever and more astute than I could ever have imagined. She had voluntarily admitted herself to the Priory clinic for observation. The very clinic I tried unsuccessfully to admit her to some years earlier. The psychiatrist from the Priory, Dr John Flood, told the court that with proper medication she was quite capable of looking after the children. This was a clever move by Veronica who came across as a highly convincing witness. She spoke with a calm assured manner giving no hint that she had any mental health problems whatsoever.

I had no idea that this custody case would turn into such a clever and bitter attack on me. Veronica's lawyer brought up stories that I displayed a devious sexual nature towards my wife, which was nasty in the extreme. I was described as a professional gambler which the court was told made me unfit to be a father. That I gambled away thousands of pounds a night. This aspect of me seemed to horrify the judge, Mr Justice Rees, who took an instant dislike to me. Many years later I would read his obituary where it was said that he thought me arrogant and untruthful.

In truth, with this particular judge that my counsel had been worried about, I had lost the case from the outset.

The judge told me that I could have access to my children every other weekend and that would be my only contact with them. I was wrecked and heartbroken. I asked my counsel if we could appeal with a different judge but they told me it would cost a fortune with little chance of success.

From this point, up until the tragic night of 7 November the following year, my world slowly fell apart. Internal bleeding, John Aspinall called it. I was drinking more heavily mixed with anti-depressants and sleeping pills. The cost of the custody case had financially wiped me out. I had to pay fees on both sides ending up with a legal bill of over £35,000. With the last of my money and selling some valuables I managed to pay the costs but I was left in deep financial trouble, which I could never recover from.

Coming to my aid, Jimmy Goldsmith invited me to his birthday party in Acapulco, and for a little while this boosted my spirits. I realised with huge relief and gratitude that my friends were wholeheartedly behind me, seeing the injustice of the court case and offering me their sympathy and support.

At least I could see my children every other weekend and I made the most of these occasions. If the weather was fine I would drive them down to the coast, Brighton or Eastbourne. We had trips to London Zoo and weekends in the country with Veronica's sister, Christina, and Bill Shand Kydd. But our most enjoyable day out was at John Aspinall's zoo, Howletts in Kent. Aspers made a great fuss of my children. After lunch at the wonderful manor house he had so beautifully restored, he would give presents to my children before we headed off for a guided tour of the zoo.

Wild animals had always been Aspinall's love and fascination. He once told me that his life was in two parts. One half was in Mayfair and the world of gaming and the other half was his desire to be close to wild animals. His collection had started early. Shortly after marrying and moving to an apartment in Eaton Square he purchased two young Himalayan bears, which he kept in cages in the back garden. Then he acquired an orphaned tiger cub he named Tara, which he insisted slept in the marital bed. Of course the cub grew fast and needed a sturdy collar when Aspers took her for a walk in the quiet hours after midnight in the streets around Belgravia.

One evening at dinner at the Clermont Aspers confided in me a little tale about Tara and an incident that took place on one of these walks in the dead of night. An Alsatian appeared from nowhere and took exception to Tara. With a swipe of her paw and a bite to the neck the dog was instantly dispatched. Aspinall then threw the corpse into someone's basement.

On our days out at Howletts, I would keep my children close to me. Aspinall was, to my mind, a daredevil with his animals often inviting his guests to enter the cages and relate to these creatures – sometimes with disastrous outcomes. (In exile I would hear of stories of keepers being killed as a result of

Aspers wishes that the staff form a close bond with their charges). This risk taking also backfired when Mark Birley's son, Robin, was horribly mauled by a female tiger and had to undergo many operations to repair his face.

Once on a tour of Howletts with the children, and knowing how desperate I was feeling, Aspers spoke quietly to me about my problems. He told me that in the animal kingdom – which he seemed to admire more than a lot of people – there was often a dominant head of the family who would deal with any problems quickly, and violently if need be. Of course, I knew what he was getting at and also that he would think nothing of taking matters into his own hands in a misguided attempt to help me and the children. I told him I would sort out my problems, but things take time.

In the summer of 74, a year after losing the custody battle, I found myself sitting in the Clermont lounge with Dominick Elwes and his friend, (whom I will refer to as Terry) a fellow artist. We were enjoying drinks and chatting before Dominick was called away to ply his charm on a new member. I was left sitting with Terry who was a man of few words. He was not unintelligent but quiet with certain faraway reserve. He was in his thirties but had a round boyish face, which made him look younger. His long flaxen hair was swept back into a ponytail fixed at the back with an elastic band. He was never dressed for a Mayfair club, looking out of place as though he had wandered in by mistake. But he was Dominick's friend and so was accepted.

Before Aspinall sold the Clermont he had always shown a certain kindness towards Terry, letting him eat in the restaurant when it wasn't busy and failing to cash his cheques on the few occasions he gambled and lost. If he should win then he walked away with his winnings. Asper's benevolence towards Terry, who he saw as a poor but talented artist, went further. He once let Terry use the club to exhibit his art. His paintings were hung everywhere, in reception, in hallways, on the staircase and in the main gaming room. I was impressed with his pictures and were it not that I already had a houseful of artworks I would gladly have purchased a couple of his paintings. Terry did well from the exhibition, selling over a dozen pictures, which would have kept him going for some time.

Chapter Seventeen

Having been left in the company of Terry I tried some small talk, which was hard going. Then, and without any sort of warning, he leaned towards me and in a sullen tone said that he would be willing to help me dispose of my wife. I was totally shocked. It was an impertinence and for a few seconds I just stared at him, lost for words and feeling my face reddening. What had stunned me more than anything was how I had allowed myself to show my desperation so openly. Had those close to me who I had confided in spoken out of hand unleashing a spread of gossip at the club?

I gave Terry a hard look and asked him what the devil he meant and where had he heard such talk – was it from Dominick I asked?

He looked hurt and apologised stating that Dominick had said nothing, that he had simply picked up on some idle talk and that he knew how unhappy I was. Out of interest I asked him what he meant when he had used the words: 'dispose of my wife.'
He apologised again saying that he should never have talked in such a way. I pressed him. What had he meant? He did not want to talk and made to leave but I made him stay in his chair.

'I only meant that I would help you,' he stammered. Then he told me almost in a whisper that he knew a fisherman on the East Coast who, would for a fee, carry out a particular service of disposing of an 'item' out in deep water. It was a sideline that had been handed down to him from his father. It was a service that was discreet, that this fisherman, and his father before him, had performed many times.

I looked at Terry aghast, and told him that his utterings were the most stupid thing I had ever heard. I then told him sharply to stay out of my affairs.

As I got up from the table, a clearly embarrassed Terry was muttering more apologies. 'I only meant that I would help you,' he repeated sadly.

After that bewildering encounter I knew I had to show a new face at the Clermont. The last thing I needed was gossip spreading that I was a broken man intending to do away with a problem wife. In the following months I put on a real show. I behaved in a friendly carefree manner to all my friends, especially Dominick who I knew was a conduit of information. If anyone knew anything about anyone it was Dominick Elwes. After all it was his unofficial job. I loved Dominick with his charm and ready wit – everyone did.

My new persona at the club had worked well. I had let it be known that I had got over the failed custody case, and as a gambler had accepted what had turned out to be a losing bet. Whenever Aspers was holding a party at Howletts, or his Mayfair home, I would be there with a smile, albeit that at the same time a festering resentment lay within my soul like an open sore.

By the summer of 1974, my financial position was catastrophic. I owed money to three of my bank accounts and had borrowed money from my family in a forlorn attempt to stay afloat. But I was going from one crisis to another, trying to keep two homes going with all the expenses that came with them. It was all unsustainable from what money was coming in. I had resorted to borrowing from friends and moneylenders with little hope of repaying these loans.

I went to see Jimmy Goldsmith in Paris, hoping that he would loan me £10,000. He said that he would not do this as he had always made a rule never to lend money to friends – as this was the quickest way of losing them – but would, instead, gift me the cash. I refused such an arrangement. We dined out that evening and Jimmy let me know that he would always be there for me – and so he would.

In sheer desperation I wrote to Marcia Tucker in New York asking that she loan me the astronomical sum of £100,000 to pay off Veronica – to provide her with a house and a substantial income for life. Marcia would not oblige. Although she could easily part with the money she stated that she did not want to interfere in a marriage dispute.

I had run out of options, and now like a drug addict seeking the next fix, I stumbled through the doors of the last chance saloons.

I would try and gamble my way out of trouble. I had won before, I told myself, and so why couldn't I do it again? I played big at the Clermont, which was now owned by Playboy. I lost and owed them £10,000, which I arranged to pay back in small monthly instalments. Having run out of credit and goodwill at the Clermont I then ambled like some hopeless drunk to the Ladbroke Club and secured yet more credit to gamble. I knew from my time and studies of betting at Eton that chasing losses rarely works. In fact it is the very worst type of gambling. It is an amazing fact that when winning it is not deemed essential how lady luck will smile on you, as opposed to when it is essential, your luck is out. Why this should be is a mystery, but I have always found it to be so.

Needless to say I lost at the Ladbroke Club and so gambling was not going to come to my rescue. Now, with additional debts to casinos, I owed something in the region of £45,000. Something had to give.

Many years previously I had befriended Ian Fleming at the Clermont and we got on well. One evening in the early sixties he gave me a signed copy of *For You Eyes Only*. It was a book of short stories and one of these stories – Quantum of Solace – had always stayed in my mind. It told of a marriage breakdown of epic proportions. When one party is so hurt that they lose all common humanity towards the other partner. It is very rare, even in the most bitter of break-ups that solace reaches zero. In this story Philip Masters, the injured party, gets his revenge in the coldest manner before divorcing his wife and leaving her penniless and friendless in Bermuda.

For me, there was no solace left. My soul was black. I had reached that zero point that Fleming had described. All that mattered in my life was my children. And this time I intended to win them back together with my home – No matter what.

My heart was full of anger and revenge. All that was dear to me, I kept telling myself, had been taken from me by a rotten judge.

By the Autumn I had come up with a plan. It was the gambler in me. When you lose you don't just stop there, you keep trying to win. I had become so worried about the care of my children that it had become a stark and deadly choice. It was either my wife or me, and I had decided that I was the best person to bring up our children. Veronica had won the court battle but, as she was soon to find out, she was about to lose the appeal. And this time I would be the judge. I did not need John Aspinall's intervention.

I had hatched an idea in my mind after weeks of careful thought but I wanted support. Someone who was prepared to commit a deadly act with me. What was it Terry had said to me that evening in the Clermont lounge? 'I only meant I would help you.' Those were the words he had used. Each night at the Clermont I looked out for him and early in October he was back, sitting alone in a silent brooding mood. I sat at his table and asked if he was still willing to help me. He looked confused but nodded his assent.

I told him to meet me outside the club on the other side of the road. Standing there in the drizzle I asked if he would be a partner in helping me with my problem. Terry stammered he might be willing, depending on what I had in mind, but it would be no more than that. He made it clear that he would take no bigger risk than I was prepared to take myself. He spoke in a firm voice, the first time I had heard him talk other than in a droll, sheepish way. I assured him on that issue and told him to meet me at my mews cottage the following evening when I would outline my plan. He was to speak to nobody of this matter.

The wheels had begun to turn. Veronica's days were counting down.

Terry arrived at the cottage at 9pm. I showed him how to unlock the back door and once out in the small yard I pointed to the rear view of my house at 46 Lower Belgrave Street, explaining to him that only two walls separated the yard we were standing in and the garden and back door to that house.

Anyone climbing those walls could then get into number 46 where my wife, a nanny and my children were resident. But it was still my home, containing many valuable heirlooms and paintings that belonged to me. I told Terry the basement back door was never locked due to two cats coming in and out of the house. (I had complained many times about this door not being locked).

We went inside and I opened a bottle of wine. With drinks in hand I told him of the plan I had thought so hard about for such a long time.

I should break off at this point and reiterate how the police, the media and most authors concluded what was planned and executed on the night of 7 November. Not one of these so-called experts – the detectives, the press, and a host of people who wrote books about the case came anywhere near getting it right, despite, as I mentioned much earlier on, clues and evidence was there for all to see. The account that all these people stuck to and which has stayed in place for the last forty years was totally wrong and it has never ceased to amaze me how these theories have held sway and been repeated time and time again.

Chapter Seventeen

This is what they said:

I had planned to kill my wife on the nannies night off – a Thursday. (They got that right). I was going to stuff my wife in a cotton mail sack, take the body out of the house, put the body in the boot of a car that I had borrowed and then drive down to the South Coast. From there, I would take my boat out to sea and throw Veronica's weighted down body overboard, where she would sink without trace. Then I would be free they said.

That is basically the conclusions arrived at, and which have been accepted without question for all these years.

I believe that now is the right time for me to come clean, to own up to everything, relate my reprehensible story and put the record straight while I can. That might be the one good thing I can do before I die.

Firstly, I did not have a boat on the South Coast or anywhere else. I had not owned a boat of any description in years. (something you would have thought the police could have checked). The mail sack in question was too small to hold a body (and in any case, if that had been the plan, one would have come up with something better than an old US mail sack). Also it will be seen why there were two murder weapons – something that was overlooked by the police and the media.

But most importantly, lets deal with the absurd and accepted notion that I intended for my wife to disappear. What on earth was I going to say to the police when they came knocking on my door wanting to know where she had got to?

My wife could not simply disappear. If that had happened who would have been the one and only suspect? Who would almost certainly have been detained by the police until she showed up? Ask yourself this question: Would it be likely that a mother, with three young children in the house, who was one minute watching TV, would suddenly get up, walk out of the front door of a house in Belgravia and vanish into thin air, never to be seen again?

And, so you see, what has been said and written about my intended actions was wrong and preposterous from the beginning and has remained so to this day.

Now I will return to my meeting with Terry.

I set out the plan with him in minute detail. Nothing would be left to chance. I had planned the perfect murder (or so I thought).

I told Terry I would pay him £5,000 up front and a further £5,000 after the deed was accomplished. (I had managed to secure a loan on the back of an impending sale that I had arranged with Christie's the auctioneers).

Terry's eyes lit up as I went through the plan. He became more talkative and spoke with a degree of confidence, which was unusual for him. Terry was not only prepared to be an accomplice but gave every indication that he was a very willing one. Perhaps it had been the money, but his keenness, while being welcome, was also a little disarming. He seemed enlivened, saying to me that I deserved to get my children back. We spoke of a murder weapon. Guns were out of the question as there must be no noise. My three children would be asleep upstairs and they were not to be alarmed in any way.

At length we decided on coshes, and Terry said that he could take care of this. In a cupboard under the stairs at the house where he rented a studio flat was an old lead pipe. He would cut the pipe to make two bludgeons. It was agreed that the murder of my wife should be a joint affair. The guilt totally equal. That way we protected each other to remain quiet ever after. We would both be as guilty as each other. (The aspect of blackmail is why I totally discounted the idea of employing a hitman). Also we needed a large bag and once again Terry said he could supply this. In the cupboard was an old US mail sack that he used for storing picture frames that he picked up cheap from street markets.

The plan was a robbery, a robbery that turned out tragically for my wife when she interrupted the intruder in the basement where we had a safe. She screamed and the burglar had attacked her with a blunt instrument as she tried to get away. He had not meant to kill her but the blows to her head were fatal.

My mews cottage, where Terry and I now discussed the plan was situated in a very quiet cul-de-sac. I hardly ever saw anyone there, not even neighbours. It would be an easy target for a robber.

This was my plan: The (hypothetical robber, robbers) had forced open the front door. Once inside he had ransacked the cottage but found little of value. Frustrated, he then went out to the back yard and realised there might be richer pickings if he climbed a couple of walls in the dark and found himself at the back of one of the fashionable houses in Lower Belgrave

Street. He did this, and easily for him, discovered the back door of number 46 was not locked. This house was a different kettle of fish than the mews cottage with many valuable items there for the taking. It was dark as he moved around the lower part of the house helping himself to whatever took his fancy. Higher up in the house he could hear the sound of a television and so restricted his plundering to the first floor and the ground floor. He then retraced his steps back to the basement where he tried to open the safe. This is when my wife came across him, fatally for her, when she came down to the basement to make a cup of tea.

How shocking I would say, when the police tracked me down to tell me of the tragedy at my former home. I might even summon up some tears. Of course I would return to the house to help the officers with their enquiries. I would tell them through my sorrow and anguish how I had always warned my wife not to leave the backdoor unlocked. I would then go through the rooms with the police pointing out what silverware and heirlooms had been stolen. Oh no, I would proclaim, one of my favourite pictures has gone. It was by Augustus John, and was most valuable. But wait, a couple of watercolours are missing which were of no value. How odd, I would add, wishing to muddy the waters. A robbery had taken place at my house and my poor wife had been murdered. You must catch the person, or persons responsible I would plead to the police.

I arranged with Terry that we do a couple of dummy runs, a complete rehearsal short of entering number 46 Lower Belgrave Street. We would check our timings, see if there was anything we may have missed. During the next few weeks we did test runs. I would collect Terry from his flat in Camden. He would have two coshes totally clean of fibres and the mail sack, which was thoroughly washed. He would keep a small jemmy in his coat pocket. We would then drive to Berkeley Square in my Mercedes where Terry would lie down in the back out of sight. On the intended night I would speak to the doorman to establish an alibi. Then we would drive to my flat in Elizabeth Street and swap cars. I had borrowed a car from a friend as my Mercedes would be conspicuous at Lower Belgrave Street. We would aim to arrive there by 8.45pm.

The dummy runs went perfectly. We set a date for 7 November. This was a Thursday, the nannies night off. We would enter the house through the front door. (I still had a key). We would go down to the basement and remove a light bulb. When my wife came down to make her customary cup of tea at 9pm we would strike in the darkness.

Having replaced the light bulb we would carry out the robbery. We would wear gloves at all times. Terry would hold the sack for me while I filled it with valuable items and small paintings. We would rob the ground floor and the rooms directly above but would not venture any further as the children would be asleep on the third floor. We would leave the basement door open for the police to see that this was how the robber gained entry. We would both leave by the front door having made sure the street was clear. I would head for the car with the mail sack while Terry would make his way round to the mews cottage. He would jemmy the door open. This would be easy, as I had already loosened some screws on the lock. Inside he would turn out draws and fake a robbery. He would unlock the back door and leave it open. All this would take no more than two minutes. He would then disappear into the night. I would only contact him again when I had the rest of his money.

At my flat I had prepared a hiding place for all the stolen articles. In time I would dispose of everything. Sad that such riches would have to be lost, but there could be no chance they turn up somewhere in the future. I would dress for dinner and be at the Clermont by 9.45pm. When the nanny returned home after her night off she would discover Veronica's body and that a robbery had taken place. She would ring the police immediately. Meanwhile I would be dining at the Clermont.

Of course I might have managed all this on my own and not involved someone else. But Terry, who like me was not your everyday killer, gave me a certain certitude to carry out this shocking crime. Using Terry was much simpler and professional I told myself. It was easier to carry out my plan with an accomplice.

The police would soon make there way to the mews cottage where they would discover a break-in and the back door open. It would now become clear to them that this was an opportunist robber, (maybe with an accomplice) a daring and violent thief climbing over walls and gaining access to number 46 Lower Belgrave Street where he had stolen items worth tens of thousands of pounds and killed my wife in the process.

Chapter Seventeen

So that was the plan that I had rehearsed in my mind a thousand times. On the night of 7 November, I collected Terry a little after 8pm. He climbed into the back seat clutching a mail sack that was wrapped around two coshes. In his coat pocket was a jemmy. We arrived at Berkeley Square in good time and I drove around before pulling up outside the Clermont shortly before 8.30pm. Terry was laying down in the back of the Mercedes out of sight. I had a quick chat with the doorman, Billy Edgson, telling him I would be back later. On the drive to Elizabeth Street I sprung a surprise on Terry, who I had paid £5,000 the previous day with the balance to come at the end of the month. I asked for a slight change of plan. Instead of two people hitting out with coshes, would he strike first and then I would strangle my wife. It would be cleaner and more decisive I said. He was sweating and showing nerves but made no objection.

At Elizabeth Street we swapped cars and drove to Lower Belgrave Street, arriving there at 8.45pm.

Terry opened the boot and removed the mail sack and one cosh, leaving the other cosh in the boot. The coshes would end up in the mail sack with the stolen goods to be disposed of at leisure.

We entered the house and went down to the basement kitchen where I removed an overhead light bulb. We waited in silence. I could feel my heart beating fast. It had been one thing planning this act but now I was trembling with fear. I thought of calling this off, for us both to leave as silently as we had arrived, to abandon this appalling plan. But it was too late; footsteps could be heard coming down the stairs. I knew immediately that something was not right but I froze. They were not the footsteps of my wife. I knew that instinctively.

The next few seconds were a blur. Sandra had seen Terry in the gloom and he had struck out like a cornered and terrified beast. Before I could stop him he had struck out again. I was screeching to him that this was the nanny and grabbed him round the neck but it was too late. The rest is too harrowing to relate in detail.

Writing about this diabolical act after all these years is very hard. I had lost my mind in 1974. Drink, drugs, not being able to sleep, revenge and outside influences had turned me into a senseless wretch.

Terry was spitting venom at me, accusing me of the shambles. He was crying and shaking and now tried to put Sandra's body in the sack saying that we had to somehow clean up everything. She would have identified both of us he was squealing. She had seen who we were he kept saying. I actually started to help him in this act, which of course was pure madness, but we were both in shock and acting in blind panic.

Then I heard Veronica coming down the stairs calling after Sandra. Terry was still raging at me. I told him to take off, to save himself. He rushed through the back door and I watched his figure disappear over the back wall and away into the darkness. I never saw him, or heard of him again.

I went to confront my wife. She was screaming and kicking out at me. I tried to calm her but she was hysterical. I grabbed her neck and she fell back and split her head. After much struggling and tears we both sat on the foot of the stairs and tried to pacify each other. Then I guided her upstairs to her bedroom. Of course I could have killed her if I had wanted to, but that was the last thing on my mind. I was already a doomed man and bereft of any further violence. My daughter was standing outside her bedroom. I told her to go back to her room and that everything would be all right. I went to the bathroom to get a flannel to tend to Veronica's head wound and here she seized her chance. She ran down the stairs and was out of the front door before I could catch her.

It was all up. I was finished and would spend the rest of my life in prison. I stood there on the pavement outside the house, my mind and body paralysed. I saw Veronica rush into the pub at the end of the street. Soon the police would arrive.

I went back into the house and just stood there in a daze. The nanny, Sandra Rivett, had been murdered by my doing and I would go to prison and bring shame on others. If Terry was caught, he would also go to prison for many years, his life shattered. My trial and condemnation would be a lasting wound on my mother, my brother and sisters and my children. I was shaking and my mind had turned to jelly. I had to try and think straight, to think fast.

With the prevailing times the courts would go out of their way to make an example of me. My friends and family would be targeted in the cruellest of fashion. Life in prison for me – a titled person that had all the advantages in life that other prisoners would never have had – would be intolerable and a daily torture. Prison life would be much harder for me than the worst criminals on this earth.

If I were to escape, the police hunt would surely be confined to me, to me alone. Nobody had seen Terry, he might still remain in the clear – to be free – to spend that £5,000 and live out his days as he wished. If I could escape the children would not have to endure the spectacle of their father standing in the dock charged with a ghastly murder. My family and friends would not be set upon by a hostile press.

Would it not be better for all concerned if this despicable man were to simply disappear?

signed
Richard John Bingham
June 2014. part 2/3

Chapter Eighteen

Back home at my flat in North London I unpacked my rucksack and placed Sidney's manuscript in a drawer. What I had read on the plane was still swimming around in my head. If the story was genuine it explained so much.

Whatever the truth, part three of his manuscript might come as something of an anti-climax. Even so, it would be good to know what Sidney had to say about escape and who helped him. Perhaps the police and the media had got that wrong also.

I texted Paul King: "Have part two. Meet somewhere neutral when you are ready." He texted back: "Nearly there Adam. Meet Friday, Noon. Sanderson's hotel, Berners Street."

That left me with three clear days, which I was glad of. For now I must forget Mr. Lucan and this treacherous escapade I was involved with and pick up the threads of my own life and routine. The following days were busy. I spent time in the garden tidying up and making repairs to fencing that had succumbed to the wind. At last it was the final acts of selling my mum's house. Before contracts were exchanged there was a last minute game of bluff – No we would not drop the price one penny – Take it or leave it we had said. They took it.

I had some meetings with my friends from the tennis club to discuss the ongoing politics. Should we sell the club? Should we cash-in and let developers build god knows how many flats on the site and allow the members to receive a handsome windfall? Perhaps £40,000 each.

I had a sneaky respect for those members trying to save the club, but times change. Changing times that had once afforded me three local pubs and now there were none.

Friday was on me before I knew it. I put Sidney's document in a sturdy bag and took the tube to Oxford Circus. It crossed my mind that I could be sneaky and photocopy his manuscript. Maybe write a book about this adventure in years to come. I decided not to. I would carry on acting as an honest messenger.

I walked along Oxford Street and turned left into Berners Street. Inside the impressive bar at the Sanderson's hotel I ordered a Bloody Mary with all the trimmings. The barman had no sooner added some Worcestershire sauce to my drink when Paul King arrived at the bar.

We shook hands like good friends. 'What are you drinking?' he asked.

'Bloody Mary,' I told him. 'Sounds good,' he said turning to the barman. 'I'll have one of those too.'

We settled into a couple of sofas in a quiet corner. Paul tucked a small briefcase down the side of his chair and placed a larger one under the table.

I resisted the urge to ask if he had the money and instead handed him the manila envelope. He placed the document on his lap while he put on his reading glasses.

'What did you make of it?' he asked softly.

'Amazing.' I replied.

'Can't wait,' he said greedily, as though about to tuck into a sumptuous meal.

'I'm going outside for a cigarette,' I said. 'I'll let you read in peace.'

I had a smoke outside the hotel and then wandered down to the shopping plaza. I mooched around trying to kill a suitable amount of time for Paul to read the manuscript before heading back to the hotel and the bar. Paul had finished reading, the document rested silently on his lap. He was staring ahead in deep thought.

I sat down bringing him out of his little trance. He turned to me his mind still preoccupied. After a few moments he tapped the document with his glasses.

'How could it be,' he said in a puzzled tone, 'that so many people fastened on to a certain type of plot?' He shook his head, smiling wryly. 'I'm an investigative journalist, but never thought twice about questioning the view that Lucan planned to chuck his wife in the English Channel and have her vanish. Of course he couldn't do that.' He flicked through the pages of the manuscript. 'All this is dead right. She couldn't simply disappear.' He shook his head again. 'How was it that nobody raised doubts about that story line?'

I took a sip of my drink. 'I think it's a case of an assumption made at the time, that gets repeated elsewhere and finally sticks. Then nobody thinks to question the story. It becomes engrained in peoples imagination.'

Paul put the document in his small briefcase that was resting by his side. 'Well, if all this is true, this story is pure dynamite Adam. I have your word that no copies have been made?'

I could not resist a little honest laugh. 'No copies Paul. Don't get paranoid on me this late in the day.'

'Sorry,' he said cheerily. 'Had to ask.'

Chapter Eighteen

He picked up the large bag from under the table and pushed it towards me. 'For you,' he said. 'Don't lose it whatever you do.'

I peered inside. There were some bundles wrapped in brown parcel paper bound with sellotape.

Paul rose and stood by my chair clutching the small attaché case hard to his chest that now contained Sidney's manuscript. He spoke in a quiet reassuring voice.

'I'm getting there slowly with the money Adam. The newspaper is edgy about releasing cash without having the whole story in their possession. Still, with this.' He tapped the attaché case, 'I should get half the amount which will enable me to pay you and Warren. I will be last in line.'

'What now?' I said easily.

Paul stared up at the ceiling doing some calculations in his head. 'This time next Friday at the Russell Square Hotel. Can you get the final manuscript by then?'

'Should be no problem,' I replied carefully. 'Let's get this over and done with. It will be a relief to get this drama out of my life.'

We shook hands gladly. I watched Paul disappear into Berners Street. I picked up the large bag and asked the barman to call me a cab. Back home in my flat I pulled down the window blinds and began sorting the cash on my kitchen table. Some packets held all £50 notes, others were mixed, tens and twenties in new and used notes. The new denominations had consecutive numbers. For no other reason than it was fun to handle such a vast sum of cash I shuffled the new and old notes together. I spent about two hours playing around like this before wrapping piles back in the brown paper and re-sealing what resembled bricks with sellotape. I now had five neat parcels of roughly the same size. Counting all this money felt totally unreal. Was Sidney really Lord Lucan? Could this money be the ultimate proof that he was that man? I did not bother to count the money. It looked like, smelt like, and felt like £60,000. It was time to decide where to hide the money. After some thought I settled on the cupboard under the stairs. I pulled out the vacuum cleaner and some suitcases. At the very back of the cupboard I discovered a stack of old vinyl LP's that I determined to get rid of one day. I inspected the floorboards. One section looked ideal. It was about two foot long. I got a screwdriver and prized the board free trying not to distort the nails. I felt underneath. Just dust and rubble. I placed the packages down amongst the dirt and hammered the board back in place. Perfect.

I had a week to kill, so checked out what flights were available to Mallorca. I had been hopping back and forth to the island, but this should turn out to be my last trip for some while. Hopefully, Sidney would tell me what he wanted me to do with his money, and then it would have to be farewell. Better for both of us that we never meet again.

There was a late flight from Luton the following day, which would get me into Palma in the evening. I booked a return flight leaving me with a few days holiday. It was early October but Mallorca should still be nice and warm. I would phone Sidney at our pre-arranged time before setting off for the airport. I had been speaking to him every other day and this had gone well. He was fine with his new mobile, but if this was to be our last meeting I would take the phone away and destroy it. All links would have to severed.

The following day I packed a small case and waited for one o'clock to come round. I phoned Sidney. There no answer and I was directed to a messaging service. I waited and tried again, but still no response. I kept trying, but Sidney was not answering. I knew something was wrong and felt troubled.

I rang again when I was at Luton airport and also when I arrived at my hotel near Palma but was repeatedly being asked to leave a message.

At the hotel I quickly unpacked and asked reception to call me a cab. I asked the taxi driver to drop me anywhere in Molinar. I went first to the Café Plaza but they were packing up for the night with just a handful of locals sitting outside. I made my way hurriedly to Sidney's apartment and rang his doorbell. I waited and then banged on the door. I wondered if he had fallen inside his flat and couldn't move. I banged on the door again and now a little old Spanish lady appeared from the next apartment. She looked at me suspiciously and then started to speak quickly, gesticulating with arms waving in the air. I could not catch a word of what she was saying so animatedly. Then she swept a hand that clearly indicated Sidney was not at home. I tried some idiotic words of Spanish, which was getting the pair of us nowhere. Then she made a sort of swallow dive pointing at the floor. I caught the meaning. Sidney had fallen in the corridor. 'Ospital,' she said.

I thanked her most warmly telling her in my best Spanish that I was a friend.

'Hospital in Palma?' I asked. There came more Spanish dialogue, but realising I could not follow she made gestures indicating an invisible man on the floor being put onto a stretcher. Then I caught the word ambulance. I understood and thanked her again.

It was late and my heart felt heavy. I decided there nothing I could do for the moment and so took the slow walk back to my hotel. First thing in the morning I would check with reception where I could find the hospital and buy a Spanish phrase book and dictionary from the hotel shop. Poor Sidney. Another fall. I felt a real sense of gloom.

I woke early and asked at reception where the hospital would be for my friend attended to by ambulance from Molinar. A very helpful girl wrote down the name of the hospital and told me it was about eight kilometres away. She phoned a taxi for me.

While I waited outside the lobby for my cab I phoned Paul King. He answered immediately. I told him Sidney had been taken to hospital and that I was on my way there. At this moment I did not care whether he could trace the call back to Mallorca.

'Shit,' came the snapping reply. 'What's happened?' he asked anxiously.

'I don't know yet,' I said. 'I will ring you when I know more.'

'Look Adam,' he said, his voice indicating something deeper was coming. 'There's been a new development at this end. The newspaper want DNA proof. It's that bloody lawyer stirring trouble and making life hard for me.'

'That's ridiculous,' I said making no attempt to hide my exasperation.

'I know it is Adam. But for now, it seems we have a much bigger problem to deal with. Keep me posted. I'll keep my mobile on me. Let me know how you get on. Good luck.'

On the drive to the hospital I reflected yet again my part in this rather unsavoury venture. What on earth was I doing? Why had I allowed myself to become so heavily involved? But maybe now events were coming to a head. I had spoken to Sidney on the phone over the last few days and he had given me no hint that he was unwell; although I was aware his health was not good. But here was another fall, and this time he did not get up and find his way to the Café Plaza for a brandy and a cigarillo.

The taxi skirted the bustling capital of Palma and the suburban sprawl of drab apartment blocks that lay far back from the tourist areas. At length we turned north. Up ahead could be seen the gleaming blocks of the University Hospital Son Dureta. The whole campus composed of modern glass and steel buildings. The driver asked if I wanted reception and we then drove a further half-mile before he parked up and pointed me in the right direction.

The hospital was most impressive. Large pictures on the walls displayed the friendly looking medical staff along with their names. I reached for my phrase book. I had written down some words and sentences I thought I might need.

I waited behind a lady at reception who was asking directions. Once she had moved on I asked the tall bespectacled man if he spoke English. The answer was a little negative. I showed him my paper where I had written down the name Sidney Ainsworth and the town of Molinar. Also on the paper, which I was glad that I had prepared, was my name and that I was a friend and not family. The bespectacled chap looked somewhat bemused, no doubt trying to decipher my written attempt at Spanish.

'One moment,' he said. He started to tap away at a computer, which seemed to make him even more confused. He then started to ask me questions in Spanish very slowly, which was a help. I could just about get the drift. I had done some Spanish lessons in London a couple of years earlier but had forgotten virtually everything soon afterwards. But I knew he was asking me when Sidney had been admitted. This was a problem. I reached for my phrase-book and found days of the week in Spanish which I sort of knew but needed to double check. Today was Sunday; Sidney had not answered my call the day before so he was probably admitted on the Thursday after I had spoken to him or the Friday. I pointed at the days, jueves and viernes.

The receptionist then asked me to wait as he disappeared into a side office. He soon re-emerged signalling that I should stay where I was. He then started to deal with the queue that had been quietly building up behind me.

I stood for a while feeling nervous before a pleasant lady approached me holding my paper. 'You are Adam,' she said with a warm smile.

I nodded, feeling relieved that I was getting somewhere. 'You speak English?' I said hopefully.

'A little,' she said, still smiling. 'My name is Margarita Rodrigues.' She looked cautiously at my paper. 'You are a friend of this gentleman?' she asked quietly.

'That's right,' I replied mildly.

She thought for a moment still staring at my paper. 'We do have a gentleman here who was admitted to the Intensive Care Unit on Friday. We do not have his details and need to contact his family.'

'He has no family,' I said. 'He lives alone.'

'I see,' she said barely above a whisper. Margarita stared past me in deep thought before turning her face to me, seemingly having come to a decision. 'Please follow me,' she said.

We sped upwards in one of the gleaming lifts to the seventh floor. I followed her in silence along a corridor to the Intensive Care Ward. She tapped in a security code and the door opened. Inside she spoke to some nurses who were manning a small station with a row of computers and files. Margarita then guided me to a bed and pointed to the occupant. 'Is this your friend?' she asked tenderly.

I nodded sadly. 'This is Sidney,' I said in a low voice.

Margarita said I could have a few minutes with him but would I see her before I left the hospital. She told me her office was next to reception.

Sidney was a sorry sight indeed. Various tubes in his mouth and nose linked him to a monitor on a bedside table. Some tubes from drip feeds disappeared up a sleeve. He was motionless, breathing just about discernable through grey lips. A nurse appeared on the other side of the bed and gave me a weak smile. She checked the fluid bags before moving on to the next bed.

I thought about what Paul King had said about DNA, but I was certainly not going to lean across Sidney and pluck some of his hair. There were places I was not prepared to go. I tried speaking to Sidney but there was not a flicker of response. I touched his forehead gently and spoke softly and comfortingly.

'I don't know if you can hear me Sidney. This is Adam. I am thinking of you and will do my best to see that your story is told. I know that is your wish. You took a chance with me and I will not let you down. Goodbye Sidney.'

I turned on my heels and left the ward. I knew I had seen him for the last time. I knocked on the office door next to reception. Margarita ushered me inside a bright airy room. Considering it was Sunday I felt lucky Margarita was on duty. Once seated at her desk she offered me her sympathy for my friend. He suffered a stroke she told me and they were doing all they could for him. Margarita gently told me in a roundabout way that Sidney was very ill. She then started to write some notes. The ambulance people had ascertained Sidney's address from a neighbour who had called them when she found him collapsed in the corridor.

She asked me Sidney's nationality and did I know how long he had been living in Molinar? Also questions as to his doctor and did he have medical insurance. I was of little help short of telling her who he was claiming to be. She asked if I had access to his apartment to perhaps retrieve his passport.

I shook my head but she had given me an idea. I needed to somehow get into his flat. 'Do you have Sidney's door key?' I asked hesitantly.

'Possibly,' she said reaching for a folder amongst a pile on her desk. 'But we can only release items to family. You understand?' she added most politely. Margarita extracted a sheet from the folder and turned it towards me to read.

It was a neatly typed list of belongings. It was all in Spanish but I could make out most of it. Items of clothing, a wallet containing 56 euros, cufflinks, a door key, a lighter and an item that caught my eye – a Rolex watch. I wondered whether to tell her the watch might be very valuable but decided not to bring attention to it.

'I don't know Sidney that well,' I lied. 'But I know the café where he is known to the staff. Perhaps I could make some enquiries.'

'If you could, that would be most helpful,' Margarita said quietly. She handed me a business card. 'My telephone extension is on the card. I will be here after 11am tomorrow.'

'You have been most kind,' I said sincerely. 'I'm grateful you allowed me to see my friend.'

'I'm pleased you came here today,' she said warmly. 'There was no identification on his person. At least now we know his name. I would ask you to keep in touch with me if you could.'

I got up to leave.

'Oh, by the way,' she said running her finger down the sheet of Sidney's belongings. 'Do you know what medication Sidney was taking? This here,' she said, pointing to an item on the page. 'Some capsules in a small bottle.' She shrugged. 'We cannot identify them. They are not what are prescribed on the label and we have no record of the farmacia that supplied them.'

I felt a cold shudder. 'I think Sidney was taking all sorts of things,' I said. 'Best destroy them.'

'Oh we will have to,' she said with a smile.

Outside the hospital I phoned Paul King. He wanted to fly out to meet me, wherever I was. The game of keeping Sidney's whereabouts a secret had changed he said. He wanted to help me. I told him to hold fire and give me a little time. Paul sounded edgy, asking what I intended to do if Sidney did not come through. I told him I was going to locate Sidney's landlord. Make up some story and try to get access to his apartment. But it was Sunday and there was little that could be done at the moment. I told Paul I would get back to him when I had some news.

Sidney had mentioned his landlord. Told me what a lovely man he was and would do anything for him. It was his landlord that bought him those trainers after his fall. I had to try and track him down. For now, I could think of no other idea. I had to get that final manuscript from Sidney's apartment before the authorities went there should Sidney not recover.

I took a cab and asked the driver to drop me off in Molinar. I went up to the second floor of Sidney's apartment block and knocked on his neighbours door. The little Spanish lady remembered me. I produced my Spanish dictionary and after much confusion on either side and me pointing to Sidney's door she seemed delighted to have understood me.

'Un momento,' she said, before disappearing inside. She soon re-appeared and handed me a business card. It was a property agency in Molinar. I felt like slapping a kiss on the old Spanish lady's cheeks. Instead I thanked her most sincerely and played with some words to say how sorry I was to have disturbed her for the second time. She was holding her hands up in a sort of prayer and pointing at Sidney's door, a worried face showing. I knew she was asking after him.

'No es bueno – Mal,' I said, knowing it was short of a satisfactory reply. She gestured another little sign of prayer. I touched her shoulder and thanked her again.

I wandered around the town and eventually found the property agency. They were closed of course, but I made a note of the opening hours. There was nothing I could do until the morning but I had made some progress.

On the long walk back to my hotel I churned over in my mind what I could say once I had tracked down Sidney's landlord. He was hardly likely to hand over the keys to Sidney's apartment to a complete stranger. My best bet was to say that I had been helping Sidney to write a novel. That the first two parts had been delivered by me to a publisher in London and that Sidney would be most upset should the final part, which was resting on his desk, did not accompany me back to London.

I would make up some tale that it was about horse racing or some such nonsense. It was a long shot but so had been everything about this bizarre affair. Now was not the time to give up. I had to try something. I would have dinner at the hotel and a couple of drinks and then sleep on it.

I arrived at the property agency at 9.30am. Three girls were gazing at computer screens at desks stationed either side of a long narrow room. One of the young girls rose from her desk and came towards me.

'Can I help you,' she asked tentatively, somehow taking it for granted that I was not a Spanish speaker. I showed her a piece of paper where I had written down Sidney's name and address.

'Can I speak to the proprietor?' I asked timidly. I pointed at Sidney's name on my paper. 'It's to do with this dirección, apartmento.'

The girl looked at me rather disconcertingly. 'What would you like to know?'

I was stumbling for the right words but at least the girl spoke English. 'Sidney is in hospital,' I said. 'He is a friend and the hospital need to locate his family,'

'I see,' she said doubtfully. 'You will need to speak to Lionel. He is not here right now.'

She seemed to think this answer was sufficient before being surprised when I then asked her the obvious. 'When will he be back?'

'Not till later,' she said airily.

I was determined to stand my ground, my voice more confident. 'I believe Lionel is a good friend of Sidney. He will want to be informed. Can you telephone him?' I said politely but with a hint of firmness.

She did not answer but returned to her desk and started tapping away at her computer. She then spoke to one of the other girls who made a telephone call. The pair of them then had a lengthy discussion, the details of which I could not discern.

'Lionel will be back at 4pm,' she said indifferently.

'Gracias,' I said. 'My name is Adam. Por favor tell him I will be back later.'

It was going to be a long day in Molinar. I made my way to the Café Plaza and ordered a coffee and croissant. Just after 11am I telephoned the hospital. I felt anxious with a heavy feeling in my stomach as I waited to be connected.

'This is Adam,' I said mildly, when I got through to Margarita. 'We met yesterday. Can you give me any news on my friend Sidney?'

'Hello Adam,' she said very softly. 'Have you managed to contact any family members?'

'I think I have located his landlord who I am waiting to see. But I'm pretty sure Sidney was all alone in this world.'

There was a long pause before Margarita spoke slowly and quietly. 'I am not really supposed to give out information other than to family, but as nobody has come forward it is with great sadness that I have to tell you that this gentleman passed away early this morning. I'm most sorry Adam. We did everything we could.'

There was silence for a while. 'It was news that I was expecting,' I said croakily.

'Can you let me have details of his landlord?' she asked gently.

I found the business card and read out the name and address of the agency. I told her that I would try and supply some more information before thanking her and ending the call.

I ordered another coffee, my mind was swimming. I telephoned Paul King.

'What news?' he said urgently.

'He's dead,' I said.

'Fuck,' he said coldly. 'I should have foreseen something like this. Tell me where you are and I'll fly out and meet you. No time for secrets now. We have to get that document Adam. If the authorities get hold of it with Lucan's name on the cover we are done for. You'll have to give all the money back. You realise that don't you?'

'I'm not thinking about money,' I said in a firm, irritable voice, as though to remind him that someone had just died.

'Look,' I said, trying to think ahead. 'There's no point in you flying out to meet me. What would you do if you were here anyway?'

'I don't know where you are Adam, but for one thing, kick down the bloody door of his apartment.'

'Great,' I said sarcastically. 'The pair of us get arrested. That's a big help.'

'Pay the landlord off,' he countered. 'I could wire some money.'

'Look Paul,' I said, my voice lowering. 'Let's hang fire. I'm meeting the landlord late afternoon. Wait and see how I get on.'

'Well good luck,' he said in an anxious tone lacking any enthusiasm.

I had many hours to kill so strolled along the front to Palma. It was low season and an easy queue for entrance to the Cathedral. The building never ceases to inspire and had a calming affect on me. I was thinking of Sidney and was not sure whether news of his death should sadden me or whether I should regard it as a relief for the man. I spent a couple of hours wandering around the Cathedral settling my thoughts.

Just after 4pm I was back in Molinar and headed straight for the property agency. The young girl that I had seen earlier pointed me to a desk at the rear of the room. It seemed Lionel was expecting me for he ushered me to his desk and offered me a very warm handshake. I guessed he was in his forties. Handsome as only Spanish and Italian men can look with thick, shiny jet-black hair swept back.

'I hear Sidney is in hospital,' he said with a look of deep concern.

'I'm afraid I have bad news,' I said haltingly. 'I phoned the hospital after I left here this morning. He passed away during the night.'

Lionel raised his hands to the ceiling, shaking his head sadly. 'That is terrible news,' he said mournfully. 'I was very fond of Sidney. I have known him for many years. I am very upset to hear this. Do you know what happened?'

'I believe he had a stroke. His neighbour found him on the floor in the corridor outside his apartment and phoned for an ambulance.'

I showed Lionel the card Margarita had given me. 'I have been speaking to this lady at the Hospital Son Dureta,' I said. 'She is very nice. I hope you don't mind but I have given her your details. She may contact you.'

'Of course, of course. We will be happy to help.'

'They need to contact any family Sidney may have but I'm not sure there is anyone. He had always given me the impression that he was very much alone.'

Lionel shrugged. 'He has never mentioned anyone to me. I think he liked to keep to himself. Can I ask Adam, how do you know him?'

'I first made friends with him at the Café Plaza. He asked if I would help with a novel he was writing.'

Lionel smiled broadly narrowing his eyes. 'Sidney was writing a novel?'

'Yes,' I said eagerly. 'It's about horse racing. He used to own horses back in England and he's a bit of an expert on the sport.'

Lionel relaxed back in his chair. 'I used to enjoy talking to Sidney but he never told me he was writing a novel. That sounds wonderful. But I was a little worried about him. He had a nasty fall a little while ago.'

Lionel came across as a really nice chap and now I had to chance my arm. 'I have delivered most of his story to a publishing house in London.' I said calmly. 'He asked me to collect the last part of his manuscript. The very last page is resting in his old typewriter. He told me that he was fearful of typing the last few words. As though he knew his time was up. Apart from the manuscript the hospital asked if I could give them some information about Sidney. Perhaps documents that would help them contact any family he may have.'

Chapter Eighteen

'Well Adam,' Lionel said smartly, 'shall we go to his apartment and see what we can find?'

My heart was fluttering. This was going well. 'If we could,' I said mildly.

Lionel went straight to a board holding dozens of keys. He took a key from a hook.

'Let's go,' he said.

I walked with Lionel across the square to Sidney's apartment block. We talked amicably on the way. Once inside Sidney's flat I showed Lionel the typewriter and the last page still to be finished. I asked Lionel whether he would mind my looking at it and maybe typing the last few words on Sidney's behalf. Sidney would have wanted that I said. Lionel waved a hand for me to go ahead. I pulled up a chair and studied the page while Lionel began looking around the apartment.

Sidney had typed a capital 'A' but had not continued to type those last few words. I had never used a manual typewriter but knew the last words would have to be typed on this particular machine with its own characteristics. It would be no good trying to do this back in London on a different typewriter. It would not be the same and would open the way for someone to cry forgery. I was aware of Lionel moving around but I had to concentrate and get this right. Using one finger I typed 'n' then 'd' then a word space. Then I typed the last few words. I managed a couple of carriage returns and put in a date.

Lionel was waiting behind me ready to have a look through the desk I was sitting at. I removed the page from the typewriter and placed it with the rest of the manuscript.

'I have checked the bedroom,' Lionel said. 'Lots of nice clothes but nothing else. He was always very smartly dressed. Shall we check the desk?'

I moved the chair out of the way and Lionel opened the top drawer. Together we looked through the paper work. It was all bills for his flat and prescriptions from his doctor. We put certain papers aside to give to the hospital. The next drawer contained written drafts of his story, which I put with his manuscript. The next drawer was interesting. It contained his passport, statements from his bank in Palma, photos – presumably of his children, utility bills and an address book. We opened the last drawer. It was full of cash.

'I will have to take this money and keep it in my safe Adam. I don't want to leave cash in an empty apartment. Will you tell the hospital that I am going to hold this money?'

'Of course,' I said. I found some large envelopes for the manuscript and what would be handed to the hospital. Sidney's mobile was on the desk. I quickly put it in my pocket.

Lionel had a last glance around the room. 'Well, I think we're all done Adam. It's very sad doing this but it had to be done. I will miss Sidney. If no family member comes forward I will have to clear the apartment. Find a good home for all those nice clothes in the bedroom.'

'He would like that,' I said solemnly while thinking what a result this had been. On the way out I told Lionel I needed to use the toilet desperately.

'No problem,' he said, 'I will wait for you.'

Inside the bathroom I grabbed a hairbrush, comb and toothbrush, which I stuffed in my pockets. Perhaps some DNA could be obtained from them. I pulled the chain.

We locked the door behind us. Outside the apartment block I shook hands with Lionel and thanked him.

Lionel held to his chest what looked like a huge wad of euros. 'You won't forget to tell the hospital I'm looking after Sidney's money? There will be funeral costs.'

'I will let them know,' I said willingly. 'They will probably appoint a lawyer to handle his affairs.'

'It's been a sad day,' Lionel murmured. I agreed and went in search of a taxi. Back at the hotel I phoned Paul King and gave him the news about everything I had managed to get hold of from Sidney's apartment. He purred out his delight until he was nearly breathless with relief. We talked at length about what I should give the hospital. He told me I must destroy the address book and his passport. If the authorities discovered his passport was a forgery they would start asking questions as to his real identity. I told him I would take care of things and ring him in a couple of days.

'Do you want to tell me where you are?' he said hesitantly. 'Not really,' I said.

The following day would be my last in Mallorca – for some time – I told myself.

I slept well that night, and after a good breakfast, asked reception to call me a cab. I asked the driver to go first to the University Hospital Son Dureta. I had sorted some documents that I would deliver to Margarita. I had enclosed a letter saying that I was enclosing bank statements and information as to his doctor. I told her that apart from the six thousand euros in his bank account the property agency also held some money on Sidney's behalf. I reiterated my view that Sidney had no family but hoped the hospital would see, that in view of his healthy finances, he would be afforded a good funeral. I had wondered whether to mention in the letter Sidney's Rolex watch that I felt sure was worth a lot of money but decided not to. I had signed off the letter thanking her for her help and that I now had to return to England. I made no mention of his passport.

At the hospital I went to reception and handed the large envelope over to the bespectacled gentleman I had seen before. 'Just a delivery for Margarita,' I said and made a quick exit.

I told my driver to take me to Calviá. It was my last day in this lovely island and I intended to make the most of it on what was a beautiful day under a clear blue sky. I would do a lovely walk from Calviá to Galilea, the highest village in Mallorca. The hike is the Vall Negre, the black valley, which I had walked many years ago.

I paid off my taxi and having found the beginning of the trail headed up to the woods. After two hours trecking I came to a clearing and a drystone water catchment that was built by the Moors centuries earlier. I continued walking uphill through woodlands and suddenly up ahead could be seen the high jagged peak of Galatzo thrusting up on the horizon behind the houses of Galilea. After walking through meadows and open fields I found a nice spot against a fence cordoning off some private land where I would have a rest and some lunch.

Behind me I could see impressive views of hills and valleys and further in the distance the panoramic coastline of Calviá. I ate my baguette that the hotel had kindly made for me and then extracted a plastic bag from my rucksack. I had another look at Sidney's passport. It had expired years ago. As it was almost certainly a fake I wondered why he had kept it. The address book had the names and addresses of various doctors in Palma and telephone numbers for letting agents in Mallorca. There was nothing in the book that connected him to London, but a lot of information had been crossed out and was no longer eligible. Other names, phone numbers and addresses for Paris and England were all jumbled up in some sort of code known only to Sidney.

I began to dig a hole with a fork I had purloined from the hotel. Once my hole was about a foot deep I wrapped the passport, address book and photos in the plastic bag and buried them. I found some rocks and made a little marker around the earth I had filled in. The documents could, at a future date, be recovered but that was not going to happen. It was all over. Sidney Ainsworth was dead and I had just buried him.

After another two hours of trekking gradually uphill through woodland paths and bushland I reached the tiny village of Galilea. I found the Bar Parroquial by the side of the church in the small square. After two much needed cold beers I asked the friendly old lady that ran the bar to call me a taxi.

Back at my hotel I packed my things ready for the journey home the next day. I had a little nap before heading to the bar for a gin and tonic. After dinner I had one more drink at the bar, as it was my last night in Mallorca. The Vall Negre, possibly the most beautiful walk on the island had been wonderfully inspiring but also tiring. It was time for bed.

My flight was on time. I grabbed a coffee near the boarding gate and soon made my way on to the plane. I had booked a window seat and made myself comfortable. A couple soon took up the seats next to me and we shared some friendly words.

As the plane roared into the sky I extracted Sidney's document from my rucksack. This had now turned into a little ritual. I would have read his whole life story at thirty thousand feet. I extracted the familiar sheets of neat type, painstakingly tapped out on his trusted old Olivetti typewriter. I leaned back in my seat and began to read the final part of this most extraordinary story.

Chapter Nineteen

THE STORY: PART THREE

MY NAME IS RICHARD JOHN BINGHAM, SEVENTH
EARL OF LUCAN.

Part Three of my manuscript.

I stood frozen as I watched my wife run down the street and
burst through the doors of the Plumbers Arm pub. I was
finished. My abominable plan was a disaster.

I went back in the house and sat on the foot of the stairs.
There were just two choices for me. I could stay where I was
and give myself up, or I could try and escape. I decided to
escape. It would be better for all concerned, I decided, if I could
somehow disappear.

I shut the door of 46 Lower Belgrave Street for the last time.
I reckoned I had a good twenty minutes before the police would
get to my apartment in Elizabeth Street. It was there I went
first in the borrowed Ford Corsair.

Inside my apartment I found a large bag to hold my blood
stained clothes. I washed my hands and face and then quickly
changed into clean clothes putting the soiled garments and
shoes into the bag, which I would dispose of later. I collected a
raincoat, scarf and cap and some cash. Other belongings in my
flat I would not need, certainly not items like my passport and
driving licence that could identify me. I telephoned my mother
telling her something awful had taken place at the house and
would she get a taxi and collect the children quickly. She
sounded shaken, asking me what had happened. I made up
some quick tale of seeing an attack taking place in the
basement when I had been passing the house and that I had
tried to intervene. I told her that I would phone her later when
she had the children safely back at her home. I cleaned the

bathroom thoroughly and with the bag of soiled clothes, wiped the floor behind me as I left the apartment locking the door behind me.

My cleaning must have been good for the police stated that I had never returned to my apartment, despite the fact that they knew I had made a telephone call from a private subscriber.

I felt more desolate and ashamed than I had ever been in my life, but I had to keep my wits about me despite the fact that my head was spinning. For now, I had to get out of London. I climbed into the car and started off to my friends, Ian and Susie Maxwell-Scott, at Uckfield, Sussex. On the way there I stopped at an industrial estate and disposed of the bag of soiled clothes in a building skip.

I arrived at Uckfield around 11pm. Susie ushered me into their beautiful home. She told me that Ian was still at the Clermont and was going to stay at the club overnight, something he did frequently. Susie made coffee and gave me a large brandy. I told her I was in big trouble feeling sure she and Ian would help me. I told her the truth aside from mentioning Terry, who I was desperate to protect at all costs. I said that I had killed the nanny, mistaking her for my wife in the dark basement. I told her how shattered I was. That when Veronica appeared on the scene I could have killed her, but could not stomach any more violence. My plan to do away with my wife had turned into a fiasco, a shambles and now poor Sandra was dead. I was no good at murder and now faced arrest and a life in prison. I told Susie that I was going to try and escape or commit suicide. That I could not handle prison life. The very thought of a life behind bars was out of the question for me. I told her that I had planned the murder of my wife so carefully. I had even made dummy runs with a borrowed car and stalked the house over many months. But I had failed in what should have been the obvious and most essential part of the plan – to check that Sandra had left the house as she would normally have done on a Thursday. How utterly stupid of me.

Susie offered me words of comfort. I should not think of killing myself. That I had been driven to despair for the love of my children. She told me that my family and all my good friends at the Clermont would support me. We would ring Ian, who would get word to John, (Aspinall) and set the wheels in motion to get me out of the country.

Chapter Nineteen

When I spoke to Ian on the phone I outlined what had happened and told him what my intentions were. I asked that he speak to nobody other than John.

Susie, who was a lawyer, wanted to go over the fine details of what had actually taken place. She was intent on probing me about every detail. To do that I would have to tell her the whole truthful story but asked her to swear that she would not mention Terry's involvement to anyone else. She gave me her word. I then told her of my failed plan and all the horrible details relating to Sandra's murder.

Her lawyer's mind started working overtime. I had not killed my wife when I could easily have done so. That was hugely in my favour she said. I told her I had quickly made up some lies to my mother when asking her to collect the children about seeing an attack taking place from outside the house. That was good, was Susie's quick response. Between us we came up with a lifeline plan should I be caught. Was it possible to see into the basement from outside the house, she asked me. I told her it was at a pinch. We then decided to stick with this rather dubious story that I had been passing the house and had seen an attack taking place in the basement. I had then entered the house, but the killer had fled. My wife immediately accused me of murder. With a top class barrister, (something she could arrange) it would be hard to convict me. In court, Veronica would be seen as a hostile witness with a history of mental illness who was only too ready to blame me.

It was a patchy, but reasonable plan for more reasons than one. I wanted certain friends and family to see me in an innocent light, especially my mother. If I should get away I would like her to cling to the belief that her son was not a murderer – that he might be innocent. And so that was the plan should I be apprehended without the opportunity of killing myself.

I thanked Susie, holding back tears. I asked if she could give me some stationery. I then wrote a couple of important letters regarding my affairs to my very good friend Bill Shand Kydd and left them for Susie to post for me. My longing wish was that my children would end up in the good care of Bill and Christina, Veronica's sister. I then telephoned my mother. She was very upset. She told me the children were safe with her and that a policeman wished to speak to me. I calmed my mother, telling her of my innocence and relating my made-up tale that I had been passing the house and had stumbled upon a murder taking

place. I said that I would ring the police the next day. I told my
mother I loved her deeply and always would.

I had left my address book at my flat in Elizabeth Street,
a big mistake. How long would it be before the police might
arrive at Uckfield? I told Susie that I should leave and asked if
she could give me some sleeping pills. She told me that I should
stay the night but I told her that would be dangerous. If the
police arrived I would be putting her in big danger. I told Susie
that my address book was still in my flat with details and
addresses of all my friends. At some point the police might
arrive at Uckfield. I told Susie that should the police interview
her she should tell the truth about having seen me after the
murder, but tell the police that I was proclaiming my
innocence. That I was going to sort things out. In that way it
would not seem as though she had entertained a murderer,
which would have burdened her with a responsibility to call
the police.

I hugged and kissed Susie and left her house around 1am. I
headed to Newhaven. After driving a couple of miles I felt dizzy
and was struggling to keep my eyes open. The sleeping pills
had taken a quick affect. I pulled into a side road and turned
the car lights off. I dozed with nightmarish dreams. When
morning light came up I continued on to Newhaven. I had been
to the town many years previously and knew a little of the
place. Arriving in the town I drove around for a while before
parking the car a little away from the centre. In the cubby
compartment I found some stationery and wrote a letter to my
friend Michael Stoop who had loaned me the car.

I walked down to the marina and stood for a while looking at
the crafts that were moored up. How easy, I wondered, would it
be if one owned a boat here to sail off to France. On the other
side of the river was the ferry port with regular destinations to
the Continent. I posted the letter to Michael Stoop addressed to
his club. Unfortunately it was minus a postage stamp but I
hoped it would be delivered. Then a thought struck me. In the
boot of the Ford Corsair was the other cosh, which was never
used. I could go back and get it and then throw it into the river.
I decided to leave it. The police could make of it what they will.
It was of no real consequence anymore. All the damage had
already been done.

Newhaven had been a good place to abandon the car I told
myself. When the car was found the police might concentrate

their search for me in this area and give me some time. (This turned out to be the case).

I walked back to the town centre and the main bus stop. I was wearing a raincoat with a scarf and a cap. I wrapped the scarf around me against the cold wind and to hide my face. Buses went to either Eastbourne or Brighton. I would take whichever bus arrived first. I decided against using the train from Newhaven as it was a small station and I might be more conspicuous there.

A bus came for Brighton. I pulled my cap down over my face. The driver barely looked at me. At Brighton station I lost myself in the crowds boarding trains to London.

At Victoria Station I found a telephone booth and looked up the number of my friends Martin and Helen. This was a huge decision. I needed to hole up somewhere but could not contact anyone closely associated with the Clermont Club. Those friends would be under the watchful eye of the police. Their movements watched, their phones tapped.

Martin was an architect who had done some work for me and John (Aspinall). He and his wife Helen had become firm friends over the years. Helen answered the phone. She told me Martin was out on his rounds. I told her I was in big trouble and needed somewhere to stay for a little while. She said that no matter what I had done she and Martin would definitely help me. I walked to their home. A lovely top floor apartment in St. John's Wood. Once there Helen made coffee and said she had left messages for Martin to return home. I told her the shocking story but said nothing of my accomplice who I was desperate to protect and hoped would never be apprehended. Amazingly, Helen took my ghastly story in her stride. She had been well aware of my torment for some time. She told me not to worry, that Martin would sort things out.

When Martin arrived I went through the story again. The true events of my guilt that I had related to Helen. He was shocked and worried for me of course but said that he had an idea where I could hole up. He made a series of telephone calls and then told me he had found somewhere for me. An American client of his had purchased a mews cottage, which was not being used. Martin had asked his client if a friend could rent the cottage for a while. The owner said he was more than happy for the place to be used. Helen insisted on making me a small parcel of food before we set off. The mews cottage was ideal. It nestled directly behind Harley Street in Park Crescent Mews and was similar to my place in Eaton Row. Martin checked that everything was working, the electricity and the boiler. There was a small lounge with a television and some comfortable furniture. Martin showed me around the cottage. The kitchen and bathroom were clean and modern. The bedroom was fine but there was no bedding. Martin told me to make myself at home while he went shopping for me.

He returned a couple of hours later with lots of bedding, towels and cutlery. Also a case of wine and spirits and more food. Martin handed me a newspaper with a grim expression. 'You've made the front pages John,' he said. Indeed I had. 'Murder in Belgravia' the headline screamed.

The police were after me, but I felt sure this cottage would be a safe place to lie low for a while. I thanked Martin, saying how sorry I was for involving him in such a shocking business, which could get him into big trouble. He told me that he and Helen were going to stand by me. I did not know it at the time but these friends, especially Helen, would be my main contact with London and a link with those allies that would support me in the years ahead. My gamble on choosing Martin and Helen to help me turned out be very good choice and probably saved me from being caught.

I asked Martin to quietly get word to John Aspinall, telling him where I was. I had a couple of brandies and then slept in an armchair.

The next day I spent on my own. The cottage was warm and cosy and I ate some food for the first time in days. I tried to pull myself together and fight off my demons.

The following day Martin turned up with more supplies and new clothes for me. He told me he had spoken discretely to Aspers (John Aspinall) at his apartment in town. The heat was on, he told me, with police crawling all over the place. Aspers had called a meeting with the Clermont Set to discuss what to do about my situation. He told Martin that the fewer people who knew where I was the better. Aspers would tell Jimmy (Goldsmith) but nobody else. For the time being, (including Helen) just four people would know I was alive and where I was lying low.

A couple of days went by before Aspers turned up at the mews cottage. He was in his usual good spirits telling me that he had driven in circles before arriving at the cottage to shake off any possible tail. He told me he was sure he was being watched and that his phone was being tapped. He made easy of my fearsome situation telling me not to worry and that everything would be sorted out.

John Aspinall was an amazing charismatic man with a will to achieve anything, and a friend that was prepared to help me no matter what. Aspers told me to get rid of my moustache but not to shave and to change the parting in my hair. I had to achieve a new look and he was going to find certain dyes to turn my hair grey. I was to stay put at the cottage until my appearance had totally changed from the pictures that were now splattered on every front page of the newspapers.

And so the following few weeks saw my looks slowly changing. With the dyes my hair was now grey and I was growing a beard, which was slowly taking shape. I had changed the parting in my hair to the middle, which also lent me a new appearance. I was gradually looking a completely different person.

Martin called on me frequently keeping me stocked up with everything I needed including sleeping pills, which I asked him to get for me. He congratulated me on my changing looks, saying that even my close friends would barely recognise me.

Jimmy (Goldsmith) came to see me, telling me that he was going to help and support me and that I was not to worry. Like Aspers, he had driven around and around to shake a possible tale before arriving at the cottage. The determination by the police to apprehend me was intensifying daily. Martin always supplied me with a newspaper and so I was well aware of the massive hunt for me and the enormous amount of publicity surrounding the dreadful murder at my house, for which I was totally responsible. The police had searched homes up and down the country but had, it seemed, concentrated most of their efforts around Newhaven, while all the time I was holed up in London.

Not a day went by when I did not contemplate giving myself up and taking the punishment that was due to me or doing away with myself. But I was just living day to day working on changing my looks, never quite knowing what to do. Give myself up, commit suicide, or go ahead with the plan to escape.

Jimmy told me that he and Aspers were working on a plan for me. That when the time was right they would spirit me out of the country to start a new life afresh. I asked him if it would be Mexico, as I knew he loved the place and had properties and friends there. He said No. Nor would it be Africa. It would have to be somewhere that I had not travelled to before. Somewhere the police would not think of looking for me. But I had to stay put in the cottage and continue changing my appearance. Wait for the dust to settle on the Lord Lucan stories that were dominating the news. I would have to be patient.

Life in the cottage became a routine I soon adapted to. I did my own washing and ironing and cooked for myself. Each night I would apply the dyes to my hair, beard and eyebrows and trim my hair in a new style.

By the middle of December I began venturing out of the cottage. I felt secure that I could not be recognised. I looked completely different, a middle aged man with grey hair and beard. As I walked the streets around Harley Street nobody gave me a second glance. A couple of times I said hello to neighbours in the mews who were pleasant but did not take any undue interest in me.

Aspers, Jimmy and Martin, called on me regularly, taking care that they were not being followed. They always came bearing gifts. I had no shortage of food, alcohol and new clothes. I was always praised on how quickly I had transformed my looks, which I worked at diligently.

On Christmas day, Martin and Helen picked me up and took me back to their home to have lunch with them. They were taking great risks on my behalf. I did not deserve such kindness from my friends. I was no more than a wretched murderer and because of me a poor innocent woman had been killed. I had thought often of taking my own life, but committing suicide is not an easy thing to do. I was not brave enough.

A few days later I read that John Stonehouse, the Labour MP, who had tried to fake his death, had been arrested in Australia. The police down under thought that he was me. The papers were full of it.

By the end of the year my excursions out of the cottage were ever more adventurous. On New Years Eve, I filled a flask with whisky and wandered through Soho and down to Trafalgar Square. I mingled with the revellers, passed close to many policemen and watched a firework display without anyone taking any notice of me. I enjoyed this outing, feeling comfortable that I could in no way be mistaken for who I really was.

Chapter Nineteen

By the middle of January 1975 I had been regularly getting out of the cottage in the evenings for some much needed fresh air and to stretch my legs. I would walk around the West End and Theatre Land, often peering through the windows of pubs wishing that I could go inside and order a drink, something I decided against. As usual, not a single soul took any notice of me.

It was around this time that the plan for my escape sprung into action. Aspers arrived at the cottage with a short, balding Italian man. He set up a tripod and camera in the lounge and hung a screen on a wall, in front of which he asked me to sit. He snapped away saying very little other than I should move my head this way and that. He then silently dismantled his equipment and signalled to Aspers that all was done and it was time to leave.

A week later Aspers and Jimmy arrived with a sort of business-like air about them. The time had come for my escape. Aspers showed me my new passport and told me to study the document and remember all the details by heart. It was a work of art. I was now Sidney Ainsworth, born in Tollesbury, Essex. Some years had been added to my real age. I was never to use my real name again. That person was no more. Jimmy then went through some papers with me. My destination was Beirut, one of the most sensitive areas in the Middle East, which came as a bit of a shock to me. (Little did we know that war would break out there soon after my arrival). He gave me my plane ticket with one stopover and showed me other papers with official stamps on them that I might need along with a one month visa. Should anyone ask, I had worked in banking and was now an aspiring travel writer. A taxi would call for me the following morning and take me to Heathrow. Jimmy gave me a packet containing some Lebanese Pounds, not too many, in case I should be stopped. At Beirut Airport my contact, Georges, would be waiting for me holding up a paper with my name on it. He would take me to my apartment. Georges would supply me with everything I might need. He would be my contact from thereon. Georges would act for me through one of Jimmy's many off-shoot companies in Paris. He would not know who I was or want to know. He would be paid generously for looking after me. Georges spoke Arabic, French and English and was a respected and influential figure in Beirut. My rent would be paid automatically and cash would be supplied to me

on a regular basis. I was to give Georges my official papers,
which he would update for me through his friends at the
Directorate Securite.

Jimmy told me to stay low and be careful who I mixed with
as Beirut was crawling with spies. If I needed to contact Jimmy
I simply had to give a note to Georges who would forward a
message on to the Paris company. But I should do that only in
an emergency. I was to keep in touch with Martin and Helen
who would forward any information or requests I might have to
Aspers. Their telephone line and address was safe. At the end
of my briefing I wrapped my arms around Jimmy and Aspers. I
was crying. They wished me luck. I had no idea when I might
see them again. They offered me a last piece of advice. Escaping
might be the easy part – staying free would be the hard part.

And so on a cold February morning my taxi sped me to
Heathrow to begin a new life.

Georges was waiting for me at Beirut Airport. I had breezed
through customs at both ends. Georges shook my hand warmly
and welcomed me to his city. He was in his forties, tanned with
a fine head of hair swept back as mine used to be. As we walked
to his car I felt the milky warmth of the sun and brightness
that I had not experienced in many months.

On the drive to my apartment Georges explained a little of
Beirut to me and where I would be staying. Tensions were high
he told me but the people went about their business as usual
and were never easily frightened. Georges gave me his business
card. A family business he told me, renting and managing
properties throughout Lebanon. His office was close to my
apartment and I should find him there should I have any
problems.

I took in the city as we drove to West Beirut and Manara.
From the airport we passed through poor districts of sprawling
ramshackle huts and Palestinian refugee camps before
emerging into the city proper. The city has been bruised and
battered over many centuries, Georges told me, and that was
my first impression. Neo-Ottoman buildings could be seen
tucked side-by-side with modern high-rise blocks and swish
hotels. Splendid cobbled street would give way to derelict
buildings and boarded-up businesses and shops. It was all
a hotch potch with war torn areas trying to rise up and start
again.

Chapter Nineteen

We soon arrived at Manara, a nice district with a peaceful feel about it. Georges showed me around my apartment, which was on the third floor of a modern block. The apartment had been aired and provisioned for my arrival. There was a good lounge and diner together with a large bedroom, bathroom and kitchen. The flat also boasted a walk-in wardrobe and a balcony. Georges had stocked the kitchen with food and generously filled the drinks cabinet with spirits and local wines.

He told me to enjoy my stay in Beirut, that despite the mix of races, religions and politics the people in this area were very friendly. But I should not stray into Palestinian areas of Beirut as trouble was slowly brewing there. He would leave me to my own devices for a while and then later on when I had settled in he would show me around. He took my visa and other papers saying that he would authorise them and that I would soon be a regular citizen.

I liked Beirut immensely. I felt free and safe strolling the streets and stopping off at coffee shops and food markets. The city had a strange vibrancy. I could sit outside a café smoking a hubble-bubble pipe and watch the world go by and nobody would bother me.

The country had been through such turmoil in its history, which had resulted in such a diverse mix in its population and cultures. There had been conquests and takeovers by the Romans, the Muslim Arabs, Crusaders and eventually the Ottoman Empire. After the First World War the region was placed under French Mandate Rule. French was the main language, which I could speak a little, although the younger people I encountered also spoke English. The people were friendly everywhere I went. In the evenings I would stroll along the famous boardwalk – the Beirut Corniche where Beirutis would come to exercise and socialise. Here were high-end shops, hotels and beach clubs and wonderful sunsets over the Mediterranean.

Georges became a good friend spending time to show me around the city in his car. He never asked anything about my past and always reminded me that if there was something I needed I should talk to him. He could arrange anything he told me.

Despite life going on as usual in Beirut there was an increasing awareness that upheaval was once again reverberating. Perversely, this made me feel even more secure in this exotic but tense city. Nobody here was interested in a certain Lord Lucan, or what he might have done. People were friendly but would never ask one's business if it were not offered as this would be seen as being intrusive.

This was my home now and my area stayed relatively calm when civil war broke out in the country in the spring. Since I had been in Beirut I had kept in touch by telephone with my friends Martin and Helen. I usually spoke to Helen who was to be my main provider of information over the coming years as to what was happening in London.

She reported that the papers were once again full of stories about me and were hounding and being nasty to anyone associated with me. The Inquest at the Coroner's Court had found me guilty of the murder of Sandra Rivett. Helen said that my friends and family had been solidly behind me in court and were disgusted at how proceedings had been handled. My wife had been portrayed as a put-upon angel.
I could not argue with the verdict but felt most relieved that my accomplice, Terry, had remained unknown and was probably now in the clear.

Later that summer I received some news from Helen that shocked me to the core. My friend Dominick Elwes had committed suicide and it was because of me. I had left a trail of destruction. Dominick had contributed to a story that appeared in the *Sunday Times*. He had painted a picture of the Clermont Set in caricature style, which was unflattering to the Set. The story that accompanied the artwork was hostile to my former circle of friends, portraying them as narrow-minded and right wing. Helen told me that private holiday snaps of myself, Lady Annabel, Jimmy Goldsmith and others had also been reproduced in the *Sunday Times* article. Dominick was blamed for all this and was blackballed out of the Mayfair circle that had once embraced him as a vital friend and the court jester. At Dominick's memorial service, Aspinall, had given a totally inappropriate eulogy. On coming out of the church Aspinall was socked in the face by Elwes's cousin Lord Rennell. Dominick left behind three young children who would be a similar age to my three children.

Dominick Elwes was one of the nicest, funniest men I had ever encountered. His death could be directly attributed back to me. It was my fault. I was sickened and could not hold back tears.

Chapter Nineteen

The following year I was to learn that Jimmy Goldsmith had launched a legal attack and a vendetta against *Private Eye* for suggesting that he had attended the meeting that Aspers had called at his home the day after my disappearance. Jimmy was not at that meeting and vented his grievances at the magazine and the editor Richard Ingrams with libel writs that almost bankrupted the popular magazine.

Jimmy won the case but his reputation was damaged. He was seen as the bad millionaire trying to crush a small satirical paper. Perhaps his disproportional anger stemmed from his new-found friendship with Harold Wilson whose wife and his secretary had also been a target of *Private Eye*. Whatever the reasons he was soon after knighted in Wilson's resignation honours list, the 'lavender list' apparently drawn up by Wilson's secretary Lady Falkender.

I stayed in Beirut for five years. When there were lulls in the fighting and intermittent ceasefires, Georges would take me up into the hills with his friends for picnics, and in the winter we would escape the city and ski at Faraya-Mzaar in Mount Lebanon. Towards the end of my time in Beirut I formed a close relationship with Sonia, a lovely girl who was part of Georges circle. She never asked questions as to my background and at the time I was in need of emotional support and friendship. Sonia was a divorcee from an American financier who had been most generous with a marriage settlement. She was carefree and independent but as time went by she wanted more from me than I could possibly offer.

The time had come for me to leave Beirut. This poor beautiful city was slowly being destroyed and was dividing between the Muslim west and the Christian east. The melting pot of diverse ideologies and power struggles had always been a part of this country and its history. But I had felt safe here. This troubled country was not interested in a displaced criminal Englishman and had been an easy place for me to melt into obscurity.

I arranged to meet Georges for dinner and told him that it was time for me to leave. I thanked him for being such a good friend to me and that I would never forget his kindness and discretion.

On 7 March 1980, I arrived in Cyprus. I travelled around the island for a few weeks staying in hotels before deciding to settle in Larnaca. I viewed various apartments before finding something to my liking to rent. This proved no problem when showing my passport. The property agency I found were willing to take my Beirut currency until I could arrange a bank account.

I went to two banks and opened accounts on the basis that funds would be transferred to me shortly. With a note from my new landlord and my passport this proved no problem.
I phoned Helen and gave her my new address and details of the banks. She would get word to Aspers who would speak to Jimmy.

Shortly afterwards when I spoke to Helen she gave me details of a contact that would be handling me from Paris. He would be known to me only as Max. Helen told me that Jimmy had snapped him up when he had been shunted out of MI6. He spoke English, French and Russian and was the sort of person that was handy for Jimmy. Helen gave me his phone number and address. I was to memorise these contact details. He would take care of regular amounts of money, which would be paid into my bank accounts. I could also contact him direct if I had any problems or needed anything. My financial welfare was being well cared for but I knew my loyal friend Jimmy was making absolutely sure that nothing could be traced back to him.

After three years in Cyprus I decided to take a chance and return to London. My passport needed to be renewed. I booked a return flight and phoned Helen asking her to get word to Aspers that I was coming back and would he put in motion arrangements to get me a new passport. I would ring her once I was in London. I had kept up with dying my hair and beard, although after these fraught years in exile, I had started to grey a little quite naturally.

I arrived in London trouble free and headed for west London. I booked into a small hotel off Queensway and telephoned Helen telling her where I was and that I would be in the hotel lounge every day at noon.

It was strangely unreal to be back in my hometown. I spent the following two days walking around London and taking in the sights that had once been so much of my former life. On the third day of my stay Aspers arrived at my hotel. It was an emotional meeting. He said that he barely recognised me. We spent the afternoon walking in Hyde Park and then ended up in a private drinking club in Soho. We had much to tell each other. He told me that Jimmy had sent his love but was holed-up in Mexico otherwise he would have loved to have seen me again. The following day Aspers took me to a small studio where I once again met the little Italian man who took my old passport and snapped some new photos of me.

While I was on this short trip in London I wanted to see my children. Not to speak to them of course, just to see them at a distance. I did manage to set eyes on them but I wished I had not done so. It hurt me more than I can say. I wanted to run to them and hug them and and tell them how much I loved them and that they were always in my thoughts. I could not hold back tears when I saw them.

A day before I was due to fly back to Cyprus, Aspers came to my hotel with my new passport. It was excellent, and must have cost a lot of money.

Aspers also gave me a Rolex watch with an inscription on the back. 'BE LUCKY J.A.' He told me that the watch was special. That it would always be a sort of insurance for me should I need money. I would always be able to use the watch as security for a loan but never to part with it permanently, as it would increase in value with time.

I thanked him, tearfully, saying I would keep the watch to my dying day.

I returned to Cyprus and stayed for a further year before moving to Greece where I lived in various places including the Greek Islands for seven years. In all these lonely wanderings I kept in touch with Helen in London, which was a great comfort to me. She was always cheerful and kept my spirits up with all the news back home.

While my passport was still valid I decided to move again. In the summer of 1992, I moved to Paris. I wanted to be back in a city and I spoke a little French. Also I wanted to meet up with Jimmy, who had interests in Paris, and spent a lot of time there.

As well as staying in touch with Helen and sending my news, and receiving news from Jimmy and Aspers, I had also maintained a close relationship with Max, who had always kept me in funds no matter where I had travelled. I contacted him again once I had found an apartment in the Marais district. He gave me the name of a bank in Saint Germain where money would be made available for me.

Whenever Jimmy Goldsmith was in Paris, he would get word to me, and we would dine out at secluded little restaurants away from busy areas. Of course we were both getting old and he told me that he had diabetes. My passport was getting near its expiry date and I asked Jimmy whether I should return to London and see Aspers to get a new one. He told me that Max could sort such things, that I should send him my passport and he would get it renewed.

While living in Paris I received the news that my dear friend Bill Shand Kydd had been left a quadriplegic after a hunting accident. I had turned to him on the night of my disappearance, writing to him and asking that he and his wife Christina, my wife's sister, would look after my children. That is what eventually came to pass, which made me so happy and relieved. A little after his accident I read that when Bill was told that he was paralysed from the neck down he said to Christina: 'Well I don't do things by half.' An incredible man with a good heart and generosity of spirit. We met as young men in St. Moritz and did the Cresta Run together. Head first down that exhilarating ice track and had formed a lasting friendship ever since. Despite his incapacity he continued to see that my children were loved and well cared for in his home.

I wished that I could go and see him and my children. I felt so incredibly forlorn when I heard of his accident and his amazing bravery.

Paris was my home for many years, but as time went by I was aware that Jimmy was very ill with cancer, that the arrangements he had financed for me over the years would soon come to an end. Once Max had provided me with a new passport I made the decision to move on. Paris was a lovely place to be in exile but it was expensive and without Jimmy I would have to be very careful in the future with what money I had. Before Jimmy succumbed to cancer he arranged through Max to pay a substantial amount into my bank account. It was a final generous gift from a great man. I decided to move to Spain, which would be a cheaper place for me to see out my days.

Three years after moving to Spain, Helen told me that John Aspinall had, like Jimmy, died of cancer. Now, only Martin and Helen knew of my existence. While in Spain, firstly in Santander, and then near Barcelona, I had a couple of scares that I was being watched. I may have been wrong about this but decided to move yet again and it would have to be my final destination.

Chapter Nineteen

I have lived on this island for over a decade. As the years have passed for this sad and fading fugitive the knowledge that I have, by and large, outlived all my old friends is a miracle, but also a depressing realisation. They have nearly all gone. The Clermont Set, and the peripheral characters that were so much of that extravagant and unreal world are no more. Martin, who was not part of that circle, died of a heart attack in 2011 and Helen, my soul-mate and main contact for nearly thirty-five years, had followed him soon after. Along with Jimmy and Aspers they took my secret to their graves.

Much has been said and written about me in the last forty years. A lot of what has been reported was wrong and ill considered. Now, old and in failing health, I came to the decision that it would be proper for me to put the record straight and come clean. I hope I have managed to do that in this manuscript.

I have always known that I can never be forgiven. That if there is a hell, then that's where I will be heading.

Inflamed by revenge, drink, drugs, debt and outside pressures, I embarked on a course of murder. I was that man portrayed in Ian Fleming's short story, *Quantum of Solace*. For me there was zero solace. My soul was black and empty. I was prepared to murder to put my life back in place. To take someone else's life to rescue mine. How monstrous.

I was the one, and only, guilty person, that led to the murder of my children's nanny and have lived as a shameful fugitive ever since. No doubt retribution awaits me. I have simply been putting off that day.

This is my story. And may God have mercy on my soul.

September 2014. part 3/3

Chapter Twenty

Once through customs at Luton airport I rang Paul King. I told him I had the final manuscript and some items that might provide some DNA. I intended to get a taxi and drop everything off at his home. Paul said that would be brilliant. That he was keen to finalise matters but could not pay me the rest of my money as the newspaper would not part with the remainder of the agreed fee until they were in receipt of the whole manuscript and were happy with it.

I told him I was not overly concerned, that he could pay me if, and when, the newspaper were satisfied with the story and the DNA was checked out. I also mentioned that because of reasons he was fully aware, the manuscript was not signed. I did not feel it necessary to tell him I had typed the last few words on the document.

Arriving in Fulham, I asked the taxi to wait outside Paul's house while I handed over these ghostly items and had a quick chat with him. He told me the anticipation of reading the final part of this bizarre story had been giving him sleepless nights. He promised to contact me as soon as he had sorted affairs with the newspaper.

Chapter Twenty

On the way to Paul's home in Fulham, I had pondered that not many would have thought Lucan escaped to Beirut. If all this were true – and surely it had to be – it would seem his friends were not only rich and powerful, but were also very canny.

That Sidney Ainsworth really was Lord Lucan might soon be proved beyond a shadow of doubt if some DNA could be extracted from items I had grabbed from his bathroom and a match surreptitiously obtained from one of his children.

Nevertheless, it was time to put this strange and dark man out of my life. I had done all I could, but now it was over. The end game had been played out.

I was glad to have handed over everything to Paul King and freed myself from the final remnants of this freaky and dangerous escapade.

Now it was time to get on with my own life. To put all this behind me.

I spent some time in my beloved garden. October had turned cold and wet and now it was time to put the garden away for the winter. I moved all the pot plants to a sheltered location and stacked away the garden furniture. Then it was clearing up masses of leaves and cleaning the pond from just about everything that had fallen into it. I had long chats with my wife and daughter and made arrangements for us to meet up for dinner when my daughter was next in London.

My tennis club had, at long last, called an EGM and the vote was overwhelmingly to sell the place. Swan Park Tennis Club, for which I had been a member for thirty years would be no more.

I met friends at the pub and did a couple of muddy walks in the country. I told nobody of the strange events that had so consumed me during the preceding eight months. It was too dangerous to discuss with anyone. When the story broke, the police would want to know who supplied Paul King with that astonishing manuscript.

I had, quite serenely, removed Sidney Ainsworth from my thoughts. This strange encounter, this strange adventure, would have to remain my secret for a long time – perhaps forever. It felt good this bizarre episode in my life was over and done with.

However, a couple of weeks after delivering the final manuscript to Paul King, he rang me and asked that I meet him at the Russell Square Hotel the following day.

I arrived before him and ordered two Bloody Mary's. He soon showed up and waved to me happily as he entered the bar. I pointed at the drink on the table that I had ordered for him.

He settled himself beside me on the leather bench seat and pushed a brown parcel towards me. 'That's for you, and well done,' he said brightly. 'You now have £100,000 and I don't want to know what you intend to do with it.'

'Thank you,' I said slowly.

'We should tie-up loose ends Adam,' he said, reaching for his drink and taking a good slug. 'Have you been using a pay-as-you-go mobile?'

I nodded.

'Can you destroy the sim, remove any link with me? I will do the same for you. Remove your number from my phone. Basically, it must be that we have never met. We have to protect each other.'

'Of course, I'll do that,' I said softly. 'Also I have got rid of the mobile I gave to Sidney, so we should have eliminated all links.'

'Good show Adam.' he said, taking another swig of his Bloody Mary.

'When will the story get printed?' I asked.

Chapter Twenty

'Well that's just it,' he said with a faint smile. 'It may never happen.'

'What do you mean?' I said, shooting him a puzzled expression.

'The paper may just hold on to it. Keep it locked in a safe with few people knowing of its existence.'

'Hold on,' I said, my voice rising a little. 'They've paid a quarter of a million quid for the story of a lifetime.'

'Listen Adam, if you knew who the proprietor was you would understand. That money is nothing to him. The same as you putting a tenner on a horse. The money is inconsequential.'

'I still don't get it,' I said tetchily. 'All this effort and it may never see the light of day. That doesn't make sense.'

'Look Adam,' he said talking purposefully. 'We have all been paid. You, myself and Warren. Don't you see it's best this way. No threat the paper risks being sued. No police from Scotland Yard knocking on my door wanting to know who the person was that handed over the manuscript. You have done a great job Adam. I can't tell you how impressed I am with the way you have handled all this. I couldn't have done any better myself.'

'He wanted his story told, that was the whole idea,' I said morosely.

'And you have done that Adam,' he said warming to his argument. 'He died in the knowledge that he had at last come clean. To write his story. To tell the whole world. You helped him in the one thing he wanted to do before he died. It's as though he knew that as soon as he finished his story he would pop off. Don't beat yourself up about it. He was very lucky to have taken a chance on you; to fulfil the one good deed he felt was left to him. Not many people would have helped him like you did.'

These words were a comfort but I had an empty feeling in my stomach. I took a big gulp of my drink.

'What about the handwriting?' I asked mildly.

'Inconclusive,' he said casually.

'And the fingerprints?' I asked.

'No definitive match,' Paul answered matter-of-factly.

'The DNA?'

'The newspaper made no comment,' Paul said, staring at a mahogany clock above the bar.

'So we don't know for sure if it was him?'

'Not really,' he murmured slowly. Paul drained the last of his drink. 'Look,' he said brightly, 'I reckon it was him, but that's just my opinion.'

Paul rose and pointed at the parcel that rested beside me. 'Be very careful with that Adam. Don't get mugged on the way home.'

I rose, and we shook hands, both offering each other a smile and a nod of the head that signalled that this would be farewell forever.

'It's been a pleasure meeting and working with you Adam. But sadly, we now have to go our separate ways.' He looked at me thoughtfully for a few moments. There was little more to say. 'Good luck Adam. Take care.'

I watched Paul disappear out of the bar and into Russell Square. He did not look back.

I sat down and placed the parcel inside my raincoat. I felt a little giddy and dispirited. Had all this been a fantasy I wondered? Was it all for nothing? Then maybe not I thought. Perhaps Sidney had heard me in his hospital bed when I told him I would do all I could to see his story was told. It was possible he passed away happy in that knowledge. I could only hope so. Anyway, I would tell myself that was the case.

I was lost in these thoughts, when suddenly an elderly gentleman approached me seemingly from nowhere. The man was smartly dressed, probably in his late seventies. He sported a bright cravat inside a smart sports jacket and was clutching a West End theatre guide.

'I wonder if you might help me?' he said in a somewhat refined voice. He tapped his theatre guide. 'Have you seen a show you might be kind enough to recommend?'

I looked at him carefully for a moment. 'I'm most sorry,' I said solemnly. 'I've made a new resolution not to talk to strangers.' He stared at me stunned, as though not quite sure whether he had heard me correctly. I got up and made to move. I gave him a cheeky smile. 'You never know where it might lead,' I said wickedly. His face was a picture as his mouth fell open. I suddenly felt awful for being so unkind. 'I was only joking,' I said. He looked at me uncertainly. I told him to see *Phantom of the Opera* which seemed to please him. He left me waving his theatre guide and casting doubtful eyes back at me.

I stood in the hotel doorway, my hand pressed against the parcel resting inside my coat as I waited for a black cab.

Back home I unpacked the parcel and did another sorting act with the cash. When I had some neat parcels bound up with masking tape I removed my secret floorboard in the cupboard under the stairs and put the packages with the others down in the dust.

One hundred thousand pounds, thanks to a dapper old boy who had grabbed my ear at the Café Plaza in Mallorca eight months earlier, having introduced himself as a certain Sidney Ainsworth. I had no idea what I would do with the money. Charities Perhaps. Might Sidney have chosen the Injured Jockeys Fund had he lived a little longer?

No matter now. Whether Sidney really was Lord Lucan or a gifted imposter was not the story. Nor was it about John Aspinall, Jimmy Goldsmith or the Clermont Set.

There can only be one story – that of Sandra Rivett, an innocent young woman who made two, easy-to-make, mistakes. The first was to apply for a position as a nanny at 46 Lower Belgrave Street and get the job, unaware she would be caring for the children of aristocratic parents locked in a bitter war. The second mistake was to change her usual night off from Thursday to the previous Wednesday. She was not expected to be in the house and paid the ultimate penalty. Sandra is the story. She is the tragic figure in this tragic tale.

To work as a nanny is a caring profession. To love and look after others. She was almost certainly a sweet woman. A woman who found herself in the wrong place at the wrong time. These thoughts flashed through my mind as I slid the floorboard back into place and got up from my knees. I had to hurry. A race would soon be off at Ascot and I was going to have a big bet on a certain horse. The nag had little chance but I was going to lump on it all the same. It was called: 'Take A Chance On Me.'

FOR SANDRA

In February 2016, one year after the Presumption
of Death Act came into effect, and amid much
publicity in the media, George Bingham, Lord
Lucan's son was, at long last, granted a death
certificate for his father.
George Bingham can now inherit his fathers title,
thus becoming the Eighth Earl of Lucan.

Sidney Ainsworth died at the University Hospital
Son Dureta, Mallorca, 12 October 2014.
He is buried at Palma Municipal Cemetery.

In the summer of 2015, at a Christie's auction in New York, a Rolex Cosmograph Daytona, Oyster Albino, watch came up for sale.

The inscription on the back 'BE LUCKY J.A.' meant nothing to the auction house or the seller. The watch went under the hammer to an anonymous buyer for a near world record of $1.2 million.

Lightning Source UK Ltd.
Milton Keynes UK
UKOW02f2054081016

284781UK00002B/3/P